# A BURST OF RIFLE FIRE RIPPED THROUGH THE SAFE HOUSE

"Soldiers!" one of the rebels shouted. "Split up and make your way to Rosalita's."

Calvin James raced through the kitchen and into the backyard. He saw Encizo reach the fence and scale it in a flash. The next man up was halfway there when he stopped dead, his spine arching.

The Phoenix Force warrior jogged hard left and hit the fence, the blunt toes of his boots finding traction. He needed only seconds, just another foot or so...

The gunner missed him, but the burst of gunfire tore through the boards supporting James's weight and dropped him six feet to the hard-packed earth. He landed on his PA3-DM assault rifle and felt ribs giving way.

The enemy troops advanced to where James lay huddled in the dirt. He knew what would follow—interrogation, names, places, dates. How much damage could he do?

The soldiers moved in close, still covering their captive, and retrieved his weapon. They were smiling when a sadist wearing sergeant's stripes reared back and slammed his boot into the bridge of James's nose.

*Other titles available in this series:*

**STONY MAN II**
**STONY MAN III**
**STONY MAN IV**
**STONY MAN V**
**STONY MAN VI**

# DON PENDLETON'S
# MACK BOLAN.

# STONY
# MAN™
# VII

A GOLD EAGLE BOOK FROM
# WORLDWIDE®

TORONTO • NEW YORK • LONDON
AMSTERDAM • PARIS • SYDNEY • HAMBURG
STOCKHOLM • ATHENS • TOKYO • MILAN
MADRID • WARSAW • BUDAPEST • AUCKLAND

First edition July 1993

ISBN 0-373-61891-3

Special thanks and acknowledgment to Mike Newton for his contribution to this work.

STONY MAN VII

Printed in U.S.A.

# PROLOGUE

*Madeira Bay, Florida*

They let him keep his belt. It was the first stupid move Dale Hargis's enemies had made all night, perhaps in days, but with some luck it could be all he needed to survive.

The blindfold he was wearing fit him snugly, but he didn't need his eyes to know the boat was turning landward, throttling down. Ten minutes minimum, a quarter hour max. Beyond that point, it wouldn't matter what he tried.

His hands were bound behind him, but his enemies had used a piece of nylon rope, instead of handcuffs. Stupid move number two. He strained his ears to pick up any sound of footsteps in the corridor outside. In addition to pure luck, he needed privacy to pull it off—the first part, anyway. Once he was on his feet, a confrontation would be unavoidable, but it was getting to his feet where every second counted.

Rolling over on his back, Hargis humped his way around until his skull made contact with the cabin bulkhead. After that, the trick was pushing with his elbows, using muscles in his back and legs. It hurt like hell as he began to work his fettered wrists across the tight swell of his buttocks, but the nylon helped a little, yielding just a millimeter here and there, when handcuffs would have simply torn his flesh.

Small blessings.

Hargis let his mind drift for a moment to escape the pain, his thoughts inevitably harking back to the dilemma he was facing. He had tried to work it out a dozen different ways, the past four hours, but he still had no idea how they had tumbled to his act. He didn't want to think about a leak, but it was something he would have to deal with later.

If he lived that long.

So far, so good. His hands had cleared his buttocks now, and he relaxed his muscles, breathing slowly in anticipation of the next move, which was bound to wake up nerves he didn't even know he had. The bastards had been smart enough to bind his ankles, which would make things awkward toward the end, but Hargis reckoned he could work that problem out, if he could only get that far.

Right now, he felt a good deal worse than helpless, lying with his feet up in the air, his shoulders straining to the point of separation, wicked gremlins working on his lower back with red-hot tongs. He hunched his head and shoulders forward, something like an awkward sit-up to reduce the strain, but his relief was marginal at best. He had to finish now while he had strength and will to go ahead, or it was all in vain.

He let his mind drift free again, as far beyond the pain as it could go. Unfortunately all that he could think of was the meet on Calle Ocho in Miami, Hargis rolling up in his Mercedes like he owned the fucking street, without a clue to what was going down. His contact had smiled with his pearly whites, a flash of gold in front, before his three gorillas leveled guns at Hargis and began to shake him down.

He wasn't carrying ID, of course, much less a wire. It didn't matter. Escalante watched while the shooters bound his wrists and ankles, making sure that it was safe before he went to work on Hargis with his fists, the beating interrupted periodically with an account of what they knew.

Too much, for damn sure.

Somehow they had lucked into the fact that he was DEA. No matter how he scanned the past two months for errors on his own part, Hargis came up empty, wondering exactly what had tipped them off. It hardly mattered at the moment, but if he survived this night, the question would be top priority, from Metro-Dade to Washington, D.C.

A leak.

The more he thought about it, Hargis had to tell himself that it was possible. The kind of money they were dealing with, it stood to reason someone would be tempted. Maybe *several* someones.

None of it would matter, though, if he didn't get his butt in gear.

Hargis brought his knees to his chest, his wrists scooting inch by inch along his thighs. The pain was wearing on his nerves, but at the moment he was more concerned with wasted time. He bent his knees and gave it everything he had, a twisting lunge that nearly finished off his shoulder sockets, hanging up for just a heartbeat on his heels, and then he made it.

The rest of it was relatively simple, once he got his second wind. The first thing Hargis did was lose the blindfold, so that he could see what he was doing for the rest of it. Unfastening his belt, he drew the two-inch buckle-dagger from its hidden sheath and smiled, fluorescent lights reflecting off the satin finish of the blade. He kept it razor sharp, no problem, but the grip was awkward, and he balanced urgency with caution, trying not to cut himself if he could help it.

The smile was back, sardonic now, as he imagined tabloid headlines. Federal Agent Slashes Wrists On Drug Yacht. Scandal At The DEA.

Film at eleven.

It took the better part of ninety seconds, working steadily, but finally his wrists were free, a few skinned patches leaking blood. He freed his ankles, then staggered to his feet on pins and needles, circulation coming back. Between stiff muscles and the rocking motion of the boat, he almost lost his balance, but he simply didn't have the luxury of falling down.

If he was going, it was time.

From this point on his one advantage was surprise. If he could make it to the rail, he had a chance. As far as odds were concerned, he didn't even want to think about it.

He thought about the safe-deposit box that he had rented in Miami Beach, the seventeen handwritten pages he had sealed inside an envelope and left there two days earlier. How long before his contact used the key that Hargis mailed him, for emergencies?

Ten days, at least.

No mercy there. The cavalry was on vacation.

He would have to do it on his own, or not at all.

The cabin door wasn't equipped with locks, but no one had a reason to suspect he would be up and moving, after all. He had no way of knowing whether there were guards outside, but he would have to take the chance. Each second counted, now that he was on his way.

He held the short push-dagger with the buckle tucked into his palm, the curved, double-edged blade protruding from between his second and third fingers. He would have to choose his targets wisely, but in haste. A heartbeat's hesitation would be all the time a gunner needed to cancel his ticket once and for all.

His left hand closed around the doorknob, every muscle in his body tensed in preparation for the move. He had two ways to go, a cautious peek or hell-for-leather, each with its potential disadvantages. A peek would let him know if there were guns outside his door, but it could also give a lookout time to draw and fire if Hargis fumbled his attack. The other route, a leap of faith, could also blow up in his face if they had guards on duty somewhere down the hall, beyond his immediate reach.

Go for it.

Hargis ripped the door open, stepping forward with his arm cocked before the sentry knew exactly what was happening. One man, as far as he could tell, and if he had it wrong then he was screwed.

No time to check it out.

When Hargis struck, the guy was turning to face him, one hand coming up while the other slid into his jacket. Too late. The blade scraped on his jawbone, sliding home an inch before his earlobe.

The gunner staggered, grimacing, his right hand still inside the jacket, groping for his hardware. Hargis followed up, a swift kick to the crotch that dropped his adversary to the carpet, blowing crimson bubbles as he clutched the family jewels.

The blade was waiting for him, sliding underneath his chin and ripping right to left. Dale Hargis realized his slacks were warm and wet now, but he didn't stop to think about it. Clutching at the shooter's automatic, Hargis shoved him backward, palmed the gun and left his adversary wheezing in the middle of the hallway like a stranded fish.

The two of them were all alone.

So far, so good.

He shifted hands, the blood-slick dagger in his left now, with the automatic in his right. It was a Smith & Wesson Model 59, which gave him fifteen rounds to play with, but he hoped to reach the deck and disembark without a fireworks show. The less attention he attracted in the next few moments, the safer he would be.

He moved along the hallway, pistol cocked and ready, just in case he met someone he didn't want to see along the way. No outside view, but he could tell from the prevailing motion of the yacht that he was headed aft, in the direction of the stern.

Hargis spent a moment at the bottom of the stairs while he tried to reconstruct the layout of the boat from memory—a weekend bash three weeks ago, with a ratio of two hookers for each man aboard. Coming out on deck, he would be just below the wheelhouse, visible to anyone on the afterdeck. It was a running gamble, once he came up from below, but it was all he had.

The stairs were carpeted, soundless as Hargis made the climb. There was a window in the door, and he took full advantage of it, scanning the afterdeck for enemies. It was a challenge, with lights behind him and the night pitch-black outside, but he would have to take the chance.

Out and moving toward the nearest rail. That made it port, five running paces on a boat this size. He kept his head down, running with his shoulders hunched as if against a killing blow. Another second now, one more...

Above him and behind, someone shouted.

"Hey!"

He swiveled, barely breaking stride, and saw a gunner bursting from the wheelhouse, sounding the alarm. The Smith & Wesson spoke three times in rapid-fire, and Hargis saw the gunner stumble, pitching headfirst down the stairs. Inside the wheelhouse startled faces pressed against the glass, with Escalante mouthing silent curses.

Go!

Somebody started firing with an automatic weapon as he threw himself across the rail. Dark water rushed up to meet him, barely time to suck in breath and hold it as he broke the surface, slicing deep into the void.

The water wasn't cold, by any normal standards, but it still surprised him, Hargis fighting the impulse to surface at once. He couldn't hear them shooting up above him, but the rumble of the engines kept him company as he began to kick toward shore. His knife was gone, but he had kept the automatic so far, just in case it functioned after soaking in the ocean for a while.

How far to shore? he didn't have a clue, but he had fixed the general direction in his mind. A hundred yards perhaps, or twice that. There was no way he could make it on a single breath, but he was counting on the darkness for his cover once he put some space between himself and Escalante's yacht.

Their destination was a mystery, but he had heard enough before they left him in the cabin to surmise that they were cruising off the southern tip of Florida, intent on dropping him someplace where he wouldn't be found until the scavengers had had a chance to feed. That meant the Everglades, a thousand different places he could hide from searchers if he made it to the swampy shore alive.

His lungs were aching by the time he struggled to the surface, breaking water with as little noise as he could manage. For a moment he was startled, fearing he had fallen in behind the yacht somehow, but then it struck him that they must have changed directions, closing in to head him off. A searchlight swept across the water, still some twenty yards away when Hargis caught his breath and dived.

Coming up for air two minutes later, he saw that he was gaining on his destination, but the yacht was still in front of him, its searchlights sweeping left and right. Before he dived again, one of the gunners opened fire on some imaginary target off to starboard, muzzle-flashes sparking in the night.

The burst of Parabellum slugs that killed Hargis came as a surprise and a relief. He sank without a whimper, bubbles trailing after him, mixed with blood. The predators would find him soon, but Hargis didn't care.

His final thoughts had been about Miami Beach, the safe-deposit box.

A time bomb waiting to explode in Escalante's face.

His sole regret had been that he wouldn't be there to see it blow.

# CHAPTER ONE

*Owyhee County, Idaho*
*Friday, 4:02 a.m.*

The Nazis never saw him coming.

Mack Bolan took advantage of the early-morning darkness, dressed in black, his face and hands darkened by combat cosmetics. The terrain was hilly, bristling with evergreens, the undergrowth alive with darting, rustling predators. He took his time. It wasn't far, and there was no point stepping on a rattlesnake if he could avoid it.

The warrior's blacksuit fit like a second skin. A Desert Eagle .44 Magnum semiauto pistol rode his hip, and a Beretta 93-R was tucked beneath his left arm in a custom fast-draw rig. His lead weapon for the probe was a Heckler & Koch MP-5 SD-3 submachine gun, the model with a folding stock and built-on silencer. Doomsday accessories included hand grenades, garrotes, a Ka-bar fighting knife...and something special in the satchel slung across his back.

The Fourth Reich was about to get a wake-up call.

As self-styled members of the master race, the Aryan Dominion's brownshirt troopers left a lot to be desired. The files accumulated by investigators from the FBI and ATF revealed that most of them were dropouts, ex-cons, deviants of one kind or another.

One in nine had been arrested on a sex-related charge within the past five years. Some of them were chronic drunks, and all of them had bottomed out in life before they found a movement that provided them with opportunities to feel superior.

At long last, love.

Or, rather . . . hate.

For thirty bucks a year they got the pleasure of despising anyone and everyone who had dismissed them as a pack of hopeless losers through the years.

The Aryan Dominion had an estimated membership of 750 nationwide, with about fifty of the hardcore haters dwelling in a rural compound north of Gransmere, Idaho. They tilled subsistence gardens, practiced marksmanship and churned out endless streams of racist propaganda from the print shop. If the reports from federal agencies were accurate, they also plotted crimes that ranged from robbery and counterfeiting to extortion, arson, bombing and assassination.

Of the estimated fifty residents inside the compound, only one held more than passing interest for the Executioner. His name was Eddie Kirk, and he was nine years old.

As Bolan understood the problem, Eddie was the grandson of a well-known California congressman. The politician's daughter had no inkling of her husband's mental problems when she said "I do." It took some time—six years, in fact—before she fully understood that he was eaten up by hate for total strangers and would never change. Divorcing Eddie's father took another eighteen months, with bitter charges, countercharges and lawyers billing by the hour. Eddie's

mom got custody at last, but Dad hung on to visita-
tion rights, one weekend out of every three. Nine
months ago, he disappeared with Eddie and the search
began.

A senior congressman has pull in Washington, and
it was no great trick to field a team of federal agents to
track Louis Howard Kirk. Uncovering hard evidence
was something else, and it had taken eighty-seven days
to place the fugitive in Idaho, holed up with his good
buddies from the Aryan Dominion. When the Owyhee County sheriff's deputies and G-men made their
search of Nazi Central, they came close to touching off
a firefight . . . but they found no trace of Eddie or his
father at the compound.

About that time the congressman began to make
some calls. It happened that he had a close friend in the
Oval Office, one who sympathized with a parent's—or
a grandparent's—sense of frustration and loss. Strings
were pulled and buttons pushed, eliciting the information that Treasury's Bureau of Alcohol, Tobacco
and Firearms had a man inside the Aryan Dominion
compound, leaking regular reports on weapons shipments, demolition seminars, the works. Said agent was
instructed to remain alert for any sign of Louis Howard Kirk and son, reporting back at once if they were
seen.

Three days earlier, the call had come—a double
bull's eye, man and boy together. The FBI wanted another crack at their target, but Washington had another idea. Two birds with one stone, as it were.

Payback time.

The Aryan Dominion had been linked with seven
murders, nineteen bombings and at least two dozen

robberies from coast to coast. So far, except for the conviction of three Nazis in the murder of a Kansas City radio announcer, none of the reported crimes had been avenged. If it was possible to rescue Eddie Kirk and take the new-wave fascists down a peg or two, so much the better.

It was Bolan's kind of job, and he agreed to take it on. A briefing from Hal Brognola, his Justice contact, and the die was cast.

Whatever happened in the next half hour, there could be no turning back.

The compound was encircled by a chain-link fence, with barbed wire on top, but it wasn't electrified. This information, and a detailed layout of the camp, had been supplied to Bolan indirectly by the ATF connection. As it happened, Treasury's informant had been chosen for a mission to Los Angeles—a volunteer, in fact—and he wouldn't be present when the hit went down.

In Bolan's mind, that gave him fifty targets, more or less, and one small boy to watch for in the middle of it all.

His infrared goggles turned everything greenish, but Bolan was used to the pale, washed-out landscape by now. The goggles kept his hands free and eliminated any need for flashlights that would tip off the Aryan Dominion's sentries to the warrior's movement through the trees.

He used a pair of insulated cutters on the wire—some cheap insurance, just in case—and slipped through a three-foot hole. No sign of sentries yet, but they were bound to be along in time. His job, if everything proceeded in accordance with the plan, would be to raise some hell, grab Eddie Kirk and leave the camp before the Nazis had a chance to seal his exit hatch.

He had the layout memorized and was headed in the direction of the CP Quonset hut, the would-be Führer's quarters. The C-4 plastique charge he planted had a detonator already attached, the red light glowing to confirm that it was armed.

His next stop was the motor pool, where Bolan found a sentry dozing at his post. A rap on the guy's skull would keep him out of play for a time, enough for Bolan to achieve his goal. The warrior left him in the shadow of a half-ton truck. The clumps of plastique he attached to every second vehicle in line were smaller, but no less deadly.

There was a chapel on the grounds, and he passed it by. If God was moved to punish these impostors, he could zap the church himself. Two charges for the mess hall, one each for the generator housing and the commo hut . . . and he was done.

Almost.

The map in Bolan's memory had singled out one barracks hut where Eddie Kirk allegedly resided with his father. Going in, the Executioner had no idea if Eddie would resist his liberation, but he had a throw-away syringe prepared, with sedatives prescribed by estimated size and weight.

Bolan gambled on the barracks being left unlocked and won his bet. He saw four cots, two of them empty. Figures huddled under blankets on the other two, one of them noticeably smaller than the other.

He moved past the elder Kirk's bed, had no choice but to put a silenced round through the man's head when he stirred and started to sit up.

Bolan made his way to where the boy lay sleeping. Eddie moved underneath the blankets, stiffening, his eyes wide open, as the Executioner pressed a hand across his mouth.

"Your mother sent me," he whispered to the frightened boy. "She loves you very much and wants you back. You mustn't make a sound, okay?"

At a shaky nod, Bolan took his hand away.

"Are you from outer space?" the boy whispered.

The warrior smiled and tapped the goggles with his index finger. "No such luck. These help me see without the lights, is all."

"My father?" He glanced toward the cot on his left, a tremor in his voice.

"He won't be coming with us, Eddie. I'm afraid we have to go right now."

"They'll stop us."

"No, they'll try," Bolan replied. "It makes all the difference in the world."

"Okay."

He thought of letting Eddie dress, but decided that they didn't have the time. A pair of sneakers and a jacket with pajamas underneath would have to do. He checked his watch and saw that they were running out of time. Before they left the barracks, Bolan dropped the empty satchel, unclipping the radio-remote unit from his belt.

"It gets a little loud from here on in," he said.

"I'm not afraid of noise."

"Good boy. Let's do it."

Bolan keyed the silent signal, waiting through a heartbeat's lag time for the first explosion. In another instant charges went off in rapid-fire around the camp. Buildings disintegrated, secondary blasts ripping the motor pool apart as fuel tanks went up in flames.

"Come on!"

He kept a grip on Eddie's hand and sprinted toward the fence, a hundred yards away. In front of them a pair of startled sentries seemed to come from nowhere, packing automatic rifles, firelight etching shadows on their faces.

The taller gunner spotted Bolan first, another beat passing before he recognized the boy and got a grip on what was going down. By that time Bolan had a target fix and loosed a burst from the silenced subgun. The gunner dropped on his backside with a small gasp of surprise.

His sidekick shouted something and squeezed off a burst that missed his moving targets by at least ten feet. The H&K did better, putting four rounds in the center ring and blowing him away. Not bad for shooting on the run, one-handed, but they still had far to go— another hundred yards, at least, before they reached the hole in the fence.

The warrior spotted other sentries racing toward the center of the compound now, all homing on the flames.

A bullet zinging past Bolan's ear told him that his luck had just run out. He veered hard left, behind the nearest Quonset hut, half dragging Eddie Kirk behind him.

"Are you all right?"

The boy nodded. "I think so, yeah."

"I need to throw them off, so we can get away."

"Be careful."

"Right."

He poked his head around the corner, jerked it back at once as bullets rattled off the corrugated metal wall. A brief glimpse, but it was enough to show him three men cautiously advancing through a pall of smoke, spread out with ten or fifteen feet between them.

Time to raise the ante.

Bolan palmed a frag grenade and pulled the safety pin. It was a sidearm pitch, left-handed, but experience and practice did the trick. Five seconds on the fuse, and he was moving as the high-explosive charge went off. A shoulder roll took him underneath the shrapnel's flight path, ready for the mop-up with his H&K.

Two gunners went down, one of them still moving as he scanned the killing round. The third was on his feet and running in a crouch, squeezing off a burst from his M-16A1 as Bolan showed himself. The bullets kicked up dust beside the Executioner, one or two of them uncomfortably close before the H&K responded with a muffled burst of Parabellum rounds.

The Nazi seemed to stumble on an obstacle that neither one of them could see. He went down on his face and stayed there. His mangled comrade got the last of Bolan's magazine, a mercy kill, as the Executioner reloaded and sprinted back to Eddie Kirk.

"Let's go!"

Confusion in the compound helped them reach the fence without another interruption, but a lookout spotted Bolan as he followed Eddie through the gap. A spotlight blazed to life and tried to follow them, but they were in the trees before the gunner found a target.

They had a lead, but that was all.

Eddie stumbled, going down on hands and knees. The warrior scooped him up and braced him in a fireman's carry, making his adjustment to the extra weight.

It was a long mile down the mountain to his vehicle, and Bolan knew that they would never make it with a hunting party on their heels. He had to stop the trackers cold, or they were finished.

Twenty yards beyond a clearing, Bolan found a tree that he could climb with Eddie draped across his shoulder, picking out a fork that offered both concealment and a fairly stable resting place. A length of nylon rope secured the boy in place.

"I'm going back," he said. "I have to stop them here, so we can get away. Okay?"

"Suppose...I mean..."

"I'll be back," Bolan assured him, hoping it was true.

"Okay."

"Stay quiet, now."

"I will."

The warrior scrambled down and doubled back to reach the clearing, picking out another tree and climbing swiftly to a vantage point that let him scan the ground for thirty yards on either side. He didn't know how many guns were tracking them, but some were bound to pass this way, and any Bolan missed would be attracted to the firefight.

He counted off six minutes, was working on the seventh when he heard them thrashing through the undergrowth, weekend warriors showing off their lack of expertise. He marked positions by the sound and estimated there were four or five, approaching in a ragged skirmish line.

The first tow broke the tree line just in front of Bolan, eager for the kill, without a thought for any kind of ambush waiting in the dark. He squeezed off two precision bursts, a whisper from the H&K at something close to forty feet. The gunner on his left went down without a whimper, like a puppet with its strings cut, but the other got a burst off from his Uzi as he fell. The aimless spray of Parabellum rounds posed no risk to Bolan, but the report brought Number Two's companions on the run.

Three men crashed through the trees, one of them shouting like an idiot that they were on their way. Surprise. Bolan lobbed a frag grenade off to his left, hunching against the tree trunk as it detonated, winging shrapnel through the woods.

One of the Nazis started to scream. On Bolan's right a solitary figure reached the clearing, saw his comrades stretched out on the ground and dropped into a fighting crouch.

Too late.

He took a short burst in the face and fell backward, his automatic rifle gone before he had a chance to fire. Below the Executioner and to his left, another rifle opened up. This one had the range, its owner doubtless sighting on his muzzle-flash.

No time to lose.

He palmed a stun grenade and pulled the pin, waiting for the rifleman to stop and reload. It was a long pitch, but he didn't need precision.

The flash-bang lived up to its name, with sudden thunder and blinding light. Bolan shielded his eyes from the blast, already scrambling down the trunk before the shock wave struck his perch. He hit the ground in a crouch, listening, picking up the sounds of someone thrashing feebly in the undergrowth.

The Executioner homed on the sounds, leading with his submachine gun, prepared for any sort of trap his adversaries could devise on a split second's notice. His index finger kept a steady pressure on the weapon's trigger, holding it at half-pull as he circled the smoky clearing, moving closer to his prey.

Both men were down, but neither one was out. The closer of the two was dazed and deafened by the flash-bang, groping blindly for his weapon. Bolan took him out with a burst across the chest.

The sole survivor had been torn by shrapnel from the frag grenade. His legs were twisted, dark blood seeping through his khaki trousers, and he clasped both hands across his abdomen, as if to keep a portion of himself inside. At sight of Bolan moving toward him through the dark, he tried to draw a pistol from its holster on his hip, but he couldn't quite manage. Bolan put a mercy round between his eyes and moved out.

Five minutes later, he and Eddie Kirk were heading toward the warrior's hidden vehicle, a year-old Blazer painted primer gray and flecked with rust in places. He put the four-wheel-drive in gear and powered out of there along a narrow logging track.

Eddie Kirk was silent on the drive to Mountain City, forty miles across the border, in Nevada. Bolan tried to see it from the boy's perspective, dating from the separation of his parents through abduction by his father, living with the Aryan Dominion, to a night of fire and blood. It was a bust, of course. He couldn't psychoanalyze a nine-year-old, but he could feel the young boy's fear, imagine something of the pain he must be feeling.

Bolan had been fully grown, a combat veteran, when his own family was torn apart by violence, and it had been difficult to cope with, even so. He only hoped that the youngster could hold it all together, find the love he needed with his mother and try, somehow, to make sense of the waking nightmare that had jeopardized his life.

The kid was still alive, and that was something, anyway.

The Cactus Inn Motel in Mountain City featured satellite TV and "magic finger" beds that shook when you inserted quarters in a coin box mounted on the wall. The coffee shop had slot machines lined up against one wall, to catch the suckers bright and early, while they waited for their ham and eggs.

"My mother's here?"

It was the first time Eddie Kirk had spoken since they hit the road, and Bolan felt a physical sensation of relief.

"Room 17," he said. "Just let me check it out first, will you?"

"Sure."

It wasn't trust, he realized, so much as weary resignation. Eddie made no move to follow Bolan as he got out of the car and walked up to the numbered door. It opened wide before he had a chance to knock, and a young blond woman raced toward the Blazer, calling

Eddie's name. Behind her, in the doorway, stood the congressman.

Next time the man spoke on television, Bolan thought the makeup crew would have to earn their money. Pushing fifty-five, the politician looked like he had aged another ten years overnight.

"Is everything . . . all right?" he asked.

"The boy's uninjured. Beyond that, I'm not qualified to say."

"Of course, I understand. He'll have the finest care available."

"I hope so, Congressman."

"I wish there was something I could do . . ."

"Just do for Eddie and his mother."

"Yes, I will." The politician blinked, a sudden memory returning. "Oh, you got a call."

It was the warrior's turn to blink.

"Say what?"

"A message, on the telephone. 'Call Leo,' I believe it was."

"That's it?"

"'Call Leo.' Yes, I'm sure that's all he said."

The Executioner brushed past him, found the bedside telephone and tapped in eleven digits from memory. It would be pushing nine o'clock in Washington, high time for Leonard Justice to be at his desk. The private line rang twice before a deep, familiar voice responded.

"Yes?"

"I got your message," Bolan said.

"Are you finished up out there?"

"Looks like."

"Okay. We've got ourselves an unexpected situation."

"Is there any other kind?"

"I keep my fingers crossed. The Man was hoping you could pay a visit to the farm."

"How soon?"

"We could have used you yesterday."

The warrior frowned, saw Eddie coming through the doorway with his mother's arms around him, tears on both their faces. Grandpa got in on the act, and then everyone was crying.

"I'm on my way."

# CHAPTER TWO

*Reynosa, Mexico*
*Friday, 10:00 a.m.*

The chicken hawk was on his way.

Carl Lyons scanned the curving stretch of desert highway with binoculars, picking out a glint of chrome in the distance, tracking until the flash of sunlight resolved itself into a sky-blue Mercedes. Figure sixty thousand dollars, with the built-in extras, and you might be close.

Crime pays, damn right.

This morning, though, it was about to pay off in a way the chicken hawk didn't anticipate.

His name was Augustin Cavillo—"Paco" to the friends who knew him best and shared his tastes. The list included politicians, businessmen and entertainers, judges, attorneys and law-enforcement officers. When they got together for the special parties Augustin Cavillo held each month at his estate outside Reynosa, they put all their differences aside and concentrated on pursuing pleasures of the flesh.

As fate or pure dumb luck would have it, all of them were pedophiles, unable or unwilling to perform with partners much beyond the age of twelve years old. They patronized Cavillo's service in the knowledge that his inventory was reviewed each month, "old" items giving way to new, and they would never have to see the same faces twice.

In fact, it was Cavillo's method of rotating inventory that had brought Carl Lyons to Reynosa, left him crouching in the shade of thorny Joshua trees and sipping tepid water while the desert temperature began to climb.

Cavillo's private parties were repulsive in themselves, but he wasn't content with servicing the so-called cream of Mexican society. Aside from pimping children to his cronies in return for cash and favors, Augustin cleared several million dollars yearly by producing and distributing a line of kiddie porn for paying customers in the United States and Canada. A relatively recent sideline was the packaging for sale of kidnapped children, stolen from the rural countryside of Mexico for shipment north, where certain well-heeled bits of human toxic waste paid anywhere from ten to thirty thousand dollars each for living, breathing toys.

The FBI and INS suspected Augustin Cavillo had been moving children north through Texas and New Mexico for more than two years. They could only estimate the numbers, based on hearsay testimony and a covert scan of Paco's many bank accounts. Conservative reports stood fast around an estimated hundred victims. Feds with more imagination hinted that the number might be double, even triple that.

No matter.

One child stolen from a loving home and sold like so much livestock would have been enough for Lyons. It was time to cancel Augustin Cavillo's ticket in the name of common decency.

"I've got him," Lyons said into the walkie-talkie. "Any company?"

There was a momentary burst of static, fading into Hermann Schwarz's mellow voice. "He's clean."

"All right," he said, "let's bring it home."

The tip on Paco's whereabouts had set them back ten thousand pesos—call it fifty dollars, give or take. It would have startled Cavillo to discover just how little he was worth.

Carl Lyons made it roughly twenty-five cents on the pound.

Dead meat.

Cavillo had been staying overnight in Matamoros, but the risks were greater if they tagged him there. An extra day would see him home, and they could have some privacy at his estate.

Of course, they wouldn't have the place entirely to themselves. Cavillo had his servants, bodyguards, and there were always two or three young "guests" in residence to keep the master occupied. Today, there should be closer to a dozen, as Cavillo had a weekend party planned for several of his closest—make that richest—friends.

Lyons had wanted to wait another day and bag the whole damned bunch, say six or seven perverts for the price of one, but Justice had turned thumbs down. It was enough, the powers that be decided, to eliminate the source and thereby shut down the pipeline, however briefly. Taking out a kiddie pimp was one thing; burning up the Matamoros social register was something else.

Case closed.

He watched the blue Mercedes, following its progress for another mile or so until the sandy foothills covered its retreat. When Paco's pimpmobile was out of sight, Lyons took his walkie-talkie and canteen, stood and dusted off his jeans, backtracking to the rental car he had concealed in an arroyo fifty yards due east.

It was a Cadillac, new model, lightly powdered with a layer of dust that cut the desert sun's reflection off of highly polished paint and chrome. The kind of car Cavillo would expect a wealthy customer to drive. In fact, the pimp was doubtless hurrying to make himself presentable for Lyons's arrival.

It wasn't every day you had a chance to deal with someone who was interested in buying stolen lives a dozen at a time. Cavillo had been gobbling the bait for two weeks now, and the big ex-LAPD detective could almost hear him drooling on the telephone each time they spoke. The deal that Lyons offered would have put Cavillo in a different bracket, if the bastard had been paying taxes to begin with.

Greed would do it every time.

"I'm rolling," Lyons said into his radio before he slid behind the Caddy's wheel.

"So, roll," Schwarz answered. He and Blancanales would be somewhere on the road by now, already moving. Reinforcements on the way.

He would have liked to do the job himself, but Lyons knew the odds. With Paco's muscle and domestic staff, he made it ten or twelve to one, and while he could remember playing worse hands, none of them had been by choice. With Gadgets and the Politician backing him, he had a fairly decent chance of coming out the other end alive.

It was all a gamble, going in. They knew the bodyguards were armed, but they were only guessing on the staff. Did Paco have a fallback option for eliminating evidence? Would there be extra muscle at the rancho, with a party coming up? Unknown.

The Caddy almost drove itself, and Lyons leaned across to reach the glove compartment, lifting out a sleek Beretta 92-F semiautomatic with a custom silencer attached. He thumbed the hammer back and checked the safety, then placed the pistol on the seat beside him, easily within his reach.

Five minutes brought him to the wrought-iron gates. A guard in uniform examined his Caddy from behind the scrollwork. Lyons left the vehicle, stretched his legs and walked up to the gates, all smiles.

*"Señor?"*

"Chad Lewis. I believe Señor Cavillo is expecting me."

The guard frowned and stepped inside the gatehouse, checking out a clipboard, finally nodding to himself. He keyed a switch, and Lyons walked back to his rental as the gate began to roll aside.

He put the Cadillac in gear and eased forward, lifting the Beretta as he pulled even with the gatehouse.

"One more thing," he said.

"Yes?"

His bullet drilled the guard an inch above his nose and just a hair off center, blowing off his cap before the guy slumped backward, sprawling with his legs protruding from the open gatehouse door.

"Siesta time," Lyons said. "Take a load off."

If they didn't dawdle, Gadgets and Politician ought to find their entry unopposed.

Lyons lifted off the brake and went to keep his scheduled appointment with the chicken hawk.

"YOU THINK HE'LL TRY to hot-dog?"

Hermann "Gadgets" Schwarz responded with a chuckle, keeping both eyes on the desert highway. "Carl? You're kidding, right?"

"Goddamn it!"

Rosario Blancanales was riding shotgun in the tail car, wishing that they hadn't given Lyons such a lead. The plan was simple, but he knew how Lyons felt about Cavillo—any child abuser—and it would be oh, so simple for the Ironman to begin without them. Two, three minutes either way, and it could still go straight to hell.

"Let's try some speed, why don't we?"

"Eighty isn't fast enough?"

"I'm in a hurry," Blancanales replied.

"We're getting there."

As if on cue, they came around a corner and the foothills seemed to melt away, the desert spreading out in front of them as far as he could see. A half mile farther, an access road branched off the highway toward Cavillo's walled estate.

"Gate's open," Blancanales said as they approached. He caught a glimpse of dust just settling in the driveway.

"Party time."

Blancanales reached under his seat and found the mini-Uzi, flicking off the compact submachine gun's safety with his thumb. Beside him, Gadgets had an Ingram MAC-10 resting in his lap.

They took it easy, passing through the open gate, both of them checking out the prostrate guard.

"One down," Schwarz commented.

"Let's move it."

They were following the blacktop driveway when a sudden, muffled beeping erupted in the glove compartment, brooking no denial.

"Switch it off," Blancanales snapped.

The beeper was their hot-line link to Stony Man, an option that was rarely used, except in bona fide emergencies.

"What's cooking, do you think?"

Schwarz frowned. "Let's stick to one meal at a time."

And he was right. Distraction at a crucial moment was enough to get you killed. The team at Stony Man would know that, going in, which made the interruption that much more disturbing.

"Check it out."

Ahead of them, Lyons's Cadillac was parked in front of Cavillo's rambling hacienda. Pulling up behind him, they could see the front door standing open, like the gate.

"He isn't wasting any time."

"Hey, suppose he does it all himself," Gadgets said, putting on a crooked grin. "We still get paid?"

"Don't worry, man. You'll get your fifty cents an hour, just like everybody else."

"Well, that's okay, then."

Moving up the steps, they had their automatic weapons ready, scanning left and right for any sign of trouble from the grounds. Surprisingly the rancho seemed deserted.

"I thought Cavillo had a staff," Blancanales said.

"Must all be inside. Let's check it out."

They found one of the staff inside the open doorway, limp and leaking on a priceless Oriental rug. His open jacket showed an automatic in a shoulder rig, but he had been too slow to reach it when Lyons took him down.

"That's two."

"Which ought to leave us nine or ten, at least."

"Would you believe they're on vacation?"

A sudden roar of shotgun blasts and automatic fire cut short their speculation. It was upstairs, by the sound, but Blancanales laid a hand on Schwarz's arm before his partner made a beeline for the spiral staircase.

"Hang on a second."

"Why?"

"Try this."

Three gunners suddenly materialized in a corridor on their left, two brandishing pistols, the middleman packing a stubby riot shotgun. Somehow, they had missed Lyons's entrance and his move upstairs, but there was no way they could overlook the sounds of combat emanating from the second floor. Now, they were facing strangers armed with automatic weapons in the master's parlor, and in such a situation there was only one appropriate response.

They opened fire.

Blancanales broke to the left, Schwarz to the right. It wasn't a maneuver that required discussion, combat reflex taking over when the guns went off. They had been fighting side by side since Vietnam, a lifetime past, and there were times when Blancanales honestly believed that he could pick up Gadgets's thoughts.

He belly flopped behind a couch that was all heavy wood and leather, feeling it absorb a shotgun blast and several rounds from someone's semiauto pistol. Wriggling on his knees and elbows, Blancanales made it to the far end of the sofa, braced himself and prepared to make his move.

Somewhere behind him, Schwarz's MAC-10 made a sound like heavy canvas ripping, and one of Augustin Cavillo's gunners bleated out a cry of pain. It was the opening that Blancanales had been waiting for, and he wasn't about to waste it.

Moving clear of cover on his knees, he found a target fifteen feet away and let his Uzi do the talking, half a dozen Parabellum manglers on their way with one twitch of his index finger. Blancanales saw the pistolero break into a jerky little death jig, crimson spouting from the holes in his chest and abdomen. He got off one more shot before he fell, but it was wasted on the ceiling, taking out a lamp designed to imitate a wagon wheel.

And that left on, the hardcase with the 12-gauge.

Whatever else he might have been, the shooter wasn't yellow. With his sidekicks down, he could have run for daylight, but he stood his ground. He stepped into the open, firing from the hip, first left, then right.

They took him down together, Blancanales stroking off a short burst when the shooter swung toward Gadgets, Schwarz finishing it as the gunner was falling backward with a dazed expression on his face.

Three up, three down.

Upstairs, silence had replaced the sounds of combat.

"Wait!" Blancanales called as Gadgets headed for the stairs. "We still aren't finished here."

"Goddamn it!"

Moving cautiously along a spacious corridor, they checked an empty den and dining room before they reached the kitchen. Half a dozen servants huddled in a corner there. Based on their clothing, Blancanales made them as a butler, a chauffeur, two maids and cooks. Both of the women were in tears, and no one showed the least desire to fight or die for Augustin Cavillo.

"Satisfied?" Schwarz asked.

"Let's go."

ALL THINGS CONSIDERED, Lyons thought the probe was going better than he had any right to expect. The racket issuing from downstairs told him Schwarz and Blancanales had arrived, and they were mopping up the troops who missed him coming in.

Or maybe, getting mopped up on their own?

No way.

He knew the Able warriors well enough to feel a twinge of sympathy for their opponents. Just a twinge, though. Not enough to wish the sleazy bastards well, by any means.

In front of him Cavillo's last two hardmen lay like broken crash-test dummies in the middle of a spacious hallway, leaking blood and brains. The pair had seen him coming, pinned him down with probing fire and tried to rush him once they had him on the spot.

Bad move.

Between the silencer-equipped Beretta and his big Colt Python, Lyons had them covered. Never mind that he was acting like a goddamned cowboy, coming out with two guns blazing. If it worked, you said a silent prayer of thanks and turned your mind to what came next.

Cavillo.

Lyons had a fix on his primary target, two doors down, a bedroom on the right. The door was closed and maybe barricaded from within, but there was no more time to waste. For all he knew the chicken hawk might have a child inside the bedroom with him, or he might be slipping out the window.

The big ex-cop checked both his weapons, making sure that each was fully loaded. He moved silently along the hallway, stepping over bodies in his path. The floor was solid underfoot, no creaking boards, but Lyons had to figure that Cavillo would be ready for rapping on his chamber door. The gunners would have told him if they had the situation well in hand, but as it was...

No pain, no gain.

He stepped back from the door a pace and hit it with a flying kick beside the crystal knob. The latch exploded, zinging shattered hardware right across the room.

The Able Team warrior went in low and fast, a shoulder roll that brought him up beside an ornate chest of drawers, the big Colt Magnum tracking, anxious for a target. Paco gave him one, a blur of motion on his left with more speed than Lyons would have given the pervert bastard credit for.

Cavillo's destination was a balcony. He pegged a shot at Lyons, missing by an easy yard, and Lyons gave one back, the Python bucking in his fist.

The man took it in the side and did a sloppy pirouette, his next shot wasted on the headboard of his king-size bed. So much for the alarm clock, as Cavillo hit the right-hand door and kept on going through the glass, a shrill cry ripped from straining vocal cords. He tried to keep his balance, but couldn't make it, slicing fingers on the jagged glass and fractured wooden slats before he fell.

He still had a survivor's instinct, even so. Almost before he hit the tile outside, Cavillo fired another shot at Lyons, close enough to make him duck his head and miss a heartbeat.

"Damn!"

The Python roared again, a miss this time, with stucco blasting from the door frame in a cloud of plaster dust. Cavillo scooted backward on his heels and elbows, firing two more rounds from what appeared to be a pocket automatic, shattering a mirror on the nearby vanity.

How many shots was that?

It was a risky business, guessing the capacity of unknown weapons. Paco might have three rounds left, or ten. In either case, though, he was short on cover, edging out of sight in a maneuver that left one knee exposed, poking around the corner of the doorjamb as a target too tempting to resist.

Lyons pictured himself on the target range, lining up a shot with all the time in the world. In fact it took him all of a second and a half, cocking the Python's hammer with his thumb to minimize the trigger pull, squeezing off the shot with loving care.

Cavillo's knee exploded, the resultant shriek of pain erupting as if from mangled flesh itself. He tumbled out of hiding, clutching himself with one hand, firing blindly with the other, peppering the walls and ceiling of his room to no effect.

The Able Team leader waited him out, hearing the hammer fall on an empty chamber before he emerged from cover. Crossing the bedroom toward Cavillo, he suddenly heard footsteps in the corridor outside and pivoted to bring the doorway under fire.

"You want to watch that," Blancanales said.

"Hey, you ought to call ahead."

"I didn't have a quarter, man. What's happening?"

"Just mopping up."

"You need a hand?"

"Not this time."

Lyons stepped across the threshold to the patio and kicked Cavillo's useless pistol out of reach. He knelt beside the chicken hawk and let Cavillo see the Python.

"Your party's canceled, scumbag. Are the children here?"

"You will let me live?" Cavillo asked.

"I'll think about it."

"They are in the basement."

"Fair enough."

As Lyons turned toward his teammate, Cavillo scrambled for his hideaway gun sheathed in an ankle holster.

The echo of the shot from Lyons's Python eclipsed Cavillo's dying scream, and there was only ringing silence in the house as he retreated toward the bedroom door.

"The basement," Lyons told them, holstering his Colt.

"Let's do it," Blancanales answered. "Gadgets has a call to make."

"What call is that?"

"We caught a page. Three guesses."

Lyons shook his head. "All this, and I thought we'd get a coffee break, at least."

"You'll get enough rest when you're dead."

"I guess."

"Let's shag," Gadgets told them, moving toward the stairs. "A house this size, they've got to have a freaking telephone."

# CHAPTER THREE

*La Galite, Mediterranean Sea*
*Saturday, 12:07 a.m.*

The Zodiac inflatable was running dark and silent, with its outboard engine muffled by a special insulated hood. The island was a jagged shadow, pitch-black with a sprinkling of stars behind it. There were faint lights showing, halfway up the seaward slope, but they weren't designed to reach the water or the five men in their speeding boat.

"Be ready," Yakov Katzenelnbogen told the other members of Phoenix Force. It was a pointless warning, but he felt obliged to mouth the words, as each of them felt duty-bound to give his gear a final check.

"I make it ninety seconds ETA," said Calvin James. He was their pointman, and the only one who didn't have to smear his face and hands with combat cosmetics to conceal pale flesh.

In ninety seconds they would be on shore. From that point, Katzenelnbogen knew that damn near anything could happen, but he would have bet his life on these men in a pinch.

In fact he had already done exactly that.

The raid had been a long time coming. Close to four years since a suitcase bomb had detonated in the cargo bay of Worldwide Airlines #106, above Kilkenny, Ireland. Six weeks had been spent picking up the pieces, another eight months passing while the President's commission plowed through reams of testimony, scientific documents, forensic evidence. Three months later a sanitized report was released that blamed the Libyans, withholding any names of individuals responsible for wiping out 267 lives. All that, and the indictments were the hard part, moving at the speed of sound inside a vacuum, but they finally got it done.

The lucky winner was a die-hard terrorist from Tripoli named Fazir Awbari. He had come a long way from his adolescent days in Black September, when he helped deliver weapons for the Munich massacre. A bust for reckless driving made him miss the show, and psychiatric profiles on the guy suggested that he had been compensating for his "failure" ever since. The grapevine had it that he rubbed shoulders with the PLO, Jihad and Hezbollah. Awbari was a killer who made up with calculated cruelty what he lacked in terms of conscience. These days, he was an idea man, letting young psychopaths act out his morbid fantasies, but he was still acknowledged as the "best" around, a terrorist who put Carlos the Jackal in the shade.

And it was the indictment handed down the previous Thursday that had brought the men of Phoenix Force so far from home. But for Yakov Katzenelenbogen, home wasn't that far away—two hours, give or take, by plane to Tel Aviv. He had long since cut his ties to the Mossad, but the war was everywhere.

This night, it brought him to a tiny speck of land a mile off the Tunisian coast, where one Awbari made his home away from home.

Katz would have been pleased to execute the terrorist on sight, but his orders were specific: seize and hold for extradition.

Rough translation: grab his ass and bring him home for trial.

It was an action calculated to provoke Tunisian diplomats, but Washington was tired of bending over backward to appease mass murderers and those who sheltered them with legal technicalities. Possession was nine-tenths of the law in his case, and the other one-tenth didn't count.

Still, killing off Awbari would have been the easy way to go. Less risk to Katzenelenbogen's men, for one thing, while reducing any chance of an escape.

Too bad.

He held the tiller with his good left hand and gripped his Uzi with the stainless-steel prosthesis on his right. For the occasion he had sprayed the custom pincer mechanism with a coat of flat black paint.

No point in taking chances, after all.

He made it something less than forty seconds now and concentrated on the shoreline, counting down the doomsday numbers in his mind.

GARY MANNING HIT the rocky beach a step behind Calvin James, helping his teammate haul the Zodiac inflatable ashore. They were 150 yards due east of the Awbari dock and theoretically invisible to sentries he kept posted on the shoreline. The terrorist was paranoid, but you could hardly blame him.

It was how he stayed alive.

The other members of the team were all on shore now, fanning out and following their orders silently, like moving parts of a sophisticated weapon. The Canadian was paired with Rafael Encizo, jogging toward a goat track etched in weather-beaten stone, their destination—a cliff sixty feet directly overhead. The other three would head downrange to take the pier before they closed in on Awbari's hillside villa.

The Uzi Manning carried had been fitted with a silencer, in preparation for the likelihood that he and Encizo would make first contact with the enemy. Officially it didn't matter who they killed on their approach, as long as they were able to retrieve Awbari still alive and kicking for the run back to their waiting submarine. From that point on he'd be someone else's headache, handled by the diplomats and prosecutors.

It was more than he deserved.

They reached the cliff, a quick flash of Encizo's penlight to confirm position, and they started up the narrow track. He made it something close to forty-five degrees, and Manning was relieved that they were climbing in the dark, instead of coming down. If all went well, they would remove Awbari by a different route.

They had a layout of Abwari's villa from a CIA informant in the PLO. It had been seven months since their informant visited the island, and the dozen guards in residence last spring could easily have multiplied, but they were counting on the floor plan of Abwari's house to be unchanged.

Above them, somewhere close at hand, came the sound of footsteps crunching stone. Encizo suddenly became a statue, Manning frozen in his shadow, index finger tightening around the Uzi's trigger. There were voices now, speaking in what sounded like Arabic. He didn't understand, but from their tone, Manning gathered there was no alarm in progress.

Not yet, anyway.

Manning and Encizo resumed their climb, and two minutes later they were at the top. The Arab voices were farther away, but still audible. The big Canadian made it something in the neighborhood of fifty feet, and definitely to their left, between his own position and the villa. There would be no circumventing these guards, once they made their move.

"You ready?" Encizo asked.

"As ready as I'll ever be."

"On three."

He listened to the Cuban counting, focused on the stone beneath his feet, the sheer drop at his back. When Encizo moved forward Manning followed him instinctively, their shadows separating to eliminate one bunched-up target for their enemies.

No freebies, this time.

There were three Arabs, dressed in army-surplus jackets, denim pants and boots. All three were packing AK-47s, but surprise took over for a heartbeat as they found themselves confronted with a pair of strangers, faces painted black and aiming submachine guns from the hip.

Too late.

The Uzis took them down in something like a second and a half, three bodies stretched out on the rugged plateau of the cliff. The loudest sound was that of fallen weapons clattering on stone, an undertone of tinkling brass as empty casings bounced away into the darkness.

Done.

Whatever happened at the house, if would be that much easier because their enemy had three less guns.

"It's time," Encizo said.

"I know."

They left the corpses where they lay and proceeded toward the villa. They had drawn first blood, and it was time for more. Ironically the only terrorist they weren't allowed to kill was the most brutal of the lot.

FAZIR AWBARI WAS AMUSED by the American attempt to frighten him. He had enjoyed the headlines, citing his indictment on 267 counts of murder, all the sound and fury in the media about the possibility of extradition and a formal trial. The running dogs of fascist Israel had to find him first, and even that wouldn't help them.

Not while the Tunisian government was forced to coexist with Colonel Moammar Khaddafi as its next-door neighbor.

It was totally delicious, when Awbari stopped to think about it. He had read the definition of a perfect crime somewhere, long years ago, when he was still a student radical. Contrary to popular belief, the perfect crime wasn't a secret from the world at large. The *truly* perfect crime was one in which the perpetrators were identified and yet remained untouchable, beyond the law.

Of course, it was inaccurate to speak of revolutionary acts as "crimes." There was a holy war in progress, whether the Americans and others of their ilk acknowledged it or not. It had begun in 1948, when scheming British politicians ripped the very heart from Palestine and gave it to the Zionists without so much as asking the inhabitants if they would mind. From that day to the present there had been no peace, would be none while the dark, malignant growth of Israel still endured.

In such a war, there were no innocents, no noncombatants. Anyone who didn't stand against the Zionist regime was automatically fair game, an enemy by definition. Terror was the only weapon readily available to broken men, and those who took their orders from Fazir Awbari used it well. Each incident produced the same attacks by Western journalists and diplomats, but that was all beside the point.

In terrorism there was no such thing as bad publicity.

Drawn from his reverie by the sound of gunfire, Awbari set down his cup coffee and took an automatic pistol from the top drawer of his desk. He stood ready when his second in command burst through the study doorway, wild-eyed, with a dazed expression on his face.

"Fazir—"

"I hear. See to the men."

He used another precious moment running down the possibilities. Israelis liked to play commando games, but he couldn't rule out betrayal by his so-called comrades in the struggle. Angry words with Arafat had left the two of them not speaking for the past three weeks, and no one with a brain would ever fully trust Abu Nidal. A major reason why the war dragged on so long had always been the childish rivalry between committed warriors of the cause.

But no matter who had chosen to attack him here, the move would fail. His soldiers were the best, and he was ready to evacuate, if need be, on a moment's notice.

Starting now.

It pleased some Western journalists to call him mad, but none mistook him for a fool.

CALVIN JAMES SQUEEZED OFF another silenced burst in the direction of Awbari's sentries and saw the last of them go down, but it was too damned late to cancel out the burst of AK-47 fire that had undoubtedly alerted everyone inside the villa, still some sixty yards away.

The dock, ironically, had been no problem. They'd come up on two gunners from their blind side, catching them as they were concentrating on the open sea. Two silenced pistol rounds from twelve feet out, and they were finished, one stretched out facedown across the pier, his partner plunging headlong off the dock into the murky water.

After that, it should have been a relatively simple move to climb the hand-hewn steps and flank Awbari's villa, taking down the other sentries one by one.

But they hadn't counted on a sleeper.

If Awbari had surprised the young man dozing at his post, the consequences would have been severe, and so the lookout found himself a sheltered niche approximately halfway up the hillside, huddled with his rifle clasped between his knees. The men of Phoenix Force would never know what woke him, but he came up firing.

The burst went wild, and he was dead a heartbeat later, but the noise from his weapon was all that mattered. After that, their hopes for a surprise attack were literally shot to hell.

The other sentries had responded quickly, three of them so far, and they had all made noise enough to wake the dead before they went down under short, precision bursts of automatic fire. It must have sounded strange inside the villa, like a weird, one-sided battle, but Awbari would be waiting for them now. The clock was ticking, any way you sliced it.

Time to move.

David McCarter pounded past James on his left, and the ex-SEAL heard Yakov Katzenelenbogen coming up the rocky stairs behind him, breathing hard.

He leaped across the body of a fallen Arab, blanking out the image of a dead face with the eyes wide open, staring sightlessly through space. Awbari's home away from home was close enough that James could make out human silhouettes behind the flimsy curtains now, their jerky haste an indication of the combat preparations being made.

From soft and silent they had gone to heavy-metal hardball in a few brief moments, but it wasn't the prospect of a fight that worried Calvin James. Their orders were specific: bring Fazir Awbari back alive at any cost. From this point on it meant that they would have to double-check each target, hold their fire if there was any doubt at all, risk everything to save a piece of human scum who should have gone down with his Black September cronies twenty years ago.

Another AK-47 opened up in front of them, steel jackets whining off the rocks and causing James to veer off course. He heard McCarter cursing, followed by the muffled sound of Uzi fire. James sighted on the sentry's muzzle-flash and fired a short burst of his own, perhaps enough of a diversion for McCarter to complete his stalk and kill.

It worked.

The Arab had a chance to recognize his peril in the final seconds of his life, unleashing a scream that eclipsed the stuttering bark of his rifle and going down in a heap as McCarter stitched him from navel to throat.

James followed McCarter toward the house, wishing the open slope afforded better cover from their enemies. They were within fifty feet of their destination when a broad picture window exploded and it all went to hell.

THE BANGS of stun grenades were slightly muffled by a set of intervening walls, but Katzenelenbogen had to squint against the stroboscopic glare of the explosions to preserve his night vision. Circling the villa in a rush, he left the mopping up to younger men, convinced their quarry would have planned against this day, anticipating danger in his own backyard.

Whatever else Fazir Awbari was, he rated high marks for survival in the past two decades. The Mossad and Israel's "Wrath of God" assassination teams had tried to kill him several times, and an equal number of attempts by "brother" terrorists had also failed to do the job. Awbari knew the risks involved and never let himself be caught without an exit hatch.

Not even here.

The rugged slope put strain on Katzenelenbogen's thighs, his muscles burning as he ran uphill, but he was gaining now. A few more seconds, and his instinct would be vindicated or disproved. He would either have the man they sought, or else he could approach the villa from behind and help the others with a room-to-room search. At worst he'd have wasted several moments on the fringes of the killing field, and there was death enough to go around.

He came around the corner in a crouch and met Awbari just emerging from the villa, with a younger gunman in the lead. Katz froze in his tracks and let them gain some distance from the house. He didn't want the terrorist ducking back inside before he had a chance to make his tag.

It would have been so easy, even now. A firm hand on the Uzi, tracking left to right and back again. Two lifeless bodies on the ground. Case closed.

Except that Awbari had a date with justice back in Washington, D.C. No matter that the trial would offer him a chance to air his poison in the media. The good news was that he'd be exposed to millions for the sadistic animal he was. The revelation of his crimes in court, with documenting evidence, would also put more heat on Libya and other sponsors of the long guerrilla war on Israel.

As for Awbari's bodyguard...

The silenced Uzi spit a burst of Parabellum rounds from twenty yards, the hardcase Arab dying on his feet, a dazed expression on his face. Awbari saw him die and swiveled to confront his enemy, an automatic pistol in his right hand, while the left groped blindly for his fallen comrade's rifle.

Katzenelenbogen ducked the first wild rounds and let his Uzi dangle by its shoulder strap, his left hand fastening around the Crossman air gun tucked inside his belt. It held a single tranquilizer dart, and a miss would mean reloading under fire, perhaps a fatal blunder at the present range.

So, he determined not to miss.

Awbari's second shot was closer, and the third round closer still. A chip of stone drew blood from Katzenelenbogen's cheek, but he was ready now, the Crossman's sights lined up for target acquisition. He squeezed the trigger gently, praying for a solid hit.

The terrorist cursed and brought a hand up to the bare skin of his neck, too late. The dart discharged its payload on impact, and removing it a second later did no earthly good at all. Awbari managed one more shot before the drugs kicked in, a screamer over Katzenelenbogen's head.

The tough Israeli waited for his target to topple forward, smiling as the man's face made impact with the stony ground. Too bad about that famous nose. Perhaps it could be reconstructed in a prison hospital.

He rose and moved to stand beside the prostrate terrorist, aware that sounds of combat had abated from the house behind him. He was ready with his submachine gun when a shadow-figure filled the open doorway, but he held his fire as a familiar voice called out.

"He's not in here," McCarter said.

"I have him."

"Still alive?"

"Damn right. The others?"

"Down and out. No casualties on our side."

"Fair enough."

McCarter came to help him lift the prostrate terrorist. It was a long walk down the hillside to their Zodiac inflatable, but there was no one left to chase them now.

In twenty minutes, give or take, they'd be back aboard the submarine and on their way. Katz found that he was looking forward to his next report to Stony Man.

# CHAPTER FOUR

*Madison County, Virginia*
*Sunday, 9:15 a.m.*

"I wish we had some kind of fix on what this squeal is all about," Gadgets Schwarz said.

Carl Lyons locked eyes with him in the rearview mirror. "Did you think they'd run it down when you were calling from Cavillo's house?"

"We could have set a call-back."

"SOP," Blancanales said from the shotgun seat. "They'll tell us what we need to know when someone thinks we need to know it."

"Even so, to call us in like this..." Schwarz let the comment trail away, examining the scenic countryside beyond his window.

They were rolling through the Blue Ridge Mountains east of Sperryville, on Skyline Drive. The Chevy Blazer was a loaner from the Justice motor pool in Washington. It wore Virginia plates and had a little something extra underneath the hood in case they needed speed, more extras tucked away discreetly out of view, if they should choose to stand and fight.

All window dressing on the present run, Lyons thought, when the chances were that they'd neither have to run nor fight. A simple briefing—maybe not so simple, given the conditions of their summons—but it wasn't like they should expect an ambush.

Not until they got their marching orders.

The Blue Ridge Mountains were a far cry from Los Angeles, where Lyons had begun the twisted trek that led him here. How many times had he been moved to ask himself "What if?"

What if his path had never crossed Mack Bolan's in those early days, when Lyons was a young detective working Homicide and Bolan was a one-man army with a hard-on for the Mafia?

What if he had decided Bolan's world was too intense the first time out, rejecting Hal Brognola's offer of a federal job that sent him undercover, working on the kind of cases where you came out bloody every time?

What if he had refused when Able Team was organized to play a role in Project Phoenix, based at Stony Man Farm?

Moot questions now, but sometimes in a quiet, contemplative moment Lyons still amused himself by playing out alternatives. Sometimes he saw himself in charge of a police division, rising through the ranks of LAPD brass. Or maybe he decided to retire and take it easy, open up a stylish seafood restaurant in Malibu. Get rowdy on the weekends with an up-scale yuppie crowd.

Sure thing.

"So what's funny?" Blancanales asked, catching Lyons's smile.

"Daydreaming."

"Beautiful," Schwarz said. "Our wheelman's in the twilight zone."

They could have flown from Washington, but they had opted for an early-morning drive, a vote of two-to-one with Schwarz dissenting. After Mexico the Shenandoah National Park was a treat for the eyes, lush greenery everywhere, with traces of morning fog still hanging in between the stately trees. A mile back, Lyons had been forced to brake while half a dozen deer had crossed the highway, a speckled fawn bringing up the rear. They were a world away from drugs and ragged beggars and the blazing desert sun.

He liked it fine.

Which didn't mean he was blasé about their summons to the Farm, by any means. He shared the curiosity of his companions, but he knew that picking it apart would get them nowhere. When the time came, they'd be enlightened . . . more or less.

The Farm was coming up, with orchards masking the perimeter, the barbed wire barely noticeable from the road. It wasn't much in terms of a defensive line, but it was never meant to be. The real defenses lay within, concealed from prying eyes. Intruders would be scanned by compact TV cameras and tracked by motion sensors, headed off by mounted guards and dogs and foot patrols. If anyone got through the orchards, they were facing open, cultivated fields where "farm hands" traveled armed by day and hidden sentries watched their turf through Startron scopes at night. In theory you could only reach the farmhouse with an invitation from the management.

Carl Lyons sometimes told himself that he could make it, if he had to, but he never really felt the urge to try.

Another time, perhaps.

This visit, they had come in answer to an urgent summons from the Man, and that meant there was work to do. No time for bullshit games.

"You think he'll be here?" Blancanales asked.

"Who's 'he'?"

"I mean the sarge," Blancanales replied.

"In a few more minutes," Lyons told him, "we'll find out."

The narrow access road had nothing in the way of signs to beckon tourists, but a few were bound to try it out from time to time. A hundred yards from Skyline Drive, they saw a cautionary notice of restricted access. Fifty more, and they were warned that trespassers would be prosecuted to the fullest extent of the law. If any strangers missed the point and kept on going, they were likely to encounter armed resistance in due course.

Lyons knew the guards were out today, as always, but they didn't show themselves to challenge Able Team. These visitors were welcome.

*Stony Man Farm*

"HEY, SRIKER," Aaron Kurtzman's deep voice issued from the intercom, "we've got a fix on Able coming in. You want to say hello?"

"I'm on my way."

Bolan rolled out of bed and retrieved his shorts from the floor, slipping into them before he reached for his discarded jeans.

"I wish we had more time," Barbara Price said, curled up beneath the rumpled sheets. "You need some R and R."

The warrior smiled at her. "So, what was this?"

"A little welcome home," she told him mischievously. "But I'm not convinced you got the full effect."

"I couldn't take much more."

"A big, strong boy like you? I bet you could."

"Don't tempt me."

Barbara knelt behind him on the mattress, both arms circling his neck, her firm breasts pressed against his back. "Would that be possible?"

He reached around and stroked her hip, picked up the makings of a tremor as his fingers did the walking. "Mmm. I wouldn't be surprised."

"So, prove it." Nimble fingers reached for his belt.

"I can't right now."

She sighed and pulled away. "I know. Can't blame a girl for trying. If Aaron asks, I'll be there in a minute."

"Right."

It had been many weeks since Bolan had worked with Able Team. He had known the three men for a lifetime—Schwarz and Blancanales going back to Bolan's tour in Vietnam, Carl Lyons from his early L.A. blitz against the Mafia. When Bolan organized his private death squad, mopping up the town with mafioso Julian DiGeorge, Schwarz and Blancanales were the friendly survivors, later teaming up and keeping track of Bolan's progress as high-tech private security consultants. Lyons, meanwhile, had drifted from LAPD into covert work with Hal Brognola's Sensitive Operations Group, later reborn as Project Phoenix with its nerve center located at Stony Man Farm.

The warrior exited his quarters on the second floor and headed toward the stairs. They took him down to the entryway and out to the front porch of the main house, where Aaron Kurtzman waited in his wheelchair.

Bolan didn't have to ask about the holdup. There had been some extra mopping up to do in Mexico, Able Team saddled with seven confused, frightened children before they left Augustin Cavillo's desert ranch. Arranging the delivery to federal officers without confessing to a string of homicides had been a trick, but Blancanales worked it out. They didn't call him "The Politician" for nothing. By this time, Bolan estimated that the stolen children were back in their homes, for better or worse, and they would have to deal with any trauma flashbacks on their own.

It was a hard life, all the way around, but there were compensations.

When you took a savage down sometimes, and knew beyond a shadow of a doubt that you were sparing future victims, some perhaps unborn, at least you had the satisfaction of a job well done.

One man *could* make a difference, even now, when satellite TV and supersonic aircraft seemed to shrink the world and thus diminish every human being on the planet. Even when the savages appeared to have control, there was a shining ray of hope that any man could grasp, with courage and determination.

Bolan watched the Blazer drawing closer, finally picking out Carl Lyons at the wheel. "They made fair time," he said, "all things considered."

"I suppose," the Bear replied. "They weren't thrilled at being called in the middle of a mission."

"They'll survive."

"I'll hold you to that, Striker."

"My pleasure."

Bolan stepped down off the porch to greet three of his closest living friends. There was a ramp to accommodate Kurtzman's chair, but he stayed where he was, giving Bolan and the Able warriors a semiprivate moment that would have to last them for a while.

A guard in denim took the Blazer after Lyons, Schwarz and Blancanales claimed their flight bags. They had traveled light, aware that no field operative hung around the Farm for very long. A day or two on average, and they hit the road again, bound for the middle of a shitstorm.

Bolan led them back to the porch and another round of handshakes with Kurtzman. Barbara Price was waiting for them in the open doorway, topping off the round of greetings with a smile for each new arrival. Once across the threshold, a mild sobering effect set in, with wisecracks briefly fading in the stretch. The steel door closed behind them, shutting out the light.

"Is Hal around?" Blancanales asked.

"On his way," Kurtzman replied. "Should be anytime."

"Somebody want to tell us what the action is?"

"In due time," Price told him. "He's saving that for when you're all together."

"Phoenix?" Lyons asked.

"They had a longer trip. Say early afternoon."

"So, what's for lunch?" Schwarz asked.

"At half-past nine?"

"I'm still a growing boy."

"We noticed," Lyons answered, poking Gadgets's stomach with an index finger.

"Hey, I'll put my pecs against yours, any day."

"You'll have to catch me, first."

Bolan listened to the men who risked their lives each time they took the field, and smiled. They had this moment coming, time to let their guard down for a while without considering the cost. A chance to physically and mentally unwind.

Before Brognola brought them back to here and now.

"TEN MINUTES," Leo Turrin said. "We'll have to wait for Phoenix."

Hal Brognola shifted in the helicopter seat, his eyes still focused on the wooded Blue Ridge Mountain peaks below. A car inched by on Skyline Drive, resembling a Matchbox toy from cruising altitude.

"No problem," he replied. "They're due within the hour."

"Too bad about Awbari's nose."

"Too bad it couldn't be the bastard's neck, you mean?"

"It crossed my mind."

"Mine, too. Prevailing wisdom is, the trail will be an international event, restating our commitment to peace in the Middle East without giving terrorists the run of the neighborhood."

"Good luck."

Brognola's mind had long since left Awbari in the dust, focused on the new problem that had landed on his desk some forty-eight hours earlier. Granted that Sunday was the earliest feasible day for an all-hands meeting, he still felt as if he were gold-bricking, wasting precious time.

It was Brognola's way to grab a problem by the neck and squeeze until it coughed up a solution he could live with. The alternative was coming up with a solution of your own and ramming it directly down the problem's throat.

Whatever worked.

His latest problem was a bitch, no doubt about it, and he had to keep his fingers crossed that someone on the team at Stony Man—or all of them together— would be capable of pulling off a minor miracle. The President had made it plain enough that countless lives would be ravaged or destroyed unless they made the puzzle pieces fit without delay.

It was the kind of crisis situation Stony Man had been constructed to accommodate, and none of Hal Brognola's handpicked personnel had let him down so far. He had no reason to believe they ever would, but at the same time, they were only flesh and blood. Each time he put them in the field, his troops went one-on-one with the prevailing laws of probability. They had sustained their share of losses—April Rose, Andrzej Konzaki and Keio Ohara killed in action; Aaron Kurtzman consigned to a wheelchair for life—but the team had survived and continued to function. Dedication kept them going, and a staunch refusal to surrender in the face of overwhelming odds.

But someday, the big Fed suspected, guts and brains were bound to come up on the short end of the stick.

Unlike the landing strip at Stony Man, the helipad was near the house. It doubled as a basketball court and looked entirely ordinary from the air, if anyone should overfly the Farm and chance to take a look below. Brognola knew it happened now and then, but landing was an altogether different proposition. Scheduled flights were fine, but unexpected drop-ins would receive a single warning to evacuate the area. If they were dumb enough to press their luck, the Farm's defensive capabilities included a battery of 20-mm Gatling guns concealed inside the barn. Six thousand armor-piercing rounds per minute was the average rate of fire, and anyone who lived through that would have Brognola's full attention, guaranteed.

He picked out some familiar faces as the chopper hovered, gently setting down. The rotors were decelerating as Brognola shed his safety harness, retrieved his briefcase and debarked.

From left to right he and Turrin shook hands with Bolan, Blancanales, Schwarz and Lyons.

"I hope you've got the coffee on."

"It's always on," Bolan assured Brognola. "What I understand, in another month or two, they even plan to wash the pot."

"I'll keep my fingers crossed."

It was a short walk to the house, and while Brognola couldn't see the guards, he knew that they were being watched. He was expected—hell, he *ran* the place, in terms of issuing commands—but the security relaxed for no man. Grim experience had taught the lesson that it never paid to let your guard down, even for a moment. If Bolan and the rest were able to relax at Stony Man, they did so only in the knowledge that professionals remained alert to any sudden threat or deviation from routine.

Some would have said it was a dreary way to live, and there were times when Hal Brognola would have readily agreed. But living in a state of siege was still one up on the alternative, no matter how you ran it down.

Dead warriors didn't pull their weight.

And right now, Hal Brognola needed all the warriors he could get.

THE TWIN-ENGINE Beechcraft was cruising at five thousand feet. Yakov Katzenelenbogen had a starboard window seat, with David McCarter sitting directly across the aisle, the other men of Phoenix Force spread out behind them to allow for legroom. It wasn't a long flight, taking off from Fort Belvoir, a few mines south of Alexandria, but Katz was tired of traveling. It would be good to plant his feet on solid ground again and let them stay there for a while.

The coded message had been waiting for them when they got Fazir Awbari to the waiting submarine and left him with a Navy medic, under guard.

When the message was decoded, it had been from Stony Man, of course. An urgent summons, wiping out the downtime they'd normally expect between one mission and the next. Cal James had said they ought to organize a soldier's union, maybe strike to win a week's vacation in between successive battles, and the joke had brought a fleeting smile to Katzenelenbogen's face before his curiosity took over.

There was no point sending back a query, asking what was wrong. If it was urgent, then by definition it was also secret. They'd hear the details from Brognola or Price when they arrived.

He thought about Abwari glaring at them as his escorts led him from the submarine. A team of federal agents had been waiting on the dock with legal paperwork and automatic weapons, an interpreter reciting the Miranda rights in Arabic, although Awbari's English was at least on par with Katzenelenbogen's own. They made the transatlantic crossing on an SST, five warriors feeling naked with their weapons left behind, and their reception had been covert VIP in Washington.

Passing over Stony Man Farm, the Beechcraft circled twice, its pilot touching base with ground control. The Farm would be expecting them, but there was still a basic protocol to be observed. Until the special passwords were exchanged, the Beechcraft was another bogey, marked for swift destruction.

The airstrip was constructed to accommodate most military and civilian aircraft, though a casual observe wouldn't know it from the air. The tarmac had been painted to resemble loose, plowed soil, and planted in the middle of the east-west runway was a beat-up mobile home. In this case "mobile" was the key, and Katzenelenbogen watched a tractor haul the single-wide away, allowing them a clear approach. The roof and front wall of the mobile home were hinged, he knew, and rigged to drop away in an emergency. Inside, a bank of 7.62 mm miniguns were manned and ready to demolish any hostile aircraft.

Touchdown.

Calvin James was on his feet as they began to taxi, grunting as he popped his back and shoulders. "Free at last." He grinned.

"You might not think so," Gary Manning told him, "when you hear what's next."

"Somebody giving you a peek?"

"It stands to reason. They didn't bring us all this way in such a rush to cut the grass."

"Somebody's ass is grass, I'll bet you," James replied, "and I'm the mower."

"A peculiar image at the very least," McCarter said to no one in particular. He finished off a can of Coke and left it tucked in the elastic pocket by his knee.

"Sometimes I get peculiar," James told him, "with the jet lag."

"Ah, so *that's* what does it."

Katzenelenbogen didn't mind the banter, but he suddenly felt driven by a need to feel the sunshine on his face and breathe unprocessed air. The day was clear and cool outside, with nothing to remind him of Tunisia, much less of the claustrophobic submarine. Up close, the runway's paint job wouldn't pass inspection, but it didn't have to. Anyone who got that far was either cleared to land or dead.

The car that came to meet them was a station wagon, and the driver stowed their lightweight bags in back, where Manning volunteered to take the rumble seat. As Katzenelenbogen settled in beside the driver, he was moved to ask, "Is everybody here?"

"I wouldn't know sir, honestly."

Like that was news.

He settled back to wait, as they began the short run to the house. There, all their questions would be answered—plus a few he didn't even want to ask.

## CHAPTER FIVE

*Stony Man Farm*
*Sunday, 1:45 p.m.*

The war room was located downstairs, on the western end of the basement level. Access to the chamber was by elevator, from the first-floor computer room, or through a coded security door from the basement level itself. Inside, a conference table built to seat two dozen delegates was occupied by slightly less than half that number.

Hal Brognola's position at the head of the table had little to do with rank, though he effectively commanded Stony Man Farm when he was on the premises. Barbara Price sat on the big Fed's left, holding her own as the established mission controller. A few feet to Brognola's right, Aaron Kurtzman manned a console that controlled a range of video displays and sound effects inside the conference room. The other seats were filled in rough approximation of the team divisions evident at Stony Man. Bolan had the next chair on Brognola's right, with Blancanales at his side, then Schwarz and Lyons, Leo Turrin rounding off the side. Facing them across the table were the men of Phoenix Force and pilot Jack Grimaldi, who had just arrived.

There was no artwork or superfluous adornment in the war room, but its walls were far from bare. Huge maps depicted every portion of the globe, overlaid in places with black-and-white glossies taken from spy planes and satellites orbiting in space. With the maps and photographs around him, Bolan always felt that he had somehow burrowed to the heart of the earth, surrounding himself with all manner of life, trying to decide which should continue and which should be destroyed.

It was the same choice predators made every day, except that Bolan left his own selfish interests out of the equation, examining each problem as it came, from the standpoint of how he could do the most good for people at risk, simultaneously inflicting the maximum possible damage on his enemies.

"We might as well get started," Brognola said. "We've got lots to talk about, and I imagine most of you are wondering why you're here. Well, I won't keep you in suspense."

A nod to Kurtzman and the lights began to dim, a screen descending from a ceiling fixture at the north end of the room. Another keystroke on the console, and a slide projector blazed to life, the soft drone of its fan becoming part of their environment in a heartbeat. On the screen a solemn face appeared—Caucasian, male, dark hair and eyes, with a mustache that hid the upper lip. It was the kind of photograph found on passports, drivers' licenses and booking sheets.

"Dale Hargis, DEA," Brognola said. "Two months ago, he was assigned to work a syndicate of Cubans and Colombians around Miami, bringing coke in through the Keys. They tell me he had nine years on the job."

The past tense said it all, and Bolan knew that he was looking at a dead man. They were making progress.

"Nineteen days ago," Brognola said, "he disappeared, lost touch with his control. They didn't want to hit the panic button right away, in case he had some kind of deal in progress, but they started putting feelers out. When he was gone a week, they pulled out all the stops."

"A little late," Lyons muttered.

Dale Hargis's photo was replaced by something pale and dappled red. It could have been a side of beef, except that it was wearing tattered slacks and one gray sock.

Before and after.

"Sweet Jesus." That from Calvin James. "What was it, shark?"

"Safe bet," Brognola replied, "but no one's really sure. He surfaced Thursday afternoon—a water skier hit him, actually. From what I understand it ruined her vacation."

"And didn't do *him* any good, I'll wager." There was no mirth in McCarter's voice.

"The ID took some time, without a head or hands, but they confirmed Dale Hargis from a broken leg he had in high school and a pelvic X ray taken two or three years ago when he got bounced around in a pursuit."

"Is there a cause of death?" Gary Manning asked.

"ME's office found a bullet wedged between two vertebrae," Brognola said. "Nine-millimeter Parabellum. Could have been a fatal shot. Without the upper torso, anything beyond the bullet find is guesswork."

Kurtzman tapped his keyboard with an index finger, and the bloody corpse was thankfully supplanted by another face. Hispanic this time, with the eyes concealed behind designer shades, long hair drawn back and tied off in a ponytail. It was a candid close-up, probably a telephoto job. The jacket this man wore was silk and must have cost him more than most Miami residents—the honest ones, at least—would take home in a month.

Brognola made the introductions. "Juan Rolando Escalante. Cuban. He was eighteen when he caught the boat lift out of Mariel in 1980. Spent time in detention, claimed political asylum from the Communists...you know the drill. They tried to check him out through INS and came up empty, which isn't to say that he was clean when Castro cut him loose. We know ex-cons and mental cases outnumbered legitimate refugees five-to-one on that scam, but there's no way to name them all."

"Was Hargis on this guy?" Lyons asked.

"Like glue. He was supposed to be a buyer from Atlanta, setting up a source for major weight. The DEA thinks Escalante broke his cover somehow, and they took him for a swim."

"You didn't call us in to cap some dealer in Miami," Blancanales said.

"You're absolutely right. Juan Escalante's not the problem. He's a symptom."

"So?"

"We're talking Panama, to start. Has anybody here kept track of things since Noriega went away?"

"They've had some demonstrations," Blancanales said. "Some shake-ups in the government."

"That's part of it," Brognola agreed, "but right now we're concerned with things that don't show up on CNN."

"Which brings us back to drugs," Grimaldi said.

"In spades. The GAO and DEA report that trafficking and money laundering in Panama are on the rise since Noriega took his dive. Bulk seizures of cocaine have more than doubled in the past twelve months, and I don't need to tell you what that means in terms of shipments getting through."

"You're saying Noriega kept the lid on?" There was something like amusement in Gadgets Schwarz's voice.

"Let's say his ego and his paranoia made him run a tighter ship than his successors. Everybody's scrambling for position now, inside the government and out. The drug cartels are going crazy. It's another gold rush, and everybody's cashing in for all they can before the bubble bursts."

Across the table Yakov Katzenelenbogen cleared his throat. "If DEA's on top of this—"

Brognola cut him off. "They know about it, but they're not on top of anything. Quite frankly State's inclined to look the other way right now, and make-believe we got it right the first time."

"Who's interested in this," McCarter asked, "if State is playing see-no-evil?"

"Let's just say the Man would rather have it handled quietly this time, without the Seventh Fleet."

"I guess we'd better hear some more," Bolan said, knowing that he spoke for all concerned.

Juan Escalante disappeared, replaced immediately by a smiling man in uniform at some kind of cocktail party, from the look of things. Perhaps an embassy affair. The soldier was approaching middle age and wore the lavish decorations common to a Third World military officer. His smile reminded Bolan of a hungry moray eel.

"Colonel Antonio Delvalle, of the Panama Defense Forces," Brognola said. "He's more or less responsible for stamping out the country's drug trade. What I hear from DEA, that translates into ripping off the small fry, executing those who give him any grief and letting heavy hitters buy a franchise. Last report, the going rate was something like a quarter mill' per month, per gang. That buys political insurance, banking privileges and a free pass when it comes to customs."

"This guy isn't carrying the ball alone," Grimaldi said.

"You got that right."

The next shot caught two men in stylish business suits, beaming at each other, and each held a cocktail glass.

"Same party?" Bolan asked.

"I wouldn't be surprised," Brognola replied. "You've got Jesus Avilla on the left, a presidential aide in charge of commerce and a close friend of Delvalle's. Word is, he's as dirty as they come. The joker on the right is one Ernesto Montalvo, CEO of the Panama National Bank. If anybody's keeping track, he's been connected to the BCCI for years."

Bolan frowned at mention of the notorious Bank of Credit and Commerce International. Chartered in Luxembourg during 1972, the BCCI compiled assets of $20 billion by the time its unscrupulous dealings were finally unveiled in 1990. That was the year BCCI paid a $15 million forfeiture and saw five of its bankers imprisoned for laundering drug money, but the scandal was only beginning. Within a year's time, BCCI had been linked with customers as diverse as Saddam Hussein, Ferdinand Marcos, Jimmy Carter, Oliver North, Adnan Khashoggi, the Medellín drug cartel and Manuel Noriega. It was no surprise, therefore, to find Noriega's corrupt successors still doing business at the same old stand.

"Montalvo runs the laundry," Bolan said. It didn't come out sounding like a question.

"Looks that way," Brognola told him, nodding. "And his biggest customers, right now, are these two sweethearts."

On the screen a mug shot suddenly replaced the cocktail party. Bolan locked eyes with a lean-faced predator. His dark hair was combed back and oiled to make it stay, and he had pierced ears—a diamond on the left, a gold ring on the right. An old scar ran diagonally from his lower lip, across his chin and out of sight beneath the jawline.

"Sergio Barbosa," Brognola informed his audience. "He hails from Cali, in Colombia. Word has it that he used to be a free-lance shooter for the dealers there, some paramilitary action on the side. He finally got too hot for the Colombians to handle, which should give you some idea of what we're dealing with. These days, he moves a ton of coke through Panama and handles contracts on the side."

Another mug shot came up on-screen, a round face this time, seeming softer at a glance...until you saw the eyes. They might have been cut glass, for all the life that they displayed.

"Carlos Velasco," Brognola said. "He's Barbosa's major competition at the moment, also a Colombian. Three years for smuggling in Bogotá, and he's suspected of a dozen murders, give or take, before he started dealing big-time. Panama agrees with him these days."

"Barbosa wants him out?" Grimaldi asked.

"Delvalle likes to keep the lid on, but there's no love lost between them. Anyway, it hasn't come to shooting yet."

"The source?" Rafael Encizo asked.

"Here we go."

A distance shot this time, a man emerging from a limousine, half-shielded by the body of his driver. Even so, they had a clear view of the dealer's face.

"He looks like Dracula," Grimaldi commented, and it was true.

"I'll take the vampire every time," Brognola said. "Guillermo Santiago, boys and girls. At DEA they rank him fifth or sixth among the richest dealers in Colombia. He might be moving up the scale, if the Ochoa Family keeps on taking hits the way they have been."

"Which gang is he dealing with?" McCarter asked.

"He covers both. They might not like it, but his prices are competitive and no one gives him any crap. If Barbosa and Velasco want to squabble on their own time, Santiago doesn't care. His trade is strictly cash and carry, all the way."

"Suppose he felt the competition heating up?"

Brognola smiled at Bolan's question. "Hard to say. My best guess is, he'd want to back the winner, but he tries to satisfy his customers across the board. I don't think he'd jump in to help one or the other right away, unless one side forgot to pay their bill.''

And that was something to consider, but the Executioner was not prepared to chart his strategy. Not yet. Hal's presentation wasn't finished yet, by any means.

''We've also got a wild card in the deck,'' Brognola said, as yet another face filled up the screen. He was a soldier, judging from the olive drab fatigues, but he wore no insignia of rank. His beard was neatly trimmed, a touch of gray around the chin, and Bolan made him somewhere in his forties. The cigar was vintage Castro.

''I know this man,'' Encizo said. ''At least I know his face.''

''Major Luis Rivera,'' Brognola stated. ''He's with the Cuban DSE.''

''What does the state security have to do with this?''

''Good question. For the answer we touched base with Langley. I don't need to tell you how the Company keeps track of old Fidel.''

''Go on.''

''Okay, I know you're current on the goings-on in eastern Europe. The newspeople say that communism's dead outside of Asia, but they missed a spot. When you put Castro underneath a microscope, he looks a lot like Stalin, even now.''

''What else is knew?'' Katz asked.

''What's new is Castro looking for a shoulder he can cry on. The Russians don't support him anymore and he's looking more and more like something time forgot. The OAS won't let him in, and now the Warsaw Pact is down the drain. What's a dinosaur to do?''

"You're saying he's in drugs?" James asked, a hard glint in his eye.

"Let's put it this way—Noriega and Fidel were bosom buddies from the time Noriega took power in 1981. We can assume that Castro knew about his good friend's link to Medellín, and there's no reason to assume he broke connections with the government in Panama when Noriega took his fall. The DEA sees Castro working through Rivera, underwriting shipments and taking his payoff in dollars, maybe laundered through Montalvo's bank en route to Switzerland or the Bahamas. Speaking of which..."

On cue Kurtzman keyed another slide, this time a black man in a custom-tailored suit. His diamond tie clasp caught the light, and he was holding a champagne glass. Yet another party for the rich and infamous.

"Byron St. Jacques," Brognola said. "A ranking cabinet minister in the Bahamas. On the record he's a mouthpiece for their tourist industry, reporting back to the prime minister. In fact he's Avilla's Bahamian counterpart, smoothing the way for shipments in transit to Miami and points north."

"Contacts?" Bolan asked.

Another black face appeared on the screen, a younger man this time, with wire-rimmed spectacles.

"The man to see for drugs in Nassau would be Thomas Mentzer. He's a lawyer, does a lot of business with the government in terms of tourism, casinos, this and that. His link with the Colombians through Panama is Julio Marti."

The last face in Brognola's hit parade was youthful in appearance, but it had the burned-out eyes of someone who had seen and done it all. His smile fell somewhere between a grimace and a mocking sneer.

"Which brings us back to Escalante in Miami," Brognola said, winding up. "You've met the players. Now it's time to change the script."

"The DEA has all this information, right?" James asked.

"Affirmative, but knowing it and having legal grounds to act are two entirely different things."

"I've heard that song before," Lyons commented.

"Then you recognize the tune. We've got a warrant out on Santiago, but the government in Bogotá won't extradite. Some crap about they don't know where he lives."

"Which is?"

"About a mile from Chigorodo. Say fifty miles from the Panamanian border."

"We could mention that to the authorities," Grimaldi suggested.

"We have. Somebody calls ahead before they stage a raid, and Santiago's never home. Surprise."

"So, what's the drill?" Gadgets Schwarz asked.

"We're giving up on piecework. The Man wants action to destroy the pipeline, end to end. Scorched earth."

"Does anybody really think we'll shut the cocaine off this way?" McCarter asked.

"One source, one channel. We take it as it comes. I'm not predicting any miracles."

"We've got a lot of ground to cover," Manning said.

"Agreed." It was the first time Barbara Price had spoken since the slide show started. Now, she had their full attention as the lights came up and Kurtzman silenced the projector. "There's no question you'll be scattered far and wide, but we're convinced that you can pull it off."

"So how's it play?" Lyons asked.

"You make the tag on Escalante in Miami, and proceed from there to Nassau. Contact's been arranged through DEA. They have a line on who to trust and who you should avoid."

"Like everyone in town, you mean?"

"It isn't quite that bad. You'll be in touch with a liaison from the police force. He'll know more about the local scene, which officers are on the pad and which are straight."

"About St. Jacques," Blancanales said. "If we're talking about a cabinet minister..."

"He's bought and paid for," Price replied. "If you can set him up to take a legal fall, okay. If not, you won't have anybody second-guessing your decision."

"Right."

"We're sending Striker into Panama," she continued, when there were no more questions from the men of Able Team. "No script, per se. Again, we have some working contacts on the ground, arranged through CIA. Feel free to use them if it suits you. David, Yakov and Gary will be close enough for backup in a pinch, but they're primarily concerned with Santiago's border traffic. Maybe they can find him hanging out around the homestead, for a change."

"Forgive my asking," James broke in, "but it appears to me you've left somebody out."

"No way," she answered. "You and Rafael are going into Kingston. Langley has a couple of their anti-

Castro activists on tap to help you make arrangements for the trip to Cuba.''

"Cuba? I don't suppose you've got a few Marines to spare?"

"They won't fit in your luggage, Calvin. Sorry. Anyway, you're fluent in the language, and it's old-home week for Rafael. We've also got a patch into the underground, in case you hit a snag.''

"We take the major out?''

"Affirmative. We don't expect a syndicate in place.''

"You meant it's just the government and army, little things like that.''

"You've got the picture.''

"I suppose it's too damn late to call in sick?''

"'Fraid so. No other questions?'' Price asked.

Grimaldi raised his hand. "Unless you called me out to make a fourth for bridge, I guess I ought to ask what I'll be doing.''

"Striker needs a pair of wings in Panama,'' she said. "You'll also be on call to Phoenix for a border hop, if necessary.''

"Now you're talking.'' Childlike joy lighted up Grimaldi's face.

"Okay,'' Brognola told them. "We're finished for the moment.''

But the man from Justice had it wrong, Bolan thought. They were only getting started.

And the finish line was still a lifetime down the road.

## CHAPTER SIX

*Tocumen Airport, Panama*
*Tuesday, 11:15 a.m.*

"I can't believe we flew commercial," Jack Grimaldi muttered for perhaps the fifth time since lift-off from Miami International. "I could have had us here in half the time."

"And risk a spotter when we cleared through Albrook," Bolan said.

"Relax. They've got your toys on standby, ready when we need them."

"It's not the same."

Bolan knew exactly what his old friend meant, in that regard. Commercial flying meant they had to come in naked, leaving all their hardware at the point of embarkation. He was carrying a fiberglass "letter opener," designed for agents of the CIA, but it would never take the place of his Beretta or the Desert Eagle. Weapons would be waiting for them at their destination, once they got that far, but in the meantime Bolan felt exposed. Like one of those peculiar dreams in which you go about your daily business, clocking in for work or showing up for school, remembering too late that you have left the house without your clothes.

Old habits had a way of dying hard...especially when they were the kind that helped a soldier stay alive.

Tocumen airport was located fourteen miles northeast of Panama City, facing the Pan American Highway. Their approach from the air was dramatic, coming in low over mountainous jungle, the canal just visible to starboard. Bolan's seat belt was already fastened, and he listened absentmindedly to the warnings in English and Spanish, his thoughts focused on the next hour or so.

The final approach to hostile ground was critical, he knew, and while Americans were welcome to the isthmus now, there was still a fair degree of local paranoia where they were concerned. Compound historic feelings with a need to camouflage the thriving drug trade, and you had a situation where the government and outlaw syndicates alike were on the alert for agents of the DEA and Interpol. The fact that Bolan and Grimaldi had no concrete links with either group was totally irrelevant.

If something blew their cover as a pair of copper buyers for a stateside wiring manufacturer, they were as good as dead.

They touched down safely, taxied toward the terminal. Around them, anxious passengers were on their feet and scrambling for their baggage in the overhead compartments. Bolan and Grimaldi kept their seats, feet bracketing their carryons, observing while the flight attendants tried to reassert control.

Good luck.

Inside the terminal they made directly for the baggage carousel, one suitcase each to claim before they hit the immigration passport desk and customs. Both men were alert to anything unusual—a camera snapping

candid shots of strangers in the airport, for example—
but they claimed their bags without a red flag going up.

So far, so good.

There was no reason to suspect a leak at Stony Man,
of course, but they were dealing with a broader network this time, sections of the CIA and DEA involved, along with native personnel. You could never
be too careful when your life was riding on the line.

Their bogus passports were the best that Hal Brognola's documents division could deliver. Bolan cleared
the immigration gate as Michael Belasko, with a smiling Jason Garrett on his heels. Their story of a two-
week business visit was routine and seemed to raise no
eyebrows. Under normal circumstances, there would be
no reason for the immigration agents to record their
names or double-check their whereabouts on any given
day.

The rental car had been reserved in Garrett's name,
and they paid for it with a credit card. The bill would
find its way back to Virginia, but the maze of paperwork would easily defeat a trace if something happened to the car or they were forced to dump it
unexpectedly.

The Pan American Highway was teeming with traffic as Grimaldi joined the flow, Bolan riding in the
shotgun seat, their bags in back. For just a moment
Bolan tried to picture other times, a ragtag band of
mercenaries, prospectors, and soldiers of fortune
starting their trek in Mexico and driving south through
Guatemala, El Salvador, Honduras, Nicaragua, Costa
Rica, into Panama. Some of the nervy bastards kept on
going; others never made it that far, lost along the way

in search of profit, romance, the adventure of a life-time.

Better days, perhaps, but they were gone.

There was little to say on the fourteen-mile drive into Panama City, Grimaldi keeping one eye on the rearview mirror all the way. If someone tried to take them on the road this soon, there would be little they could try beyond evasion and escape, but as it happened, they appeared to have no tail.

The streets of Panama City were crowded with vehicles and pedestrians, but Grimaldi took his cue from native drivers, leaning on the horn at frequent intervals and shifting lanes erratically to gain a jump on drivers to his left or right. It crossed Bolan's mind that the pilot was frustrated at being earthbound, handling the compact rental like an F-15 in combat. He was somewhat relieved when they pulled up in front of their hotel and left the car with a valet.

"So, what's the drill?" Grimaldi asked him as they made their way inside.

"We wait awhile," the Executioner replied. "If no one's been in touch by sundown, I go hunting on my own."

"That's what I like. Precision strategy."

He understood Grimaldi's sentiment, but at the moment there was nothing he could do. He had agreed to wait for contact from their allies in the city, but he didn't plan to waste the night, if no one got in touch.

When it came down to staging a campaign, the hell-fire warrior had some notions of his own.

*Kingston, Jamaica*
*Tuesday, 12:00 p.m.*

IF ANYONE WAS WAITING for them at Palisadoes International Airport, Rafael Encizo couldn't spot the tail. They claimed their bags and found their rental car reserved under the name of Curtis Jones, Calvin James taking the wheel for the ten-mile drive into Jamaica's capital city. The Palisadoes peninsula served as a natural breakwater for Kingston harbor, and Encizo had his first glimpse of the city from a distance, with green water and sailboats in the foreground.

"Always thought if I came down here, it would be on a vacation," James said, checking the mirrors every hundred yards or so to verify that they were clean.

"Consider this a rest stop, if you like."

"Some rest. It must feel weird, like, going home again.

The same thought had been on Encizo's mind since lifting off that morning from Miami International. The goal of "coming home" to Cuba, helping liberate his motherland from Castro's tyranny, was something in the Phoenix warrior's blood, as much a part of him as genes and chromosomes. And yet, the time for action always seemed to be mañana, losing definition as the waves of Cuban refugees made new lives in America, their anger and commitment to the cause of "Cuba Libre" handed down through generations while they made no concrete move to see it realized.

In fairness it wasn't the fault of refugees per se. Some thirty years ago, the government in Washington had been committed to removing Castro from the Cuban seat of government at any cost...or so the

White House spokesman said. Then came the Bay of Pigs, with crucial air support withdrawn to leave the exile soldiers on their own, outnumbered, hopelessly surrounded on the beach. Attempts to surgically remove Fidel were likewise fruitless, running out of steam when journalists caught on to Washington's flirtation with the Mafia on contract murders in the Caribbean. A burst of rifle fire in Dallas changed the nation and the world forever, leaving Cuban refugees to struggle for themselves in a forgotten cause.

For many the frustration had propelled them into groups like Omega 7, which struck out blindly at Soviet embassies, international airlines, even the United Nations building in New York. Others nurtured the dream of returning home to Cuba while they went about the business of their lives, for good or ill. The Mariel boat lift of 1980 brought more refugees but little hope, too many of the new arrivals drawn from prisons and lunatic asylums as Castro found a way to cut his own crime rate at America's expense. Today, many of the Marielitos were deeply involved in narcotics trading, prostitution, extortion, following in the historic footsteps of Eastern European immigrants at the turn of the last century.

Encizo didn't sympathize with those who lived outside the law, but he could understand their choice. Most of them had grown up with Communism from the moment they were born, drifting into crime at home from a combination of poverty and personal character flaws. In the United States they found a world of boundless opportunity beyond their wildest dreams, and they began to grab for all the gusto they could manage.

Rafael Encizo had selected an entirely different life-style—education followed by the military and clandestine service—but his private choice wasn't the reason he waged war against the predators in his community. In his view, every man and woman had a range of choices open in their lives, regardless of the poverty or affluence inherited at birth. A rich man could be honorable and maintain his wealth without infringing on the human rights of others. So, he thought, a poor man could preserve his dignity without adopting the behavior of a predatory beast and victimizing those who shared his troubled times.

The fact that he had grown up hating Communists in general and Castro in particular didn't make Rafael Encizo sympathize with right-wing terrorists, narcotics traffickers, or other outlaw scum who hid their crimes behind a facade of "patriotism."

As for going home...

"I'm not sure if it is home anymore," he said.

"Say what?"

"I don't remember much about Havana from the days before we left, and most of what I do remember will be gone. It's not like I can just walk in and pass for someone who's been living there for twenty years."

"Is that supposed to put my mind at ease?"

Encizo forced a smile. "At least we have our contacts on the ground."

"That's something else," James said. "With all the shit that goes on at Langley, how come we're so cozy just like that?"

"It's called not having any choice," Encizo replied. "We've used their operatives before."

"That doesn't mean I have to like it. Anytime we step outside the family, I get nervous."

"So, we'll have to watch out backs."

"I'm watching, bro. You bet your life on that."

*Miami, Florida*
*Tuesday, 1:05 p.m.*

MIAMI'S EIGHTH AVENUE runs through the heart of Little Havana, where the Cuban refugees and their descendants call it Calle Ocho. For a mile or two, a tourist can forget that he is still in the United States, imagining himself transported to another time and place. The signs are all in Spanish, Cuban restaurants and shops on every side, with traffic interrupted periodically for Catholic festivals. In the botanicas the wax or plaster saints bear many names, depending on the buyer's preference.

And it was here the men of Able Team began their mission.

"I see it," Lyons said. "A half block, on the left."

"Affirmative."

Schwarz had the wheel, with Blancanales sitting in the back. Their target was a supper club where Juan Escalante operated from a back-room office, organizing shipments out of Nassau and distributing his poison to dealers on the street.

"Suppose he isn't there?" Schwarz asked.

"We'll know him by the Jaguar," Lyons answered. "Cherry red. We miss him here, Plan B."

"I always hate Plan B."

"So, keep your fingers crossed we get it right the first time."

"Coming up."

The shiny Jaguar occupied its place of honor, near the club's back door. There were five other cars in the lot, but they all kept their distance, a kind of vehicular caste system. Lyons guessed that anyone who scratched the boss's ride was gator bait, and made a note to kick the fender coming out.

Assuming that he came out.

Considering the scope of what they had in mind, the tag on Escalante was a relatively minor thing, but it could still go sour, blow up in their faces. All it took was one wrong move, a glitch they couldn't plan for, and their game in the Bahamas would be called off on account of blood.

He felt like saying something, but his friends were doubtless having similar thoughts of their own. Each time they took the field, there were reminders of their own mortality. It wouldn't help for Lyons to raise the point now, when they needed every ounce of concentration to survive the next few moments.

Gadgets pulled in close behind the Jag and left the engine running, reaching underneath the driver's seat to draw his mini-Uzi with a silencer attached. He cocked the submachine gun, left the safety off and placed it in his lap.

"Five minutes," Blancanales announced, his voice almost disguising the soft, metallic click as he drew the bolt back on his own weapon.

"I'm on it," Schwarz replied.

"Don't hang around if anybody calls the heat."

"No sweat."

Lyons palmed his own Uzi, holding it close to his thigh as he stepped from the car. It was a short six paces to the door, no guard outside, but once across the threshold they'd have to watch each step.

The door was unlocked, telling them that Escalante still expected company. It set his teeth on edge as Lyons stepped inside, with Blancanales on his heels. If they had dealers dropping in before they finished up their business, Schwarz would have to take them in the parking lot, and that would surely blow whatever chance they had of making this a simple in-and-out.

The first guard met them fifteen seconds later, emerging from the kitchen as they moved along the hall toward Escalante's office. Taking in their weapons at a glance, he thrust a hand inside his jacket, reaching for a pistol he'd never find in time.

Lyons hit him with a 3-round burst from something like a dozen feet and slammed him back against the wall. The gunner left a crimson smear behind him as he slithered down into a seated posture, slowly toppling over on his side.

So much for simple.

"Let's motivate," Lyons said, moving swiftly toward the door marked Private at the far end of the corridor. The dining area was somewhere on their left, the kitchen on their right.

"Hey!"

The voice came from behind them, and the shooter might have scored if he had been more disciplined. Instead of crying out in shock at finding his companion slain, he should have drawn his piece and fired at once, but it was too late now, with both men pivoting to bring him under fire. The gunner tried to duck back under cover, breaking for the kitchen, but a silenced burst from Blancanales drove his face into the doorjamb, dropping him a few feet from his friend.

"God*damn* it!"

They were running out of numbers now, uncertain whether there were still more soldiers snacking in the kitchen, having no time left to double back and check. Whatever shot they still had at surprising Escalante, it required a swift, decisive move, before somebody else barged in and started raising hell.

"Let's do it!" Lyons snapped, already rushing toward the office door.

"On two!"

They were about to kick it, right feet raised in unison, when one of Escalante's people opened the door, lips forming a command to the guards who could no longer hear him.

The double blast of Parabellum manglers lifted him completely off his feet and hurled him backward, sprawling in the middle of the room. The Able Team warriors entered side by side, their weapons tracking, automatically dividing up their field of fire.

Six faces, one of them familiar from the briefing photos. Escalante lounged behind a spacious desk, a cheroot tucked in the corner of his mouth. The others stood or sat around him, formerly engrossed by what appeared to be a two-foot stack of greenbacks on the desk. The sudden death of their companion had distracted them from money for the moment, five hands groping after weapons while their leader dropped from sight behind the desk.

Lyons took the left-hand side, his finger locked around the Uzi's trigger, laying down a solid stream of fire. The fat man closest to him took six or seven rounds, the impact spinning him like a demented would-be ballet dancer, lacking only grace and talent. Lyons had quit watching by the time his face collided with a nearby filing cabinet, cutting short his awkward pirouette.

The next man up was tall and slender, with a scraggly mustache. The big pistol in his hand was probably a .45, but Lyons hit him with a burst across the chest before he had a chance to use it. Going over on his back, the shooter managed two wild shots, one of them blowing out a long fluorescent fixture while the other drilled a hole in an acoustic ceiling panel.

Number three saw Escalante drop behind the desk and tried to join him, but the dealer shoved his gunner out to stand alone. Lyons caught him on the rebound, stitching him from throat to groin with the remainder of his magazine.

On his right Blancanales took the other pistoleros down with a blazing figure eight, the two of them collapsing in a heap. One had an automatic in his hand, but there had been no opportunity for him to fire before he fell. Blood pooled around their bodies, oozing toward the desk where Escalante hid himself.

And that left one.

Lyons fed a new magazine into his weapon, holding it aimed at the desk while he drew back the bolt. Beside him, Blancanales also had the cringing dealer covered, if he tried to make a move.

"You've got three seconds," Lyons told the man. "One..."

A scuffling sound came from behind the desk, shoes scraping on the vinyl floor. They had to figure Escalante had a weapon, something.

"Two."

He risked a glance at Blancanales, found his comrade standing firm with both hands on his submachine gun, primed to see it through.

Escalante's high-pitched shriek was one part fear and one part anger. Lurching to his feet, he managed one shot from a snubby .38 before converging streams of fire ripped through him, hurled him backward, pinning him to the wall. They let him have it all, three seconds' worth, and watched him drop back out of sight behind the desk.

Good riddance.

"Works for me," Blancanales said.

"Fair enough."

A woman's scream erupted from the corridor outside, and they emerged from Escalante's office to discover several members of the kitchen staff examining the first two gunners they had killed. Blancanales shouted a warning in Spanish, and a glimpse of their weapons did the rest, cooks and dishwashers vanishing in a rush.

"They're bound to have a phone in there," the Politician said.

"I wouldn't be surprised."

They hurried past the kitchen door, no point in saying that there might be guns in there, as well as a telephone. If so, nobody chose to try his luck.

Outside, the sun was bright and warm. Schwarz, waiting for them in the rental car, beckoned them to hurry, pointing at his wristwatch. Blancanales ran ahead, but Lyons hesitated, turning back to face the shiny Jaguar. Fifty thousand dollars sitting there, easy.

"Well, shit."

He let the Uzi rip, a magazine of thirty rounds at something close to point-blank range. The tinted windows shattered, bullet holes like giant acne scars appearing on the driver's side. The left-front tire exploded, followed swiftly by its mate in back. When he was empty, Lyons turned and slid into the car, pressed back into his seat by the acceleration as they pulled away.

"You know," he said, "they just don't make 'em like they used to."

# CHAPTER SEVEN

"I'm getting a feeling of déjà vu," McCarter said, scanning the hectic street scene from his hotel room. Despite the air conditioner, the can of Coca-Cola that he held was sweating in his hand.

A grunt from Manning, seated on the sofa, was the only answer he received. Katz had stepped out for a moment, to try their contact number from a public telephone, without a recorded link to their room.

"We should have taken three rooms," McCarter griped.

"Too much trouble sweeping all the time," the big Canadian replied.

He meant for "bugs," of course, not dust, and it was true. Three rooms—or even two—meant that much extra time consumed with basic aspects of security, the sweep for listening devices each time they returned from any kind of outing.

The team had secured armaments immediately. Their first stop, after checking in at the hotel, had been a dealer recommended by the Stony Man computer. He dealt in cash and asked no questions, holding confidentiality more sacred than the profit he recorded on clandestine deals. The dealer wasn't interested in the specific politics of any customer, as long as he or she could pay the going rate for military hardware.

Katz had done the shopping, picking out five identical AKS-74 assault rifles. The newest version of the venerable AK-47, these weapons featured folding skeleton stocks and were chambered for a new round, the 5.45 mm projectile with a steel core, designed to mushroom and tumble in meat, thereby inflicting catastrophic wounds. Unloaded, the rifles weighed less than four pounds each, with 30- and 40-round magazines stamped from distinctive tan plastic to minimize additional weight. Best of all, a trace back on the weapons, if lost or discarded, would provide no link to the United States.

The same was true of Katzenelenbogen's choice for side arms, with Browning double-action semiautomatics packing 14-round magazines, their muzzles threaded to accept professional-quality suppressors manufactured in Italy. With a live round in the chamber, the Brownings were equal in quality and firepower to the M-9 Beretta 92-SB that was now standard issue for all U.S. military forces. A supply of Dutch V-40 "minigrenades" completed the package, leaving the Phoenix warriors prepared for anything short of an engagement with hostile armor.

The chances were, McCarter knew, that they would need it all.

Their last trip into Panama had been a scorcher—and a victory of sorts—but no success was permanent in any sort of holding action. Predators replaced each other, like a deadly spider regenerating lost legs, and sudden power vacuums often produced a population explosion of would-be masters. Sometimes, if your luck held, they devoured one another in a feeding frenzy. Other times, like here and now, there seemed to be enough loot for a breeding colony of parasites to take root and survive.

Which meant that it was time to wipe the slate. Again.

The coded knock was right on schedule, but McCarter drew his Browning just in case. Each time one of them left the room alone, there was a chance he'd be spotted, grabbed, perhaps interrogated for the kind of information enemies could use to their advantage.

Katzenelenbogen was alone, the corners of his mouth turned upward in his stoic approximation of a smile. "They're in," he said.

McCarter felt himself relax a little, knowing it was premature. Confirming Bolan's and Grimaldi's safe arrival was a small step toward their common goal, but it felt good to be in motion, all the same. The former SAS commando's tolerance for killing time was marginal, at best.

"When do we start?" he asked.

"Right now."

THE SECOND PHONE CALL in an hour quickened Bolan's pulse. The first had been from Yakov Katzenelenbogen, posing as a local businessman, confirming his appointment with "Señor Belasko" for tomorrow at 10:00 a.m. In fact they had no meeting scheduled, but the brief exchange told Katz that Bolan and Grimaldi were in place with no apparent tails. A reference to "merchandise" on Katzenelenbogen's part told

Bolan they had backup weapons waiting for them if their contact failed to get in touch for any reason.

Bolan wasn't counting on a letdown yet, but it was always nice to be prepared. In case.

The second call, by definition, had to be good news or bad. The good would mean a solid contact with an ally fixed by Langley. Bad would mean that they were blown before they started, forced to scramble for their lives.

The problem, Bolan knew, was that the call could still go either way. A breech in their security could burn the native contact, leave him open to interrogation, and sufficient time or expertise would guarantee that he spilled everything he knew. It wasn't much, but the Executioner's false identity would be included, with the name of his hotel.

But if they had his name and working address, would they bother with a call? A sudden blitz against the room would do as well, unless they were concerned with missing any backup Michael Belasko might have brought along.

These thoughts went through his mind before the telephone could ring a second time, and Bolan scooped up the handset without apparent hesitation. Either way it played, he had to see it through.

"Hello?"

"Señor Belasko?"

"Yes."

It was a woman's voice, the note of caution audible.

"I am Maria Calderone, from PanAm Copper."

While the company was real enough, he wasted no time on the alias. It didn't matter if the caller was an ally or a hostile plant. She wouldn't use her real name on an open line, in either case.

"Good afternoon, *Señora.*"

"*Señorita.*" This time, underneath the caution, there was something like amusement in her tone. "I wonder if you might be free to meet me for a drink?"

"Just tell me when and where."

"Perhaps right now? I'll meet you in the hotel lobby. There's a club nearby, where we can go and talk."

"Sounds fair. How will I recognize you?"

"Never fear."

The line went dead, and Bolan cradled the receiver. When he reached Grimaldi, Jack was hot to check the meeting out, a cautious shadow, but the Executioner declined. The two of them were still unarmed, and there was little that an extra pair of fists could do in the event that he had been set up. Conversely, by exposing Jack to a potential enemy, he stood a chance of doubling their casualties and crippling the operation on the starting line.

"I don't like this at all," the pilot told him.

Bolan smiled at that. "I'd have been disappointed if you did."

He used the stairs. It was a small thing, but if hostile guns were waiting for him in the lobby they'd watch the elevators first, a chance to catch him in a box and keep him there. It made no sense to Bolan that his enemies would call him down to die in front of witnesses, when they could storm an upstairs room without an audience. Leaving the hotel was something else, but he could only cope with one risk at a time.

The lobby entrance to the service stairs was unobtrusive, almost hidden in a corner. The door was steel, a foot-square window mounted in the middle of it, wire mesh pressed between two panes of glass. From Bolan's vantage point, he had a fair view of the lobby—elevators, registration desk, some potted plants and easy chairs for those who liked to sit and watch the other guests walk by.

A young woman standing near the house phone mounted on a pillar caught his attention and held it. She seemed preoccupied with studying a posted advertisement for the hotel's current lounge act, but he noted that her eyes kept flicking toward the elevators every ten or fifteen seconds.

Waiting.

Bolan placed her somewhere in the early twenties. Her dark hair glimmered on her shoulders, and she had the dark complexion of a native. She was nervous, standing there, but that shouldn't surprise him even if she was his contact. Either way, she had to know the stakes were life-and-death.

She wore no jacket over a clinging silk blouse and knee-length skirt. If she was carrying a weapon, it would either be inside her handbag or concealed about her person in some suitably imaginative way. The other bodies visible from where he stood included the desk clerk, a bellhop and a middle-aged couple lounging on a velvet love seat, twenty feet beyond the woman.

Outside, then, if there was a plan to take him down. And Bolan knew that there was only one way to be sure.

He managed to surprise her, coming from an unexpected quarter, and he mentally subtracted points for failure to observe the obvious.

"Miss Calderone?"

She almost jumped, but caught herself and turned to face him with a smile that flickered briefly, like a faulty neon light, before it caught and held.

"Señor Belasko?"

"In the flesh."

She glanced behind him, understood at once. "You like the stairs?"

"It helps me keep in shape."

"Of course. Americans enjoy the exercise."

"Let's say we're interested in staying healthy. When you consider the alternative..."

There was a healthy dose of caution in the lady's smile.

"I have a car outside," she told him. "Shall we go?"

*Kingston, Jamaica*
*Tuesday, 3:30 p.m.*

THE VICTORIA CRAFTS Market was crowded with tourists and locals alike. Stalls offered leather goods and handmade jewelry, intricate wooden carvings and coconuts with grinning faces, clothing in an infinite variety of styles and colors. Haggling over prices was the rule, and most of those involved apparently enjoyed the game, but its appeal was wearing thin for Calvin James.

They had been browsing—trolling, really—for the best part of an hour, pausing here and there to scrutinize a piece of merchandise, shaking their heads when a craftsman began his pitch, adjusting the inflated prices downward as he felt the sale slipping away. The items ranged from full-fledged works of art to junky souvenirs of dime-store quality, but James and his companion weren't in the mood for buying anything this afternoon.

Their mission in the marketplace was far removed from commerce.

They were looking for a man.

Or, rather, they were waiting for an unknown man to seek them out, provided he could spot them in the milling crowd.

The worst part of a high-risk mission, James decided, was the waiting. In the heat of combat there was seldom time to think beyond the needs of a specific moment, taking each new challenge as it came. When you were marking time, though, each moment seemed to last forever, giving the imagination ample room to wander and investigate dark corners of the mind. A warrior who allowed himself to worry was in trouble, granting his opponents an advantage they would otherwise be forced to win by strength of arms.

And waiting for a total stranger in the open, in an unfamiliar city, took the cake. James had an inkling how the targets in a shooting gallery might feel, if any of them were alive.

"How long are we supposed to hang around, again?"

Encizo frowned, eyes shifting restlessly from face to unfamiliar face. "If nobody shows by four o'clock," he said, "we're out of here."

The nameless caller had been vague, instructing them to try the marketplace between three and four o'clock. Someone would be in touch within the hour, he said. The password was supposed to be a reference to Montego Bay, the kind of thing a tourist normally wouldn't encounter while haggling over prices for a pair of sandals or a bracelet.

Half an hour to go, and James was uneasy with the knowledge that their contact, to effect the planned connection, must already know their faces. That meant someone had been tailing them without their knowledge, or their photographs had been leaked somehow, without a tip to Stony Man. In either case it made him feel more vulnerable than he would have liked.

A sitting duck, in fact.

The Rasta moving toward them through the crush was average height, with classic dreadlocks hanging down like tentacles around his face. He wore a brightly colored shirt and faded jeans, old sandals on his feet. His eyes were hidden by a pair of inexpensive shades. The white-bread tourists parted to allow him room.

James shifted his position, nothing obvious, enough to give the Rasta ample space. Instead of passing by, however, he veered left and stopped in front of James, perhaps a foot between them.

"You lookin' for a first-rate guide, mon?"

James glanced at Encizo and shook his head. "No, thanks."

"Aw, sure you are, mon. How you goin' to find Montego Bay without you have a guide to show you there?"

It clicked, and James could feel his spirit sinking. At his side Encizo also picked up on the cue.

"Montego Bay, you said?"

"Where else two gentlemen like you be goin', then? You take your journey one step at a time, I think."

"We haven't picked out all our gear," Encizo said.

"Hey, mon, I got exactly what you need. You come with me, I show you all the wonders of Jamaica, mon, and then some. Make you glad you came."

James glanced at Encizo again before he said, "I guess we're in your hands."

"And safer hands you never goin' to find in Kingston, mon. Andrew Morant don't let you down, no. Come with me this way. We goin' to take a little ride."

"Terrific."

If Morant picked up on Calvin's skepticism, he declined to make an issue of it. Turning on a well-worn heel, their new guide started back in the direction he had come from, winding through the crowd with James and Encizo close behind.

When they were safely on their own, without an audience, James meant to find out how Morant had known their faces. Failing that, he meant to keep a close eye on their guide, against the possibility of treachery. A little paranoia never hurt when you were living on the edge. In fact it helped to keep you living.

Damn right, mon.

The game was on, but they had far to go before they even caught a glimmer of the finish line. And any fumble on the way could still mean sudden death.

One thing James promised to himself: if this Morant turned out to be a Judas goat, he wouldn't live to draw his salary. In that case, the ex-SEAL thought, their "little ride" would be a one-way trip for all concerned.

*Nassau International Airport*
*Tuesday, 3:47 p.m.*

"YOU'VE GOT THE CAR on standby, right?" Lyons asked.

"Affirmative."

In front of Blancanales, half a dozen blue-haired tourists clogged the 727's aisle, all dragging luggage from the overhead compartments, wheezing and complaining, dentures clicking audibly as if an unseen hand were snipping off their syllables with scissors. Finally the jam broke up and they began to inch in the direction of the jet bridge, shuffling along like convicts in a prison chow line.

"Anyway," Lyons muttered in his ear, "the scenery can't get any worse than this."

Inside the terminal they had a chance to stretch their legs and make some time. The baggage claim and immigration took nearly half an hour, but the car-rental booth was clear, and Blancanales showed an AmEx gold card to the young man working on the counter. Moments later, when the mandatory paperwork was done, he palmed a set of keys and led his teammates toward the parking lot.

A black man in a floral shirt and mirror shades waited for them at their rental car, reclining with his back against the driver's door. When Blancanales slowed, the stranger tried a cautious smile.

"You're clean, don't worry. I've been watching you."

"Is that supposed to give me confidence?" the Politician asked.

"It should. In Nassau you can always use an extra pair of eyes."

"I brought my own."

The man shrugged. "Consider this a present from the DEA."

They were expecting contact sometime after they arrived, but Blancanales hadn't counted on a welcoming committee at the airport.

"You're alone?" he asked.

"I was, until you got here. Perry Tate."

They shook hands all around, Blancanales resisting the urge to ask for credentials.

"So, you've been watching us," Schwarz said. "I don't suppose there's anybody watching you?"

"No way. I've had more practice shaking tails than any five Miami strippers you can name."

"I can't name any, right offhand."

"Well, there you go."

"You have a car nearby?" Lyons asked.

"Nope. I taxied out. My luck, I figured I could find someone to drive me back."

"Your lucky day, I guess."

"Looks like."

"We're new in town," Blancanales said, handing him the keys. "You drive."

"Suits me."

When they were underway and rolling east toward Nassau proper, Blancanales kept a close eye on the nearest mirror, watching out for any shadows they picked up along the way. Tate noticed his reaction, frowning as he drove.

"I told you we were clean."

"You don't mind if I check the scenery?"

"Be my guest."

"So, what's on the itinerary?" Lyons asked.

"First thing, we'll get you settled into your hotel, on Paradise. First-class, you'll like it. Close to the casino, anything you need. You feel like going for a ride from there, I'll show you where the bad boys spend their time."

Still checking out the highway in his mirror, Blancanales spoke. "I don't know what you've heard about our mission—"

"Need-to-know," Tate interrupted him. "Assist where possible, in an advisory capacity or otherwise."

"It could get ugly down the road."

"Seems like I've traveled down that road a time or two."

"We're mainly looking for an introduction," Blancanales said. "Beyond that point, you're free and clear."

"Depends on how the shit goes down, I'd say. The folks you're after, if it blows up in your face, they'll want to have a word with me before it's over."

"Maybe you should think about a change of scene," Lyons suggested, "once you set us up."

"And miss the main event? No way."

"Your choice," the Politician told him. "Just so everybody knows the score."

"I'm covered."

"Speaking of which..."

"No sweat. The hardware's waiting for you, safe and sound."

"Would you have the inventory memorized by any chance?" Schwarz asked.

"We've got your basic smorgasbord. Glock-17s for casual wear. If you need a little something extra, we've got MP-5s, AR-18s, street sweepers."

"What about explosives?"

"I'll see what I can do. You won't be needing any tanks, will you?"

"We'll let you know," said Blancanales.

"Many thanks," the man from DEA replied with a sardonic smile. "I'd be obliged."

# CHAPTER EIGHT

*Panama City*
*Tuesday, 3:30 p.m.*

Colonel Antonio Delvalle had his mind on revolutionaries. They weren't his first concern, in ordinary circumstances, but the past twelve months would hardly qualify as ordinary. Taken further, he'd have to say that nothing had been truly normal since the American troops invaded Panama and arrested President Manuel Noriega to complete their Operation Just Cause.

As a career soldier and patriot, Delvalle had been outraged by the violation of Panama's sovereignty, a return to the old days of gunboat diplomacy when the United States still viewed Central America as a kind of private game preserve. However, when he thought about the situation as a businessman, Delvalle had a rather different view.

With Noriega in the presidential palace, business had been good for smugglers and the authorities who offered them protection. Even so, El Presidente's ego was a stumbling block to any kind of major wealth for his subordinates. While Noriega ruled the roost, Delvalle and a hundred other officers with equally expensive tastes had seen the limits of their own ambition etched in stone. If only that one stumbling block could be removed...

And so it had been, courtesy of the United States.

These days, the cocaine trade in Panama was free to spread and grow without the interference of an egomaniac whose cult of personality determined every other aspect of the national experience. The power vacuum left by Noriega's passing guaranteed that politicians would be forced to scramble for their jobs, relearning some of the survival skills they had long since laid aside. If that meant making deals with traffickers in contraband, it was a buyer's market. Dealers from Colombia and other countries to the south were free to shop around and spend their money on the statesmen who appeared to serve them best, without a strongman laying down the law at every turn.

And while the politicians scuffled for donations, underbidding one another, the professionals in national security and law enforcement were allowed to concentrate on getting rich. Patriotic fervor aside, it struck Delvalle as a sensible solution, all around.

Unfortunately, when the profits multiplied, his risks did likewise. It was known that agents of the DEA and FBI were focusing attention on the Panamanian connection, gearing up for action on another front in America's so-called war on drugs. No matter that the "war" was hypocritical, halfhearted and predestined to fail. Any foreign effort to restrict the drug trade was danger to Delvalle, since it pointed out his own long-running failure to succeed in that regard. He didn't think that the Americans would bother extraditing *him,* of course...

If they were so inclined, the Yankees could bring pressure on the president to find himself another watchdog. Foreign aid meant more to Panama, right now, than covert payoffs from Colombia, and no one in the government was anxious for a second Just Cause Operation. If it came down to threats of military action in the next few months, Delvalle knew that someone would be sacrificed, and he wasn't prepared to fill that role himself.

The colonel shifted in his chair and watched Avilla's secretary as she finished typing a letter and checked it for errors. When it came to office staff, Jesus preferred them young and slender. Flexible. Delvalle thought about the woman in Avilla's bed and felt himself begin to stiffen, thankful when the soft tone of the intercom distracted him.

"Mr. Avilla will see you now," she told him, putting on a smile reserved for VIPs. She pressed a button on the intercom and held it down until Delvalle reached the tall connecting door that opened on Avilla's inner sanctum.

"Thank you."

"You're welcome, Colonel."

The door eased shut behind Delvalle and he found Avilla smiling at him from behind a massive desk of polished teak. He had a fat cigar between his teeth, and blue smoke formed a halo just above his head.

"A new one, eh?" Delvalle nodded toward the outer office as he spoke.

Avilla smiled and shrugged. "Juanita was becoming careless and demanding. They are easy to replace."

"Of course."

Delvalle found himself a chair and settled in. The desktop lay between them like a giant game board, where the fate of men could be decided over whiskey and cigars.

"You've heard from Santiago." It wasn't a question.

"Yes," Delvalle said. "He's interested in moving larger shipments. Naturally he understands that it would mean a higher price."

Avilla frowned around the bulk of his cigar. "And greater risk for all concerned."

Delvalle shrugged. "With the Americans, who knows? The DEA expresses some concern, but even their television networks have dismissed the war on drugs."

"We've seen what happens when we take their apathy for granted, Colonel."

"That was personal. If Noriega had been smart enough to play the game, instead of waving swords in public, threatening the White House, he would still be sitting in the presidential palace, rather than a prison cell."

"Perhaps."

"We know that Santiago will continue shipping merchandise to the United States, no matter what we say or do. At least this way, we profit from the trade."

"Greed kills," Avilla pointed out.

It was Delvalle's turn to smile. "We all die when our time arrives, Jesus. The question is, how do you wish to live?"

The man considered it for several moments, then finally nodded. "Very well. You handle the arrangements. I will brief the president."

Delvalle doubted that, but it wasn't his problem. Rising from his chair, he leaned across the desk and helped himself to a cigar. The minister regarded him with vague amusement through a veil of drifting smoke.

"Be careful with these friends of yours, Antonio."

"I always am, Jesus."

THE LADY'S CAR WAS PARKED half a block from his hotel, and Bolan waited while she slid behind the wheel, then leaned across the seat to let him in. If they were being shadowed, he couldn't pick up the tail.

Which didn't prove that he was home and dry, by any means.

"My real name is Miranda," she informed him as she put the compact car in motion.

"Calderone?"

"Limachi."

"Ah."

"You understand the need for caution?"

"Absolutely."

Bolan understood it well enough, in fact, that he wasn't about to drop his guard. Legitimate or otherwise, the woman might be subject to interrogation in the future, and the less she knew about him now, the less she'd be able to reveal.

"I'm with Democracy in Action."

"Come again?"

"We lobby for a greater share of what you call the civil rights. Removing Noriega helped our cause, but there is still much to be done."

"Locking horns with the Colombians could get you killed," he said.

"Protesting in the streets could get me killed," she answered. "Even now, it is a chance we take in Panama, to win our freedom."

"How's it going?"

"We make progress. If you are successful, maybe it will help."

"You link the drugs with this administration?"

"But of course. If the police and military were instructed to prevent the traffic in cocaine, it would be stopped. Instead, they turn their backs, and politicians bank the profits of corruption. Do you not have men like this in the United States?"

He had to smile at that. "We've got our share."

"Then we are not so different, after all."

She drove him through a maze of streets, with Bolan noting landmarks in his mind for future reference. If she was taking him to meet his scheduled contact, there would be no problem. Otherwise, he just might have to kill the lady and as many of her comrades as he could. If he survived and wound up stuck without a taxi, he would have to find the hotel on his own.

So far, so good.

Her destination was a residential district in the suburb of Balboa. Bolan kept his mouth shut while she pulled into a narrow, littered alleyway behind a row of houses that were universally in need of paint and various repairs. A scrawny dog staked out his territory, standing fast until the bumper of Miranda's compact came within a foot of cracking yellow teeth, and then he fled without a backward glance.

Survival of the fittest in an urban jungle. Somehow, it made the Executioner feel more at home.

A small garage faced on the alley, and the door swung open from the inside when Miranda tapped her horn. The man who stood aside to let them in was average height, midthirties, with dark hair and eyes. He was also carrying an automatic pistol in his hand.

"What's this?" Bolan asked.

"Security. You understand?"

"I've been there."

There was no sign of the pistol as they climbed out of the car. The dark man had both hands free when he closed the door behind Miranda's car and latched it from inside. A single naked bulb suspended from the rafters cast their faces into shadow, making moods impossible to read.

"This way," Miranda said, and Bolan followed her inside the house, their one-man reception committee bringing up the rear. He half expected an assault at that point, but they made it through a fragrant kitchen to a smallish sitting room without a sudden rush of hostile movement on his heels.

When Bolan glanced around to check, the man was gone.

But they weren't alone.

A man approximately Bolan's age was waiting for them in the sitting room. The draperies were tightly drawn, to frustrate private eyes, and several lamps were burning to illuminate the room. An inefficient cooler, mounted somewhere on the roof, worked overtime to cool the stuffy house.

"Señor Belasko." Bolan's host stepped forward and shook his hand. "My name is Angelo Rodriguez. Welcome to my country."

"Thanks. It's not my first time."

"So, you know the city?"

"Bits and pieces. I could still use help to find the things I need."

"Of course. My network is at your disposal."

"Network?"

"I assumed Miranda would have told you. Please, sit down."

He chose a swaybacked couch and settled in. "Democracy in Action?"

"That is but our public face, you understand?"

"It's not required for me to know your business," Bolan said. "In fact it's not a good idea at all."

"Then know that this house has been borrowed from a friend without his knowledge or consent. When we are finished here, all traces of our presence will be swept away."

"Suits me."

Rodriguez smiled. "In that case, how can I assist you?"

Bolan thought about it, frowning to himself. "We might as well start at the top. What about Jesus Avilla and the government connection?"


"HERE HE COMES."

McCarter barely moved his lips, no radio in hand to give his game away. The tiny microphone was fastened under his lapel, but it was sensitive enough to catch a whisper from a range of six or seven feet. The cordless earpiece had begun life as a standard hearing aid, revamped at Stony Man to serve as a receiver with a one-mile active radius.

"I read you," Manning answered, speaking from a block downrange.

The Rolls-Royce was a tank designed with luxury in mind. However Sergio Barbosa felt about security, he didn't skimp on dollars where his private comfort was concerned. They'd require statistics from the factory for any kind of detailed rundown, but McCarter guessed the Rolls would glide through .50-caliber—and maybe even 20 mm—rounds without a hitch. If they were forced to stop Barbosa on the road, some kind of antiarmor round or high explosives would be called for.

"Coming your way, Katz," McCarter said as the Rolls turned left. A curt acknowledgment from Katz-enelenbogen told him they were covered.

He was crouched beside a motorbike across the street from Sergio Barbosa's office building, juggling wrenches while he waited for the dealer to appear. Katz had the stakeout on the east, with Manning on the west, prepared to trail Barbosa any way it played. The key was versatility and timing, nothing to upset their man or tip his driver off that anyone was shadowing the Rolls.

A moment later, while McCarter stuffed his wrenches in the open saddle bag, Manning breezed past him in a compact rental, giving Katz and the Rolls a respectable lead. McCarter kicked the bike to life and swung around to follow in his own good time, resisting any urge he felt to rush it and produce a pileup on the limo's tail.

For now, Barbosa was a lead and nothing more. They had his major operations spotted from the briefing back at Stony Man, but it remained for them to get a feeling for the man. If all they had to do was take him down, a simple visit to his office would have done the trick. Come through the door with automatic weapons blazing, take down anyone who gave them any shit, and nail Barbosa in his office, maybe still behind his desk.

Instead, it was a game of watch and wait . . . at least for now.

They were coordinating moves with Bolan and Grimaldi, more or less, to synchronize the play. When they had checked out Barbosa and done the same to his competitor, Velasco, they'd be prepared to strike. Meanwhile, the Executioner would be securing the necessary information for coordinated moves against the government officials who permitted cocaine traffic through the capital of Panama.

If they could bring it all together, it would be a triple play.

Clean sweep.

McCarter didn't like to think about the possibility of failure, but it was always there. Bad luck, a fumble on the one-yard line, and they were history.

From the direction they were traveling, he knew Barbosa must be headed for his supper club. Another wait, and it was Manning's turn to watch the street this time. Barbosa's goons weren't exactly rocket scientists, but even they would grow suspicious if a bike broke down across the street each time their boss pulled in to check his books or grab a bite to eat.

Coincidence could get you killed, McCarter knew. It was a fundamental rule of making war against the odds.

And from the supper club, if Stony Man's prediction held, they'd be following Barbosa to a nightclub where he ran a small but plush casino in the back, remaining long enough to check out the action to see if there were any women that he fancied on the premises. From there it could begin to come unglued.

No sweat, McCarter told himself. They had experience at tailing bigger fish than this, in cities where security and curfews made it difficult to move about, much less keep up an organized pursuit. In Panama, at least, there was no state of martial law to slow them down.

And once they started turning up the heat, what then?

He thought about the ruling government's cocaine connections, wondering what kind of opposition they should look for when it hit the fan. Removing one man from the presidential palace hadn't cleaned the slate in Panama, by any means, and if Brognola's briefing was an indication of the total picture, they were bound to ruffle some important feathers when they put the ball in play.

Which fazed McCarter not at all.

If there was heat to come, so be it. He was ready for the worst his enemies could do. The sooner the better, in fact.

A clean sweep started with a single stroke, and he could feel it coming. Anytime now.

They were on their way.

# CHAPTER NINE

*Pedro Point, Jamaica*
*Tuesday, 6:15 p.m.*

In fact, Andrew Morant had driven them twenty miles beyond Montego Bay, his old converted taxi sounding like a rattletrap that might break down at any moment, leaving them on foot. From what James could determine, it was meant to sound that way, an auditory complement to its appearance—rusty patches like psoriasis, with primer gray applied too late—which validated the impression of a junker going nowhere fast.

If Calvin had to make an educated guess, he'd have said the Rasta's taxi had sufficient power underneath its hood to blow most standard-issue squad cars off the highway in Jamaica, maybe even in the States. The rust and primer paint were ugly, as intended, but the bodywork was sound, the bumpers reinforced for ramming in a crunch. There was a pistol hanging underneath the dash, though James couldn't be sure about the make and model.

If Morant made any unexpected moves in that direction, James was prepared to punch the man's ticket from his place behind the driver's seat. No weapon needed, when a simple clutch and twist would do the job just fine.

But so far, it was cool. Their guide assured them that the car was clean, and he made no complaint when James confirmed it with a compact scanner, designed to resemble a pocket transistor radio. Actually it *was* a radio, its primary function fulfilled by dialing the tuner to an open channel and sweeping the telescopic antenna around the desired perimeter. A listening device within a range of twenty feet or so would set off one hellacious squeal, but there was nothing in the car that he could find.

Except that piece beneath the dash.

En route from Kingston to their destination, Morant talked nonstop, except when he was interrupted by a question from his passengers. Jamaican folklore and natural history were interwoven with tales of the "posses"—brutal, drug-dealing street gangs—that had lately surfaced in America, beginning with importation of ganja and expanding from there to include cocaine and heroin. In Kingston and environs, half a dozen posses struggled for control of the narcotics trade, Morant involved in tracking their progress for domestic and foreign authorities.

In short their guide was playing both sides of the street. Not strictly mercenary, but he was adept at juggling, keeping several balls in the air without losing his own. The posses saw him as a free-lance dealer, con man, sometime source of information and equipment. The police in Kingston paid him well for timely tips and "lost" their paperwork on minor scams he operated on the side. From time to time Morant struck bargains with the DEA, but he was doing this job for the Company.

The CIA's continuing grudge against Castro was legendary. It transcended shifting administrations and philosophies, defied detente and *glasnost*. Fidel was the last of the hard-line, unrepentant reds, and there were ranking officers at Langley who would never rest until he was deposed—and preferably dead.

James knew that they'd have to watch their step on this one, taking care to avoid the snares of Company intrigue. If Langley had its own agenda working, it would have to wait. The Phoenix force warriors had a mission to perform, and it didn't involve a broader war against the Cuban government per se.

Their destination was an isolated house, well screened by trees and separated from the coastal highway by a hundred yards of tangled undergrowth. Its giant picture windows faced the cliff's edge and a blue expanse of water stretched to the far horizon.

"Cuba over there," Morant said, pointing north beyond the glass, "but you can't see him, no. Be ninety miles, about there, to the nearest point of land. I have the maps and charts you need, compass, climbing gear, all kinds of things."

"Let's check it out," James suggested.

"Sure thing, mon."

They could easily have flown into Guantanamo and thus eliminated the necessity of crossing open water, but the risks outweighed the rewards. The U.S. naval station was observed around the clock by Castro's DSE, and slipping out unseen would be a virtual impossibility. And once the Cubans got a fix on them, they were as good as dead.

Morant led the way downstairs to a basement carved out of the rock. Storm doors opened on a rugged path that led down to the beach, a hundred feet below. Inside the basement bright fluorescent lights showed off a combination storage area and workshop where their gear had been collected.

"This one, she be hard to find on radar," Morant said, directing their attention to the crate that held a fifteen-foot inflatable. "Get where you going, you can hide her out somewhere or slit her up the belly with a knife. She sink real fine."

The outboard motor was a compact model with a special cowling to reduce its noise. In spite of the precaution, James knew, they'd be rowing for the final mile or so.

"What else?" Encizo asked.

"The goods be over here."

Morant moved toward a workbench where two stacks of peasant trousers, shirts and sandals were arranged. Each pile was anchored with a faded duffel bag. Inside each bag they found a PA3-DM 9 mm submachine gun made in Argentina, plus an Argentinian copy of the Browning Hi-Power automatic pistol and extra magazines for both. A pair of folding knives and plastic bags with their forged ID inside completed the ensemble.

James found his partner watching him, a strange expression on his face, as if expecting the ex-SEAL to renege. The Phoenix Force warrior took his PA3-DM and tried the action, pleased to find that it was smooth and well maintained.

"So, what the hell," he said at last. "We've done with less. Let's get it on."

*Paradise Island, Nassau*
*6:40 p.m.*

THE CASINO WAS DOING fair business when Lyons arrived. He spent a moment at the cashier's cage and turned five thousand dollars into chips before he started trolling, making his way toward the baccarat tables.

It was a Vegas layout with a Monte Carlo crowd, no faded jeans or loud Hawaiian shirts to mark the tourists. Tuxedos and formal evening gowns were the rule, presenting the image—however erroneous—of a quality, upscale crowd. In fact the dress code seemed to modify behavior, toning down the raucous laughter that was normally a fixture of the carpet joints in Vegas or Atlantic City. These gamblers had come to risk their money, the same as anywhere else, but they meant to do it with style.

It was ironic, Lyons thought, considering the origins of the Paradise Island casino. Meyer Lansky and the Mafia had done the groundwork a quarter century earlier, trying to recoup their losses after Castro closed the Mob's casinos in Nevada. Lansky's brainchild was an innocuous-sounding construction company called Mary Carter Limited, designed to lull suspicious locals while their legislators were seduced with bribes. By 1967 Lansky and his pals were raking in the skim and cashing in on "liberal" Bahamian banking laws. For ranking leaders of the syndicate, the islands were a profitable hybrid of Hawaii, Switzerland and Vegas, all rolled into one.

Lyons spotted his man at the second baccarat table, gold-rimmed glasses bright against his ebony skin. The

tux that Thomas Mentzer wore had set him back an
easy grand, but from the pile of chips in front of him,
it looked like he was doing well enough to buy the tai-
lor out.

A middle-aged woman on Mentzer's left was handling the shoe when Lyons bought into the game. His
first two cards were perfect—queen of spades and nine
of hearts—and Lyons bet the limit, clearing two grand
on the play. The next deal left him with a red jack and
a deuce, which added up to two points in baccarat,
where nine is the ideal. He drew an eight of clubs and
busted back to zero, watching half the winnings from
his first hand disappear.

Mentzer won the next two hands with an eight and a
natural nine, respectively. He was a man who liked to
win, from all appearances. A thousand-candlepower
smile turned on each time the sweet cards came his way.
The pile of colored chips in front of him had taken on
the likeness of a child's toy fortress, towers rising on
either side.

The shoe was running low, and everybody took a
break while six new decks were shuffled, then slotted
into place. The lady who was dealing took the opportunity to cut her losses, and the shoe was passed to
Mentzer, bringing on another smile. No way for him to
cheat in these surroundings, but the man had confidence enough for half a dozen gamblers as it was.

Lyons made a point of meeting Mentzer's gaze this
time around, a hint of challenge in his eyes. He waited
for cards, a four and a three, deciding that it wouldn't
hurt to test his luck.

"Again."

The deuce came through on schedule and he flipped the others over, watching Mentzer's smile lose wattage.

Gotcha.

There were two more players at the table, both of them to Lyons's right. One had a diamond pin on his lapel and the twang of down-home Texas in his voice. The other was a gray-haired Englishman who played with grim determination, covering his cards and chips with slender, hairy hands. The two of them were losing steadily, and while it seemed to irritate the Englishman, the lanky Texan grinned and threw his chips away like they were going out of style.

The next four hands were split right down the middle, two for Lyons, two for Mentzer. The Englishman bailed out when Lyons took a seven-thousand-dollar pot the fourth time out, and Texas lasted two more rounds before his well ran dry. He made a little joke as he excused himself, but Lyons missed the punch line, concentrating on his adversary's face.

And it was down to one-on-one, the way he wanted it, with Mentzer dealing. Perfect.

Mentzer had a clear-cut lead as far as money was concerned, some forty thousand dollars stacked in front of him, compared to Lyons's seventeen. He could afford to take a chance when the Able Team leader was forced to be conservative, but Lyons knew that he'd have to play with cast-iron nerve if he had any hope of pulling off a sweep.

Beginning now.

He caught a four of diamonds and a three of hearts to make it seven. All the rule books said that he should stand and hope the dealer busted out. Instead, he took another card and fought to keep himself from grimacing as it fell faceup on the table.

Four of clubs. His three cards added up to one. A deuce would beat him now, with seven thousand dollars on the table, if the dealer didn't blow it.

Mentzer drew on five and caught the five of spades. A zero for his hand. The money came to Lyons, and he felt a new rush of adrenaline kick in.

His adversary let him have a natural the next time out, a nine to Mentzer's eight, and Lyons closed the gap to fourteen grand between them. Mentzer's smile was history, his full attention focused on the cards and his opponent's face. Whatever he was seeing there, Lyons hoped it left him ill at ease.

The next round went to Mentzer, beating Lyons's seven with another eight, but the enjoyment had begun to pale. The dealer lighted a cigarette and left it burning in the ashtray, instantly forgotten as he started thumbing more cards from the shoe.

A six and a deuce to Lyons, for a solid eight. The dealer played it safe and stood on seven, losing two grand for his trouble. When he tried to make it back by doubling his bet next time around, the queen and nine of hearts that Lyons held defeated him.

Ten grand between them now, and Lyons knew that it was time to make his move. Another hand or two could do it, if he kept his nerve and played with skill.

In fact the next hand came to Lyons courtesy of his opponent, with a six and three unbeatable. He bet three thousand, and saw the dealer draw to help a six and wind up holding deuce.

No time like the present.

Mentzer dealt him a five of diamonds and the ace of spades. With six in hand, the game could still go either way, but Lyons had a feeling now. It wasn't luck, or even confidence, so much as a conviction that the game was his.

He made a show of counting chips, frowning to himself in mock concentration before he pushed twenty-five thousand across the green field. A murmur rose from the circle of spectators, and Mentzer blinked once in surprise. The croupier was red-faced, forced by house rules to inquire if Mentzer would consent to waive the limit in a special case.

The dealer thought about it, nodded grimly, and began to shovel chips across. No fortress now. The pile of plastic wafers suddenly reminded Lyons of a model city gone to ruin in the wake of World War III.

He met the dealer's gaze, unblinking, as he said, "Another card."

It could have been most anything—a four to bust him out, or any other card besides the ideal, absolutely perfect three that fell across his hidden cards. Lyons showed the other two and watched his adversary wince, almost a grimace.

Mentzer had been sitting on an eight.

The rest of it was anticlimax, mopping up the dealer's last four thousand dollars with an easy nine that left the big ex-cop sitting on a profit in the neighborhood of fifty large. He tipped the croupier five hundred, waited for security to bag his winnings and prepared to leave the table. Half a dozen strangers stood in line to shake his hand, congratulating Lyons on his luck and hoping some of it rubbed off on contact. He was feeling like a candidate for city council when a black hand wrapped around his own.

"Congratulations," Mentzer said. "You play courageously."

"I do my best. Chad Lewis, from Chicago."

"Thomas Mentzer. May I ask if you are here on holiday or business?"

"Some of each. I deal in pharmaceuticals around the Midwest region. Rumor has it the Bahamas are the place to be for major deals."

"With all the manufacturers you have in the United States?"

"They don't turn out the merchandise I need," Lyons said.

"Ah."

"Thing is, it's not that easy making contact."

Mentzer's smile was working on a comeback. "There's a possibility," he said, "that I can help you there."

"You think so?"

"I'm convinced of it.'

"In that case," Lyons said, "why don't we have a drink? My treat."

*Panama City*
*6:50 p.m.*

THE KEY TO RATTLING an enemy, Bolan thought, was to find his weakest point and hammer it relentlessly until you had a breakthrough. In the present circumstances he assessed the common weakness of his adversaries as their competition, breeding paranoia and a passion for security. If he could plant a wedge between the city's major dealers, drive it deep enough, they just might turn on one another and proceed to do a measure of the soldier's work.

If nothing else, it was a chance for him to thin the hostile ranks.

He flipped a mental coin, deciding he'd start with Sergio Barbosa. The dealer made his home in Balboa Heights, north of Panama City, but his business headquarters occupied the top floor of an office building near the waterfront, symbolically watching over the port where much of his merchandise entered the country.

Considering the Latin trend toward a siesta in the afternoon and dining late, it came as no surprise to find Barbosa's office occupied in early evening. Bolan had no way of knowing if Barbosa would be there in person, and it made no difference. For the moment it was adequate to know that he'd get the message one way or another, something for the smuggler to think about while Bolan cinched the noose around his neck.

He wore a set of workman's overalls emblazoned with the logo of a nonexistent plumbing company and packed a three-foot toolbox as he locked his van and left it in the alleyway beside another office building, facing Barbosa's from the opposite side of the street. No one challenged Bolan en route to the service elevator, and he had the car to himself, riding it all the way to the roof. Emerging into early dusk, he circled toward the street and found his vantage point two floors above the office complex where Barbosa's people kept the books, dispensed their bribes and calculated profits on their shipments of crystalline death.

Kneeling, Bolan opened the toolbox, removing a superfluous tray of drill bits and screwdrivers. Underneath, the Walther WA-2000 sniper rifle nestled snugly in its place with less than a half inch to spare.

The German rifle was unique in both appearance and design. A "bullpup" model with its 6-round magazine behind the pistol grip, it had a fluted 26-inch barrel clamped at either end to minimize the loss of accuracy when a shot was fired. Recoil was further reduced by the weapon's semiautomatic action and a heavy muzzle brake. The Walther was chambered for .300 Winchester Magnum rounds, and its standard telescopic sight from Schmidt & Bender offered a 10-power zoom, which was more than adequate for Bolan's present needs. With the supporting bipod bolted into place, he had a sturdy, compact killer in his hands.

A quick scan of the lighted office windows showed him six men on the job, no women visible at any point. Barbosa's machismo was showing, to Bolan's relief, eliminating any need for him to pick and choose. Another sweep confirmed that Sergio wasn't among them, and he settled on a squat hardman near the window, riffling through the contents of a filing cabinet. Bolan's sniper scope picked out the bulge of hardware underneath his target's coat before the cross hairs settled on a pockmarked cheek.

The warrior took a deep breath, let part of it go and held the rest. At this range there was no correction necessary for the bullet's rise or drop, 220 grains of death prepared to bridge the gap between the marksman and his target on command. His finger curled around the Walther's trigger, gently taking up the slack.

There was a chance the window would be bullet-proof, but Bolan didn't think so. Even with the fortune that he paid in bribes, Barbosa still aspired to the appearance of legitimacy, something he'd sacrifice if he began to fortify a standard suite of offices against attack. His men were packing guns, and there were doubtless other weapons in the office, but the Executioner was betting that the walls and windows had been left alone.

The Walther pushed against his shoulder, and Bolan held steady on the scope, watching as his Silvertip Super-X round drilled the glass and ripped into his target's face. One moment the gunner was standing there, absorbed in his work, and the next he was down. The empty Magnum cartridge spun away and clattered on the rooftop, several yards away.

The Executioner swiveled to the right a few degrees and caught a second member of the team still gaping at his dead companion, trying to make sense of what he saw. Another squeeze, the Walther's thrust against his shoulder, and he watched the gunman's lower jaw disintegrate, explosive impact punching him backward in his swivel chair.

The four survivors knew they were in trouble now, but there was still initial shock to overcome, a natural confusion as their comrades fell among them, nothing but the sound of broken glass to tell them what was happening. Two of them dropped instinctively and scrambled under nearby desks, reactions typical of soldiers with experience. The other two were green, one of them actually reaching for a pistol on his belt, as if he thought the gun could help him now.

This time the Silvertip took out a fist-size segment of Barbosa's window, ripping through the quick-draw artist's chest and slamming him against the nearest wall. He hung there for perhaps a second and a half before surrendering to gravity, his passing marked by crimson smudges on the wall.

Three down, and three rounds still remaining in the Walther's magazine. The only gunner still remaining on his feet had reconsidered his decision, ducking toward a bank of filing cabinets with his shoulders hunched, head down. A Magnum bullet helped him get there, boring in beneath one shoulder blade and flattening to shred a lung before it lifted him completely off his feet. The gunner's forehead struck a cabinet with sufficient force to dent the middle drawer, and he rebounded like a cartoon figure, sprawling on his back.

The other men were safely out of sight, and Bolan used his last two rounds on target practice. One punched through the office water cooler, spouting liquid in a double stream. The other stopped a wall clock dead and left it dangling by a snarl of wires.

Enough.

He packed the Walther, left the scattered brass behind and headed for the waiting elevator. It would take a few more moments for the two survivors to recover and alert police, but anyone who heard the shots could place a call, and Bolan knew that he was running out of time.

Barbosa would receive the message, but he wouldn't understand at first. The dealer would begin to cast around for enemies, and he wouldn't have far to look.

Within the next few hours, Bolan hoped there would be enemies enough to go around for all concerned.

# CHAPTER TEN

*Stony Man Farm*
*Wednesday, 5:30 a.m.*

It would be the best part of an hour before the sun lighted up Virginia's Blue Ridge Mountains, but Aaron Kurtzman was awake and on the job. His console in the Stony Man computer room was fashioned in the aspect of a giant horseshoe, with a master keyboard and auxiliaries, four monitors, a laser printer and a battery of telephones. The room at large was something from a hacker's high-tech fantasy, with sophisticated hardware on-line to the Pentagon, Langley, the Justice Department, and a satellite surveillance network that could count the trees in someone's backyard.

This morning, though, Kurtzman's thoughts were far removed from any problems in the Eastern Hemisphere. The troops were working relatively close to home, but their proximity didn't mean they were safe, by any means.

The battle had been joined—on one front, anyway—and Kurtzman hated knowing there was nothing he could do but watch and wait.

He heard the elevator coming, swiveled in his chair to face the sliding door. When Barbara Price emerged, he noted dark rings underneath her eyes, the clear mark of a sleepless night. She raised a hand in greeting and came around to join him at the console, peering over the computer wizard's shoulder at the several screens.

"What's happening?" she asked.

"It's quiet at the moment, but they had a busy night. Five hits against Barbosa and Velasco that I'm sure of, close to twenty hostiles down. The locals think they have a gang war on their hands."

"They will before he's finished."

Kurtzman nodded, recognizing Bolan's plan. It was divide and conquer all the way, made easier by the suspicion that prevailed between Barbosa and Velasco in their world of subterfuge and double cross. It didn't take much agitation to provoke a fight between two jackals, and the executioner was skilled at rattling his enemies. With any luck at all the dealers might dispose of each other, or at least reduce the odds by thinning out the ranks.

Whatever else went down in Panama in the next two days or so, the local cops and coroner would have their hands full counting bodies, trying to control a situation they'd never fully understand.

"How's Able doing?"

"Contact with the money man," Kurtzman replied. "It's early yet for any kind of deal, but they'll be pushing. Lyons doesn't like to wait around."

"I wish we had a better fix on Mentzer's contacts," Price said. "He has to have an in with the police. The way it is, we're damn near working blind."

"Their contact from the DEA should have a line on that end of the game. He's got enough time in to know the players on a first-name basis."

"Still no comeback on Miami?"

Kurtzman shook his head. "Escalante wasn't anybody's favorite citizen. They aren't exactly lighting candles down at Metro-Dade, and DEA's been falling on his operation like a ton of bricks. Whoever's taking Escalante's place, he'll have a hard time moving any merchandise the next few days."

And if they caught a break, Kurtzman thought, those few days could be enough to shut the pipeline down. One pipeline, anyway.

No lasting victories, but what the hell.

"That just leaves Rafael and Calvin," Barbara said.

"En route. They should be landing anytime within the next half hour, but we can't depend on any contact after that, until they wrap it up."

And Cuba was potentially the joker in the deck, he realized. At least in Panama and the Bahamas, their respective governments were still on speaking terms. The very act of penetrating Cuban territory raised the kind of diplomatic questions Washington would rather sidestep and ignore. It was essentially an act of war, and while precautions had been taken to reduce the risk of any demonstrated link to the United States, Kurtzman's primary concern lay with James and Encizo. They could easily be lost without a trace in Cuba, and pursuing them would be a no-win proposition all around.

"How solid are their contacts on the island?"

"According to the Company, they're granite," Kurtzman replied. "Of course, the Company was certain everyone in Cuba would revolt against Fidel and kick his ass in '61, when they set up the Bay of Pigs."

"I like your confidence."

He frowned, the silent screens and printer preying on his nerves. He wanted action, something—anything— to tell him what was going on beyond those insulated, soundproof walls.

"Truth is," he said at last, "the information network in Havana is about the best that Langley has. I mean, they've had the net in place for over thirty years. They're working on a second generation of devoted spooks. I think we'll be all right."

"I'm sure we will. It's Rafael and Calvin I'm concerned about."

Me too, Kurtzman thought, but he kept the words inside. It was a bit of superstitious nonsense, but he always shied away from voicing private fears, as if the very act of speaking out could make the nightmares come to life.

"They'll make it," Kurtzman said.

But even as he spoke, he wondered whether he was reassuring Barbara or himself.

*Cabo Cruz, Cuba*
*5:50 a.m.*

THEY HAD BEGUN their run at half-past ten, and they were pushing daylight even so. On solid ground, with any kind of decent vehicle, they could have made the transit in an hour and a half, no-sweat, but this was different. Traveling by night on open water, navigating by the stars and stopping twice to fill the outboard engine's tank with gasoline, they managed barely eighteen miles per hour for the trip. The last mile and a half, without the engine, had been even slower, rowing toward the darkened coastline, constantly alert to any sound of engines that would mean a Communist patrol.

Encizo had to trust the fact that they were underneath the coastal radar. Otherwise, there should have been patrol boats massed and waiting for them, maybe helicopters in the air. The Fidelistas were as conscious of security as the Israelis, moving swiftly when perimeters were breached and uninvited visitors set foot on Cuban soil.

Those visitors were prone to disappear without a trace, Encizo knew, though some of them were kept alive for propaganda purposes—a captured agent now and then, whose presence on the island could embarrass Washington sufficiently to satisfy Fidel's colossal ego, make him think that he was one up in the game of national diplomacy. These days, the satisfaction of a nuisance victory from time to time was all that Castro had.

It was incredible, Encizo thought, the way the man hung on in spite of everything that happened in the world around him. In the recent past Communism had been repudiated by Moscow and the nations of Eastern Europe. Germany was reunited, with the Berlin Wall reduced to scrap and chunk souvenirs for Western tourists. Hungary's dictator had been executed by firing squad and Russian moderates had defeated a short-lived coup attempt by hard-line reds.

Still, for all the worldwide changes, Castro's Cuba seemed to exist in a political vacuum, divorced from the reality of international events. Gray hair aside, he might have been the same Fidel who tried to bluff America with Russian missiles thirty years ago. Imprisonment of dissidents was still the rule, with cruel interrogation teams and firing squads still gainfully employed at the Principe Prison in Havana. Censorship remained a fact of life, and government reports proclaimed that Castro still enjoyed a widespread popularity among his people, but the truth was difficult—if not impossible—to judge.

This morning, with the predawn darkness giving way to faint light in the east, Encizo dared not let himself be sidetracked by the broader cause of Cuba Libre. He was pledged to a specific mission, with precise and limited objectives. In and out, if everything went well.

Someone had written that you can't go home again. Of course, it wasn't literally true, but Rafael Encizo understood the sentiment. Your life, the lives of those around you, changed irrevocably each and every day. Once years had passed, returning to your roots became an exercise in preordained futility. And yet, some men were bound to try, against the odds, determined to reverse the course of history.

Encizo had decided it was one thing to repay old scores and punish enemies, another to expect that what you did for private motives would eventually change the world. In joining Phoenix Force he had accepted and acknowledged his responsibility to stand against the savages in any form, forsaking private grudges for the most part, working for a common cause.

But if the two should intersect . . .

When they were fifty yards from shore, he let himself believe they had a chance. The final run took everything he had, in terms of strength and concentration, leaving on the oars and battling the surf that broke against a rocky shore. Their target was a stretch of open beach, and making it required a pull against the current, straining until the muscles in his back and shoulders cried for mercy, perspiration mingling with the salt spray on his face.

There was a flooded cavern close to where they landed, carved out of the cliff by several million years of wind and water working constantly on polished stone. They carried the inflatable inside and weighted it with stones, against the possibility they might be able to return and use it for their getaway.

And if it blew up in their faces, they'd have to find another way. Assuming they were still in any shape to leave the island once their work was done.

"That's it," James said, retreating to the nearby rocks where they had left their duffel bags of gear. "You ready?"

It was a long walk to Niquero, where their contact would be waiting, but discretion was the better part of valor, and they had specifically requested that they not be met. In fact the man they were supposed to meet had no idea of how or where they would be entering the country.

Just in case.

Encizo frowned and nodded. "I'm as ready as I'll ever be."

And he hoped that it was true.

*Panama City*
*6:15 a.m.*

IT WAS EARLY for the jackals to be stirring, but in Bolan's estimation they had passed a restless night. Before he broke off contact, shortly after two o'clock, he had allowed both major gangs to feel the heat, a switch-off that would make Barbosa and Velasco realize that both of them were under fire. All things considered, with the atmosphere of competition they had cultivated during recent months, the logical result would be suspicion aimed at each other, hopefully igniting sparks that could be fanned into a full-fledged shooting war.

In fact he was prepared to fan some sparks right now.

The shipping office was Velasco's pride and joy, a point of entry for approximately half of the cocaine he moved through Panama and the Bahamas and Miami. Other shipments traveled overland or came by air, diverse routes utilized to frustrate customs and the DEA, but oceangoing traffic from the east coast of Colombia to Panama was fairly constant, with official payoffs minimizing interference from the law.

So far, the information Bolan had received from Angelo Rodriguez and Miranda had been accurate in all respects, but he reviewed each target in advance, allowing for the possibility of error or deliberate deception. Anytime a soldier worked on hostile ground with unfamiliar allies, he was well advised to double-check incoming data prior to making any lethal moves. He had no reason to mistrust the dissidents as yet, but he had seen how personal agendas sometimes skewed perception and produced erroneous reports. The last thing Bolan needed was to find himself caught up in any kind of local power play.

His mission was essentially divorced from politics, except where politicians had allied themselves with Bolan's targets, selling out to leaders of the drug cartels. As such—at least in Bolan's mind—the "statesmen'' had surrendered any special privileges they had as chosen spokesmen for the people.

When you wallowed in the sty, you came out smelling like a pig.

And it was time for makin' bacon, yes, indeed.

According to the best intelligence his allies could accumulate, Velasco was expecting—or had just received—a major shipment at his warehouse on the waterfront. For Bolan's purposes it hardly mattered either way. If he could torch a load of coke, so much the better, but his goal was simple havoc, come what may.

He wore a knee-length overcoat that covered up his hardware—a Beretta 92-SB autoloader slung beneath his left arm in a quick-draw rig, and the stubby Heckler & Koch MP-5 K submachine gun carried on a swivel mount to Bolan's right. The outer pockets of his coat were heavy with M-68 impact fragmentation grenades and spare magazines for the H&K stuttergun.

The warrior believed in preparing himself, leaving little or nothing to chance.

Gray dawn was breaking on the waterfront as Bolan left his vehicle and walked the long block to his target. Even with the night's turmoil, there were no guards posted in the warehouse parking lot or on the loading dock. Velasco was apparently intent on broadcasting the image of business as usual, biding his time until he could identify his enemies and move decisively to mete out punishment. Meanwhile the Executioner had no doubt that there *would* be guards inside the building, but the absence of perimeter defenses gave him room to operate.

A metal ladder had been bolted to the warehouse wall beside the loading dock, and Bolan took advantage of it, climbing swiftly to the broad, flat roof. Skylights had been employed to save on electricity, and the warrior used them now to scan the indoor killing ground as best he could. Below him, crates and cartons were arranged in east-west rows with aisles between them, forklifts standing off to one side like a pair of drowsy dinosaurs. He couldn't see the office, but he counted four armed men and doubled that to play it safe.

The warehouse was a spacious structure, tall and broad. Inside, the crates of merchandise were stacked up ten or twelve feet high, an easy fifteen feet below the ceiling. Bolan didn't fancy the idea of leaping through an open skylight, trusting crates of unknown merchandise to bear his weight instead of dumping him with twisted joints and broken bones. It was a way to go, but he preferred a more conservative approach.

Like flushing out the rats, for instance, and allowing them to help him with his job.

He started at the west end of the warehouse, farthest from the ladder, with a frag grenade in one hand and his MP-5 K submachine gun in the other. Impact fuses meant that he couldn't risk pitching through the plate-glass skylights. He'd have to clear the way before he made each drop, and that meant timing, right on down the line.

Four skylights, four grenades.

He fired a 3-round burst at point-blank range and dropped his M-68 before the echo of the gunfire died away, racing on toward the next skylight in line. Behind him, the muffled *crump* of an explosion rocked the warehouse, startled voices rising from inside. Another burst, another drop, and he was moving on. He repeated the procedure twice more before he reached the west end of the building, pausing only long enough to feed the stuttergun a brand-new magazine.

He took the ladder in a rush, fairly sliding down the last ten feet or so before his feet touched solid ground, and he was waiting with his submachine gun when Velasco's troops erupted from the warehouse, shouting questions, cursing, waving guns.

Bunched up that way, the seven of them never really had a chance. He swept them with a stream of Parabellum manglers, left to right and back again, the MF-5 K laying down a steady line of fire. Three seconds emptied out the magazine, and Bolan palmed his side arm, closing in for mercy rounds to finish off the two men still alive.

Inside the warehouse, echoes of a secondary blast told Bolan one or more of his grenades had sparked a fire, the hungry flames exploring, looking for a place to feed. He didn't know what kind of merchandise Velasco had inside the building and he didn't care. His point was made.

Until the next stop, right.

The Executioner was only warming up, and he had much to do before the main event. Along the way, he meant to give his enemies a taste of hell on earth.

It was the very least that he could do.


*Havana, Cuba*
*7:15 a.m.*


MAJOR LUIS RIVERA was an early riser by disposition and training. A child of peasant stock, he grew up working in the cane fields from the crack of dawn to sundown, a compulsive regimen that followed him into the military service of his country some years later. These days, when his rank and duties would have normally allowed him to relax a bit, he found himself controlled by force of habit, instinct—call it what you will. He rose near dawn each day, regardless of the season or the work at hand, and rarely went to bed before the stroke of midnight, even on his rare days off.

It happened, therefore, that Rivera was on duty, working in his office, when the call from Panama came through. It was his private line, reserved for sensitive communications, theoretically unmonitored by his superiors within the DSE.

"Hello?"

"We have a problem."

He didn't expect the caller to identify himself. Indeed, it would have been superfluous, because Rivera recognized his voice. It was Delvalle, doubtless calling on a line he felt couldn't be traced. Rivera smiled and hoped he was correct. If not, the colonel had a lot to lose.

"Explain."

"A war of sorts," Delvalle said. "Our friends are killing one another in the streets."

Rivera frowned. Again, there was no need for names. He knew the major drug cartels in Panama as well as anyone, their rivalry and simmering mistrust. It was a fact of life with scum like that, the threat of violence over an imagined insult.

"I believe enforcement of the law is your department," he replied.

"You have a sizable investment in the operation," Delvalle said petulantly. "I thought that you should be informed."

"And what is it that you would have me do?"

The colonel thought about it for a moment, taken by surprise. He called sometimes to ask advice, more often to complain about the risk that he was taking in return for getting fabulously rich, but their arrangement was a relatively simple one. Rivera and the Cuban government agreed to underwrite the traffic in Colombian cocaine and share in any profits made in Nassau. If the DSE was needed to facilitate a shipment, calling on its covert sources to resolve occasional emergencies, Rivera was prepared to go the extra mile. But there was clearly nothing he could do about a gang war in the capital of Panama.

"I thought you should be told," Delvalle repeated. "If it continues, there will be investigations. Should your link to the arrangement be disclosed—"

"It will not be disclosed," Rivera interrupted, tight-lipped, feeling angry color burn in his cheeks. "I have your word on that, unless I am mistaken."

"No, of course not." Suddenly Delvalle sounded worried. Fair enough. "I simply meant—"

"A revelation of the sort that you suggest would surely point to you, as well," the major said. "And if you somehow managed to escape detection, I would still be forced to reevaluate our contract."

"As I said—"

"There would be diplomatic protests, I imagine," Rivera said, cutting off Delvalle's words, "but in the absence of compelling evidence, the president would hardly recognize such blatant propaganda as established fact. We would be forced to cut our losses, as the Yankees say.''

There was a momentary silence from Delvalle as he registered the message, taking it to heart. He got the point, but it could do no harm to emphasize.

''Remember Salazar,'' Rivera said.

''Of course.''

''And please feel free to keep in touch if you have any more concerns.''

''I will.''

The line went dead, Rivera cradling the handset as he leaned back in his swivel chair. He *was* concerned about the prospect of disruption to the trade through Panama, since he was banking on that traffic for his own retirement fund. Beyond the personal concern, Rivera's guarantee of safety had persuaded his superiors to let the scheme proceed, and any failure now would place his own neck on the chopping block.

He would begin to monitor the situation closely through his eyes in Panama, but he would take no action yet. Direct involvement would be premature, potentially disastrous if the game went sour.

He could wait awhile before he made his move.

And if Delvalle weakened, showing signs of strain...well, there were ways around that problem, too.

In fact no matter how the game played out, it might be wise to look for new associations. Insurance, as it were.

Rivera lighted a fat cigar and blew smoke toward the the ceiling fan that slowly twirled above his head. The flat blades went to work and tore the smoke apart like shredded dreams.

It could be just that easy, he decided, if he had to pull the pin.

And it was always good to be prepared.

# CHAPTER ELEVEN

*Panama City*
*7:45 a.m.*

*Remember Salazar.*

Antonio Delvalle didn't have to rack his brain on that one. He could spell the details out from memory, with no refresher from the covert files he kept locked in his office.

Reuben Salazar had been a Cuban operative in Panama, a go-between of sorts when Noriega was in power, handling payoffs, running messages between the presidential palace and the DSE when there were matters that required extreme discretion. He had served for eighteen months before he lost his mind and thought that he could play both ends against the middle, holding up his masters with a threat of airing their dirty secrets, scuttling the Panamanian connection with America if he revealed the Cuban bond.

It was a gamble, and the agent lost. Rivera had no tolerance for fools, and he reserved a special hatred for the kind of traitor who would sell out his country for private gain. Not that the major's communistic principles prevented him from banking money on the side, by any means, but he demanded loyalty from his troops at any cost.

When Salazar went missing on a Friday night, Delvalle knew he was as good as dead. The shock had come when he surfaced three days later, bound with barbed wire to a telephone pole on the outskirts of Fort Clayton, overlooking the canal. According to the medical examiner's report, he had been tortured brutally, nonstop, for most of the three days that he was missing. Shock and blood loss had eventually spared him further agony, and he was then discarded as a public warning to Rivera's other agents in the field.

Betrayal had a price, and there was no escape.

Delvalle thought that it had been an error to involve Rivera in his current problem, but the news was bound to reach him, either way. At least in this scenario Delvalle demonstrated loyalty, full disclosure of the facts before Rivera heard the story from his spotters on the street. And if the Cuban was uncomfortable with the night's events, so much the better. He might actually be moved to help Delvalle for a change, instead of simply waiting for his bonus payments to arrive.

Or, did he really want the Cuban's help?

It crossed Delvalle's mind that DSE involvement meant a loss of personal control, intrusion by a band of foreigners who took their orders solely from Havana. Intervention by the Cubans placed another wild card in the deck, when he was faced with two rogue players as it was. Barbosa and Velasco had to be controlled, and that would mean involving Santiago.

Damn it!

Overnight, Delvalle's neatly ordered world was threatening to fall apart, and at the moment he had no concrete idea of how to put it right. His first attempt—the phone call to Rivera—now appeared to be a grave mistake. His next move, calling Santiago, would be calculated in advance, to guarantee the desired result.

Santiago enjoyed his privacy, avoiding contact with business associates whenever possible, but this qualified as an emergency in Delvalle's mind. Barbosa and Velasco were on the verge of open war, if they hadn't already crossed the line. Both purchased their supplies from Santiago, and he had to understand how much a shooting war—with the resultant heat of an investigation—stood to jeopardize his safety. No one was untouchable these days if thrown into the eye of publicity.

There was a chance that the Colombian might turn his back, refuse to help Delvalle out, but you didn't become a multimillionaire—some said a billionaire—if you were stupid. First and foremost, Santiago was a businessman who kept watch on his empire, from the tracts of forest where the coca leaves were harvested, through jungle laboratories and the transport caravans, to shipment, sale and distribution on the street. At any point along the way, a relatively minor problem could become exaggerated, growing over time if it wasn't examined and resolved.

Guillermo Santiago had a reputation for resolving problems, and Delvalle hoped he'd agree to intervene between Barbosa and Velasco, make them understand that all this killing would be bad for business. Bad for all concerned.

If they refused to listen, one or both of them would have to die.

It was a drastic step, Delvalle realized, but as the bodies started piling up, there would be public calls for justice, restoration of the peace. Arresting either of the dealers and subjecting him to trial would be like opening Pandora's box. Who could predict what either man might say if he was called to testify—the payoffs he had made to ranking members of the government since Noriega's fall, the links with Santiago in Colombia and other friends in the Bahamas, moving drugs to the United States. It would be scandalous, disaster for them all.

Of course, such felons had been known to struggle and resist arrest. In that case no one would be startled if a gun went off and blood was shed. The officer who pulled the trigger would become a hero, earn promotion. The dealer who replaced Barbosa or Velasco—maybe both—would learn from their mistakes and make an effort to avoid embarrassing his friends.

Delvalle was beginning to enjoy the fantasy, but logic told him he should strive for a more peaceable solution first. Barbosa and Velasco paid their bribes on time, and they had caused no major problems up until the past few hours. It was premature to think of killing either man before they had a chance to talk.

But he would speak to Santiago first. A point of courtesy or protocol—and personal insurance, just in case things went from bad to worse.

Besides, Delvalle liked to share his troubles. It was so much nicer than attempting to discover the solutions on his own. And if he failed, by any chance, there would be blame enough to go around.

*Chigorodo, Colombia*
*8:30 a.m.*

THE SWIMMING POOL was lined with tile imported from Venice, hand-painted with erotic scenes that would have made the *Kama Sutra*'s author stop and stare. Below the surface of the water, they were magnified, distorted slightly, so the figures almost seemed to come alive.

Guillermo Santiago liked to dive and hold his breath, imagining the several thousand figures come to life, all coupling frantically around him as he watched. Sometimes, it made him so excited that he had to call for one of his women and possess her, right there in the pool.

It was a privilege that came from owning money, land and people.

Power was the key, and Santiago never tired of bending peasants to his will. The fact that he considered nearly everyone else in the world as peasants didn't endear him to his fellow man, but popularity had never been the drug lord's first concern.

In fact it never ranked as a concern at all.

His father had worked on a coffee plantation near Bello, north of Medellín, but they were caught up in *La Violencia,* Guillermo's parents and two older brothers killed by left-wing guerrillas in a Sunday raid on the village.

Or had they been right-wing guerrillas?

It was hard to remember after twenty-six years, and Santiago had only been fourteen at the time. Still, he was old enough to remember faces glimpsed from his hiding place in the forest, along with the names their attackers had called back and forth to one another while they killed the men and boys, dragging some of the younger women and girls away for their pleasure.

It took Guillermo Santiago nineteen months to find them all and kill each one in turn. Before he finished, he was almost seventeen and he had earned a reputation as a ruthless killer. In the neighborhood of Medellín, that background either got you work or got you killed.

Santiago took the work.

For seven years he executed contracts for the Medellín cartel, collecting information all the while and memorizing the mistakes his masters made, so that he could avoid them in the future. By the time he was twenty-five years old, Guillermo Santiago had a nest egg that allowed him to acquire a shipment of cocaine. He also had the necessary skill and nerve to smuggle it through the Dominican Republic to Miami, where he tripled his money. That shipment led to another and another, until he had a different sort of reputation. Now, he was a ruthless killer with a growing fortune on his hands, and those who wished to deal with Santiago didn't snap their fingers anymore.

They showed respect.

Which is to say, they were afraid.

Respect and fear were flip sides of the coin in Santiago's business. You couldn't have one without the other, when you dealt with jackals every day. A show of weakness on the smallest matter was enough to get you killed, and there were always several dozen would-be leaders waiting in the wings to take your place.

So far, pretenders to the throne had had no luck with Santiago. When the leader of the Medellín cartel got jealous and dispatched assassins to his rancho in the north, Guillermo sent the genitals of his attackers home in plastic sandwich bags. When the guerrillas pressured Santiago for extortion money, he invested in a pair of military helicopters, tracked them to their village and destroyed them in the middle of the night, together with their families.

It was the only way he knew to play the game.

Beyond a certain point, the money was irrelevant. It hardly mattered if he had six hundred million or a billion dollars stashed in safe-deposit boxes, scattered far and wide from Bogotá to Nassau and Lucerne. A year from now, he might have twice as much, considering the American appetite for drugs, and that was fine. Guillermo had more money now than he could ever spend, unless he chose to buy himself a continent, and there were none for sale.

It was the power that he craved, a poor boy's compensation for the early deprivations of his life, the things that he was forced to do and witness as he grew to manhood. Now, when Santiago snapped his fingers, women knelt to do his bidding, politicians kissed his ass and hard-eyed soldiers asked him who should be the next to die.

And any man who tried to strip Guillermo Santiago of his power was as good as dead.

He surfaced in a rush, his dark hair plastered to his scalp and shoulders. Clinging to a ladder in the deep end of the pool, he saw one of his servants approaching with a cordless telephone in hand.

Guillermo frowned. In his experience the unexpected calls were mostly trouble, seldom news that anyone would want to hear. Still, trouble was a part of power, and its resolution was the final test.

He scrambled halfway up the ladder, heedless of the fact that he was naked.

"A thousand pardons, sir," he servant said. "The telephone . . ."

"Who is it, Esteban?"

"From Panama, sir. The soldier."

"Ah."

There were perhaps a hundred people in the world who had the number for Guillermo Santiago's private line, and one of them was Colonel Antonio Delvalle of the Panama Defense Forces. Santiago didn't like the man, but he was useful in his way, especially since Noriega's downfall. More specifically, Delvalle knew it was unwise to bother Santiago at his home with trivia, which meant the call would be important.

"Leave the telephone."

"Yes, sir."

Santiago found a towel and dried his hands. He didn't ask the naked woman on the chaise longue by the pool to leave. The headphones covering her ears would give him ample privacy, and Santiago liked the view.

"Antonio."

"I must apologize for calling you at home, Guillermo."

"Never mind."

"We have a problem here...."

"Go on."

"Our friends are quarreling. There are casualties."

Guillermo felt a knot of apprehension forming in his gut. "How many?"

"Seventeen, so far. More wounded, I suspect."

"The cause?"

Delvalle hesitated. "It is difficult to say. The trouble started overnight. I have not spoken with them yet."

"But you are calling me."

The colonel paused again, aware of his mistake now, anxious not to make it worse. "I thought that you should know in case I cannot reason with them. If I must take steps..."

"Of course. I'll see what I can do, meanwhile. If there are any further difficulties, use your own initiative."

"I will."

Guillermo cradled the receiver, no goodbye or fare-thee-well to speed the colonel on his way. Delvalle had a job to do, and every moment he spent on the telephone was wasted time.

The drug lord had a job to do, as well.

Barbosa and Velasco were subordinates, but they weren't his men per se. Both dealers came to Santiago for their merchandise, and so he exercised a fair amount of influence, but they could always turn to Medellín or Cali if they didn't like his rules.

At least they thought so, anyway.

In fact Guillermo Santiago rarely let a customer escape. He was a reasonable man, where business was concerned, and did his best to look out for the interests of his customers. When they betrayed him, though, or jeopardized his safety, there was hell to pay.

He wouldn't judge Barbosa or Velasco on the basis of a phone call from Delvalle, but it was enough to make him seek more information on his own. A shooting war in Panama was bad for business, worse than all the killing that went on in Medellín and Bogotá. At home the violence was accepted as a fact of life, a means of helping Nature weed out her defective specimens. In other countries, where the Yankees had expressed an interest, random bloodshed in the streets could bring on punitive reactions that were bad for all concerned.

Guillermo meant to find out what was going on and solve the problem for the benefit of all concerned, but mostly for himself. He didn't like intrusions on his quiet life at home, and he would punish those responsible.

Beginning now.

*Panama City*
*9:05 a.m.*

THE CROWD HAD STARTED turning out by eight o'clock, responding to the flyers circulated over several days. Miranda had been hoping for a group of six or even seven thousand people, but she estimated nearly twice that many in the ranks when they began their march downtown. The organizers soon ran out of placards, but a number of the demonstrators brought their own, and others were content to simply chant or sing in time with those who carried signs.

It was Democracy in Action's largest protest demonstration in the past three months, and she could see that they were gaining bodies all the time, new marchers falling into line with every block they traveled. Traffic snarled on side streets, blocked by the procession, and police were out in force to keep the peace. So far, they hadn't tried to stop the march, but she expected opposition well before they reached the presidential palace.

And from that point on, it would get interesting.

Miranda marched and sang the old, familiar songs, but she couldn't help thinking of the tall American and the explosive violence he had triggered overnight. If there were less police along the line of marchers than usual, it was because their officers had called them off to pick up bodies, scouring the urban battleground for evidence.

She understood that it wouldn't be possible to root out the cocaine dealers by peaceful means, and yet the latest violence left her feeling guilty. Never mind that it was only killers who had died, so far. Her struggle with Democracy in Action was an effort to eliminate the kind of strongman government so common in Latin American countries, where human rights traditionally took a back seat to privilege and so-called national security. It seemed incongruous that violence would be necessary to achieve their goal, but there had seemed to be no other way.

Worse yet, they were relying on Americans to solve the problem, when they should have done the work themselves. Again, Miranda understood the reasons, all about the link between Colombian cocaine and the United States, but she couldn't escape a feeling that the Yankees had to be laughing at her people, viewing them as childlike peasants who could never quite get out of trouble on their own.

The Great White Father rides again.

She didn't get that feeling for the man who called himself Belasko, but she understood that he wasn't alone. There would be other men who pulled the strings and gave the orders, men in Washington who felt they had the right to raid her country anytime they had the urge, abducting presidents or peons for a trial in the United States.

Someday, when she and all the thousands like her had a chance to prove themselves, perhaps that view would change.

And in the meantime, they would demonstrate at every opportunity.

A cry went up along the line. Miranda, near the middle of the crush, jumped up on tiptoe long enough to see the armored cars approaching two abreast. With just a glimpse she recognized the AMAC vehicles that had been purchased from America, their windows screened with heavy wire. Each car would have a dozen riot officers inside, but they were weapons in themselves, equipped with ramming bumpers, water-cannon and grenade launchers, water-cascade pipes to keep the sides slippery and douse petrol bombs, electrical wires in the hull to shock any unwelcome hangers-on.

Behind the vehicles she saw a line of riot clubs and helmets steadily advancing, easily a hundred officers. They were still nearly half a mile from the presidential palace, and the gauntlet had been thrown.

A loudspeaker on one of the cars gave the challenge, a disembodied voice commanding the marchers to cease and disperse. The rest was as predictable as any movie watched a hundred times before. No matter how Miranda or the other organizers tried to caution their marchers in advance, they couldn't change the script.

From somewhere in the crowd a rock was thrown. It missed the armored cars and rattled in the street, more missiles following within perhaps a second and a half. Miranda called for them to stop, but no one heard or listened. In a public demonstration, when the troops arrived, you started throwing rocks. It was the thing to do.

And when the rocks began to fly, the water cannon opened up.

Again, it was a standard move, but many of the demonstrators managed to appear surprised. Some of the men were shouting curses, women screaming, everybody dodging as the high-pressure nozzles commenced firing. One swept the ranks with a continuous stream, sweeping marchers off their feet, while the other blasted away with rapid-fire pulses of water, each striking home with a force enough to knock a large man down.

The vehicles advanced, and Miranda was jostled by the crowd as it began to break and turn. Another moment, and she heard the popping sound of the grenades as they were launched, pale clouds of nauseating "pepper" gas erupting where the shells touched down. Miranda started pushing through the crowd, not running from the vehicles so much as making for the sidewalk, knowing she could easily be trampled if she tried to stand fast in the middle of the street.

The armored cars were closer by the time she reached her destination, butting slow, disoriented marchers with their special bumpers, rolling over one man's leg when he fell down and wasn't quick enough to wriggle clear. Miranda didn't hear the sound of snapping bones, but she couldn't escape his high-pitched scream of agony.

She found the recessed doorway of a shop, stayed long enough to catch her breath, then plunged back into the frenetic, churning crowd. There was an alley up ahead, perhaps an exit from the riot scene if she could get that far. The hot tears in her eyes weren't entirely due to CS gas.

What kind of government preferred to gas its people rather than sit down and listen to their justified complaints? How could she champion nonviolence when the state replied to every peaceful protest with a show of force?

The riot troops were charging now, their truncheons flailing, cracking skulls. Behind the tinted plastic shields, their faces were invisible. For all she knew they might be robots programmed for destruction, stored in basements underneath the palace until their services were needed on the street.

She ran, half blinded by the gas now, almost to the alley when a hand fell on her shoulder, spinning her around. The club was two feet long, at least, black plastic gleaming with a bright steel knob at either end. Miranda lost her footing and fell against the wall. She saw the club drawn back, prepared to strike.

The man came out of nowhere, stepping past her and delivering a swift kick to the soldier's groin. The riot stick went flying, clattering on the pavement. Her attacker clutched himself and went down on his knees. The stranger turned to face Miranda, one hand reaching out for hers.

Belasko.

"Time to go," he said, and jerked her to her feet.

A moment later they were running.

# CHAPTER TWELVE

*Rio Atrato, Colombia*
*11:15 a.m.*

Yakov Katzenelenbogen estimated they had crossed the border sometime shortly after half-past nine o'clock. The drive from Panama City had taken four hours, including the river crossing at El Real, and they had left their vehicle on that side of the border, hiking their equipment across without displaying any paperwork for customs and immigration. There was no way to explain the hardware, so they didn't even try.

American relations with Colombia were strained already, given Washington's insistence of a cocaine crackdown Bogotá couldn't—or wouldn't—implement, and covert efforts to disrupt the country's leading cash-and-carry industry were bound to raise some eyebrows. Drugs were a domestic problem to the government in Bogotá, and politicians had been "working on" the problem for a decade, getting nowhere fast. Still, American intervention was regarded as an insult.

They had long memories in South America, but looking to the future was a different story. If you came up short on grazing land, burn down the jungles and to hell with global oxygen supplies, endangered species and erosion. Massacre the native Indians to build a superhighway through their territory, eight lanes running from the capital to stop dead in the forest, ten or fifteen miles away. Think first about a business partner's ethnic background, rather than his acumen or honesty.

There came a time when it wasn't enough to shrug and say mañana, hoping that a problem would resolve itself and simply go away. Cocaine was such a problem, and today was such a time.

Their course lay overland, and it had led them into marshy ground an hour earlier. The swamp would slow them, but they had planned ahead, allowing extra time to make the trek. Their greatest danger at the moment would be quicksand or the slim, flat-headed vipers that could kill a man in minutes if their venom reached a major artery or vein. Bushmaster. Fer-de-lance. Jararaca. Katz knew that there were several other species, but the names meant nothing to him. He was busy watching for their subtle movement in the undergrowth, a hint of warning in advance.

Before much longer, when they laid their ambush on the jungle trail, they'd be watching for a different kind of snake. This breed of reptile walked on two legs like a man and made his living from the misery of others, dooming thousands to a slower, more degrading death than any serpent in the forest.

And he did it all for cash.

They wouldn't strike the viper's nest today. Instead, they were about to send a message back and let their adversary mull it over for a while. It was absurd to think that he'd make the right decision, suddenly decide to close up shop and take his millions off to Switzerland or who-knows-where, but they were buying time. A setup punch before the knockout, while their comrades fought on other fronts.

"There."

McCarter blocked the narrow trail in front of him, but Katz could hear the river now. The bridge would be nearby. The Israeli checked his watch and found that they were running short of time.

Assuming that the caravan left Chigorodo right on schedule and met no opposition on the way—a safe assumption, in Guillermo Santiago's own backyard— the trucks should be along within the next half hour, give or take. That left them time enough to do their work, but only if they started now and did it right the first time. No mistakes and no delays.

"Let's do it," Katzenelenbogen said, already moving as he spoke.

The plan was relatively simple, given the terrain. Their targets would be slowing down across the bridge from force of habit, and the Phoenix warriors would allow them to reach the west end before springing their trap. Claymore directional mines would bracket the trucks and help close the back door, but it would all come down to firepower from there, after the initial surprise.

Like always.

Three against how many?

Their intelligence said two trucks rolling, with a point car and another bringing up the rear. Perhaps a dozen guns, if they were lucky, but they couldn't count on luck. That first punch had to be a killer, so the rest of it was only mopping up, a message to Guillermo Santiago from an enemy he didn't know existed. It was overdue, and there was no time like the present for delivery.

Katz watched his men and covered them as they began to place the Claymores, listening for any sound that would betray the caravan arriving early. Every second counted now, to get them in position and concealed before their enemies came on the scene.

It was a grim, familiar feeling, making ready to annihilate a group of total strangers, but it didn't prey on Katzenelenbogen's mind. The men he meant to kill were murderers themselves, some killing with the guns they carried, others with the drugs they sold. By any standard of morality they were the lowest breed of scum. A well-paid lawyer might debate their rights until doomsday, but he wouldn't have the chance with these.

It was payback time, or getting there at any rate.

IT WAS A PLEASURE being on the road. Orlando Cruz enjoyed the border runs, a taste of power, even though he knew the border sentries showed respect for Santiago's guns and money, rather than for Cruz himself. He was an emissary, nothing more, but it was still a vast improvement over living in the mountains with his family and picking coffee beans until his hair turned white.

Each time Orlando thought about his parents, he was unsure whether he should laugh or cry. One signaled disrespect, the other weakness, so he mostly kept his feelings to himself. It was a man's way, and it served him well enough, except in private moments when the past crept up and took him by surprise.

It was a long way from the Cordillera Oriental, south of Bogotá, to Chigorodo and the post he held in Santiago's empire. Cruz had been a simple peasant when he left his home and crossed the mountains, bound for Medellín. He was attracted by the tales of men grown rich on selling coca to the Yankees, who could kill themselves with drugs for all he cared. It made no difference to Orlando what went on in other countries, just so long as he could rise above the poverty that was his birthright, find a way to hold his head up like a man.

And so he had.

The easy part was making contact with the drug cartels. They were impossible to miss in Medellín, with flashy cars and women, the palatial homes, the suits that would have cost a simple working man his yearly income. The drug lords always needed errand boys, and that was how he started, volunteering as a gunman once he realized it was the quickest way to get ahead. The first time out, Cruz nearly wet his pants when it was time to pull the trigger on a human target, but the feeling passed and he discovered the rewards of violence went beyond a simple paycheck.

There was something in the act of killing that allowed Orlando Cruz to view himself with new respect, imagining that others felt the same. And if they only feared him, that would be the next best thing. In either case they looked at him with different eyes, and women sought his company. Above all else, he felt a rush of godlike power every time he pulled the trigger. It was more than he had ever hoped for, better than his wildest dreams.

Unfortunately there would be no killing on a run like this. He almost wished the jungle bandits or guerrillas would forget themselves and try to steal the shipment, sacrifice themselves for his enjoyment just this once. It was a fantasy, of course. Between the bribes that Santiago paid and his established reputation as a killer, it would take some kind of lunatic to challenge him this close to home.

Too bad. But Cruz could always dream.

Once they had cleared the bridge, it was another forty minutes to the border checkpoint. Crossing into Panama was a formality. The guards received a pittance, their superiors a more substantial sum delivered in advance. In Pinogana they would drop their cargo, turn around and go back the way they came. When they were safely back in Chigorondo, Cruz would start to think about the evening, new ways to amuse himself.

But they would have to get there first.

He stayed alert despite his knowledge that it would require a madman to attack the shipment, for there were such men. In fact Colombia bred more than her fair share, as witnessed by the rate of violent crime and random, senseless homicides reported every year. Colombia had more murders per capita than the trigger-happy United States, and no one but the victims seemed to mind.

Riding in the open military jeep that led the convoy, Cruz was ready when the bridge came into view. He had an Uzi submachine gun in his lap, two men behind him armed with AK-47s. There were more guns in the trucks and in the trailing jeep. Enough to handle any sudden threat.

The bridge had always struck him as the perfect place to mount an ambush. It had never happened—they had never even met another vehicle, in more than forty trips—but Cruz imagined gunmen hiding in the jungle, watching as his jeep approached, the trucks bunched up behind. Once they were on the bridge, their options for escape were strictly limited. Advance or put it in reverse, assuming they weren't boxed in. Perhaps a wild leap from the bridge, if they weren't cut down before they left the vehicles.

It made Cruz nervous, and he always compensated with a smutty joke, protracted long enough to see them safely on the other side before he dropped the punch line, making everybody laugh. Today, it was a variation of the padre and the farmer's daughter, adding little twists to make the priest seem more perverse, the virgin more seductive. They were chuckling in their seats behind him, waiting for the good part as they rolled across the bridge.

Orlando Cruz felt better.

He was smiling when the world exploded in his face.

THE CLAYMORES WERE command-fired by remote control, each mine containing hundreds of ball bearings fixed in plastic, primed to cover a sixty-degree arc at the maximum effective range of 270 yards. The present range was more like forty feet, with two mines set to go off simultaneously, one on either side.

The jeep in front was dead on target, rolling at an estimated twenty miles per hour when McCarter keyed his mines from twenty yards away. There was a double puff of smoke, a crack of thunder and he watched the jeep disintegrate. A hundred shotgun blasts couldn't have done such damage, vaporizing glass and shredding rubber, ripping through the open jeep, its engine block, the four male passengers.

McCarter saw the jeep stop dead, its punctured radiator draining in a liquid rush. The first truck back in line was peppered by the double blast, its driver swerving to avoid collision with the jeep, but his reaction was too little and too late. The bumpers came together with a loud metallic crunch, and then the truck stalled out as well.

There was a screech of brakes downrange, the tail car's driver trying to reverse when Gary Manning fired his Claymores at the other end. One of the gunners in the second jeep had risen to his feet, a futile gesture of defiance, and McCarter grimaced as the man disintegrated in a cloud of crimson spray. His three companions were protected slightly by the jeep itself, but none of them were spared.

McCarter had the lead truck in his rifle sights before the echo of the secondary Claymore blasts had died away. He saw the shotgun rider scramble from his seat and drop into a crouch beside the vehicle, an automatic weapon in his hands. The gunner had no targets, and a gash above one eye had drenched the left side of his face in blood, but he was ready to defend his cargo to the death.

Almost forty yards stood between them when he fired a short burst from his automatic rifle, aiming for the gunner's chest. The 5.45 mm rounds were dead on, tumbling after impact, driving McCarter's target back against the body of the truck. The gunner squeezed off a burst as he fell, but it was wasted on the asphalt at his feet.

The driver was next, still hunched inside the half-ton's cab. McCarter stitched a burst across the windshield, hoping it would rattle him, but there was no response. More fire from Katz and Manning on the flanks, and someone was responding from the second truck in line. Both of the larger vehicles were trapped, immobilized by wreckage, but a number of their occupants were clearly armed and able to resist attack.

McCarter rose from cover, moving in a crouch as he approached the bridge. The gunners in the second truck were busy with Manning and Katz, defending their flanks, and the ex-SAS commando concentrated on his main objective, holding the AKS-74 braced against his hip.

The four men in the jeep were wasted, fresh blood mingling with gasoline and motor oil in a pool beneath the riddled vehicle. McCarter crouched beside the point car, wondering if the truck's driver might be hit after all. It would simplify matters no end, but he had to be sure . . . and that meant confirmation.

He palmed one of the minigrenades, pulled the safety pin and wound up for the pitch. An easy fifteen feet or so, and he was counting on the half-ton's bodywork to help contain the blast. Whatever happened after that, McCarter would be on his own.

The shattered windshield made it simple, up and over in an easy lob. He saw the egg bounce off the dashboard, dropping out of sight, and then a strangled-sounding cry of panic issued from the truck. The driver's door flew open and a man leaped out, all flailing arms and legs, intent on putting space between himself and the grenade.

No time to tag him as McCarter ducked back under cover, counting down the last two seconds on the Dutch V-40's fuse. The blast was somewhat muffled, clearing out the half-ton's two remaining windows, shrapnel ripping through the firewall, roof and doors.

Somehow, the driver saved himself from the initial blast, sprawled facedown on the pavement, but his comeback was a problem. Dazed by the concussion, shaken by his brush with death, he lost it when he scrambled to his feet, remembering his automatic pistol much too late. He was stooped over, reaching for it, when McCarter took his head off with a short burst from the AKS.

All done at this end, but the sharp, staccato sound of automatic weapons told him there was still a battle to be won. A number of their enemies were still alive and standing fast.

McCarter went to join the fight and see what he could do about those odds.

HE MADE IT three guns in the truck, at least, and that without the two men still alive in front. From his position on the shoulder of the highway, thirty yards and then some from his targets, Manning was afraid that there was little he could do to flush them out.

The Claymores had eliminated any danger from the trailing jeep, but he had fired them both as planned, and now he had no more to play with. Manning knew that he would have to close the gap if he was going to eliminate the gunners firing from the truck.

He pulled the pin on one of his V-40 frag grenades and lobbed the bomb toward the middle of the bridge, already moving as the blast threw smoke and shrapnel out to cover his advance. He made it halfway to the silent jeep before his adversaries opened up again, and Manning had to belly down against the asphalt.

Now the jeep provided cover. Katzenelenbogen laid down a screen of fire as Manning wriggled closer, digging with his knees and elbows, holding the AKS-74 in front of him. Up close, he heard rounds glancing off the jeep, some punching through and finding flesh or padded seats. A fuel can mounted on the tailgate of the jeep had taken several dozen Claymore hits and spilled its contents on the roadway. Manning crawled through a slick of gasoline and breathed the heady fumes the last few yards.

Terrific.

All he needed was a spark now, and he had a chance to go out with a bang. More reason why he ought to wrap it up as soon as possible, before the gunners in the truck got lucky with a ricochet.

Did they have tracers?

It was doubtful, but the thought set Manning's teeth on edge. He had a mental flash of smoke and flames, a blind rush toward the nearby river, bullets ripping through him as he ran.

Enough!

He had a job to do, and there was no avoiding it. He risked a glance around the body of the jeep in time to see a gunner step down from the cab, the side away from Katz, and advance toward the rear. His enemies were tired of sitting still and taking hits like targets in a shooting gallery, and that was fine, if their impatience made them careless.

Manning drew another grenade from his web belt and yanked the pin, lobbing the deadly egg toward the open back of Santiago's truck. He gave it too much altitude and cursed as the V-40 struck the canvas tarp, spun once and wobbled off the side . . . to land directly at the shotgun rider's feet.

By that time there was about a second and a half remaining on the timer fuse, enough for Manning's enemy to freeze and try a scream for size. The sound of the explosion covered any noise he made before he died, the close-range blast of shrapnel tearing him apart and scattering the ragged pieces like confetti.

In the truck his three surviving comrades opened up in unison, two of them spraying the jeep, one firing toward the undergrowth where Katz had taken up position prior to the attack. A frag grenade went off inside the forward truck, immediately followed by a burst of 5.45 mm rounds, McCarter closing in. The odds were better with a pincers movement, but the Briton's presence in the line of fire restricted Manning's own approach.

One way to do it, if he meant to do it properly.

"Grenade!" he shouted from behind the jeep. "Stand clear!"

It didn't matter, at the moment, whether his intended prey spoke English. If they did, the warning might cause one or more of them to show himself in Manning's line of fire.

He palmed another frag grenade and pulled the pin, correcting from his last pitch for a lower angle, aiming for the open tailgate. One should do the job, if he could make the pitch.

One of the gunners opened fire with a submachine gun as he rose, the jeep absorbing most of it. A hot round ripped through the lifeless driver's skull and spattered the Phoenix warrior with his brains. The lob was overhand, deliberate and precise. Forget about the momentary panic of a weapon smoking almost in your face, and get back to cover in the shadow of the jeep.

He heard a startled cry, and then the lethal egg went off. The shock wave rippled past him, Manning on his feet and firing with the AKS as he advanced. One gunner draped across the tailgate, dead or dying, dark blood soaking through the denim fabric of his shirt. Two bodies remained in the truck, and he shot them both, though neither one was moving.

Stepping to the side, he found McCarter checking out the cab. The driver slumped across the seat, blood trickling from a neat hole in his forehead.

It was almost finished.

Katzenelenbogen joined them on the bridge. "We're running late," he said to no one in particular. "Let's finish it."

They had no thermite, and they needed none. Plain wicks of fabric did the job, inserted in the place of gas caps, Manning backing off before McCarter struck a match. They watched the vehicles catch fire and waited for the secondary blast of fuel tanks from the trucks before they turned away.

McCarter caught a whiff of Manning's clothes and said, "You're lucky someone didn't light *you* up."

"It crossed my mind."

"You don't mind if I smoke," McCarter asked.

"You don't mind if I kick your ass?"

"Another time," Katzenelenbogen said. "We're expected in the city."

"Maybe you should grab a shower first," the former SAS commando said to Manning, "just in case you meet a *señorita.*"

"I don't know. They like their hombres hot, I understand."

"That doesn't mean deep-fried."

They kept the banter up as they retreated from the killing ground, and Katz ignored them, concentrating on the trail. Behind them, underneath a cloudless sky, the hungry flames consumed four vehicles, a dozen corpses and eleven million dollars' worth of pure cocaine.

It was a start.

# CHAPTER THIRTEEN

*Niquero, Cuba*
*Wednesday, 12:00 p.m.*

The produce truck had been a lucky break, all things considered. Three other vehicles had passed them by, suspicious drivers fearing they were thieves or worse, and Calvin James had braced himself to walk the fifteen miles if necessary. It would blow the best part of the day, but there was no alternative . . . until the grinning, almost toothless farmer came along.

In other circumstances James would have tipped him for the ride, but they were traveling as peasants looking for a job in town, and so couldn't afford to show their money. As it was, a round of thanks and handshakes seemed to leave the farmer satisfied, and he continued on his way.

Niquero is a coastal town, 170 miles due west of the U.S. naval station at Guantanamo. Many of the residents are fishermen, but others scratch a living from the earth, growing sugar cane and other crops in the western foothills of the Sierra Maestras. The average Cuban earns less than two thousand dollars per year, and it shows in Niquero, where the shops are small and often poorly patronized. On market days the fishermen and farmers bring their goods to sell from makeshift stalls or wagons parked around the central plaza, but a visitor will look in vain for anything resembling modern stores.

"So this is Castro's revolution."

Rafael Encizo spit into the street. "You know about Fidel and baseball?"

James shook his head. "Can't say I do."

"A year or two before the revolution, in the 1950s, Castro went to New York City. He was famous as a baseball player then, if you can picture that. He tried out for the Yankees, as a pitcher, but he didn't make the cut. Instead, he came back home and entered politics."

"I always leaned toward basketball, myself."

"In some ways I believe he never moved beyond those times...what you would call his glory days. Fidel still dreams of Kennedy and Russian missiles, fighting exiles at the Bay of Pigs. Today, he finds himself alone and doesn't understand the changes in the world, because he can't change himself."

"Sounds like your people need another revolution."

"I believed that once."

"And now?"

Encizo shrugged. "What would happen if Fidel was overthrown tomorrow? Do the millions from America run home and pick up where they left their lives in 1959 or 1980? What about the generations born in the United States?" The Cuban shook his head. "I have no answers now."

"So, let's try different question," James said. "I'll start. Why don't we try to find our contact?"

"Right. We have a job to do."

Their destination was a leather shop, located on a side street two blocks from the central plaza. Stopping at a newsstand for directions, they continued on their way with caution, James imagining suspicion in the glance of every Cuban citizen they passed. He was intensely conscious of the pistol underneath his lightweight jacket and the submachine gun in his faded duffel bag.

They paused again outside the shop. If they were being set up for an ambush, this would be the time. An easy shot for gunmen stationed on the roof directly opposite, or lounging in a small café across the street. Or would the shooters wait until they stepped inside the leather shop? Perhaps the plan included taking them alive for questioning.

James caught himself before his paranoia ran amok. There were no snipers on the roof, and two old women occupied the café's window seats, engrossed in gossip. Neither of them gave the Phoenix warriors so much as a second glance. The few pedestrians in sight appeared to have no interest in the two men standing on the sidewalk, and he would have bet that none of them were armed.

Inside the shop, a young man wearing denim and an apron made of oilcloth huddled at a workbench on their left, putting the final touches on a hand-tooled belt. A cowbell mounted on the door frame clanked twice to announce their presence, and the young man raised his eyes to greet them.

"Yes," the man asked in Spanish.

James let Encizo do the talking and checked out the shop. A faded curtain screened the back room from his view, and he began to drift in that direction, checking out the wallets, shoes and belts on sale, his right hand ready for a draw if there was any indication of a setup.

"I have boots on order," Encizo informed the craftsman, using the code phrase supplied by Andrew Morant. "Vaquero style."

The young man stared at each of them with narrowed eyes, another moment slipping past before he laid his tools aside. "I have them in the back," he said at last. "This way."

It would be now or never, James thought, his fingers resting on the pistol grip as Encizo preceded him. They were alone inside the tiny office-storeroom, and he let himself relax a bit.

"I am Raul Guererro," the young man told them, shaking hands. He didn't ask for names, and none were offered. "I did not expect you to arrive for several hours."

"We got lucky," James replied, surprising Guererro with his command of Spanish.

"So. I call for transportation now."

The young man stepped behind an ancient wooden desk and lifted the receiver on a black, dial-model telephone. Encizo moved to stop him, one hand settling on the man's arm.

"What transportation? Are we going somewhere?"

"You will meet our leader," Guererro replied, "but he cannot come here to see you. The police and DSE, you understand?"

"Where is he?"

"That is not for me to say." There was a measure of defiance in his eyes. "The trip will take some time. You should begin as soon as possible."

Encizo glanced at James and saw him shrug.

"So, make the call."

*Nassau*
*12:25 p.m.*

HERMANN SCHWARZ had earned the nickname "Gadgets" when he served in Vietnam, a tour of duty that included service with Mack Bolan's Penetration Team Able. Schwarz's specialty included bugging, booby traps and any other gadgetry or dirty tricks that helped to put his unit one up on the enemy.

In private life, teamed up with Blancanales as security consultants and investigators, it was only natural that Schwarz would call the operation Able Team. The truth was, Gadgets had missed the war sometimes, when he'd been stuck behind a desk or analyzing data for a corporate security account. He had never missed a chance to grab himself a piece of Bolan's private war, and Hal Brognola didn't have to ask Schwarz twice when he began recruiting soldiers for the Phoenix Project, based at Stony Man Farm.

No one with half a brain would ever call his life smooth sailing, but the easy road had never much appealed to Gadgets Schwarz. When he ran out of time and luck, as every man inevitably does, the Reaper wouldn't find him drooling in a rest home, blank eyes staring at a game show on the tube. He was prepared to trade those "golden years" for living on the edge, right here, right now.

Which brought him to the offices of Byron St. Jacques, Bahamian minister of tourism, identified by DEA as the man to see for permission when it came to moving through Nassau. Anywhere in the Bahamas, when it came to that.

St. Jacques was out to lunch just now, with meetings afterward, and not expected back before late afternoon. His absence was a bonus, and the Able warrior meant to take advantage of it while he had the chance.

The minister's receptionist was black and beautiful, potential cover-girl material if she could tear herself away from answering the telephone and typing memos. Self-assurance and surprise were mingled in her gaze as she glanced up at Schwarz in his workman's coveralls.

"I'm here about the telephones," he said before she had a chance to ask.

"Indeed?"

"We got a call. Somebody couldn't reach you. I believe you'll find the line is dead."

She tried it, and of course it was. Five minutes earlier, a visit to the basement had insured the fact.

The secretary looked perplexed. "I know that it was working earlier."

"It happens," Schwarz told her, putting on a smile. "I'll need to check your other phones, before I hit the trunk line."

"Well..."

"Or, if you'd rather wait," he said, "I'll take my lunch break now and take some other calls I've got lined up. I could be back by half-past five or six o'clock."

The thought of staying late and missing calls made up her mind. "You'd better do it now."

"Suits me."

She let him into St. Jacques's office, where paneled walls showed mounted photos of the great man shaking hands with politicians and celebrities.

"Nice place."

"You'll find the telephone—"

"Right over there," he finished for her, moving toward a desk that could have doubled for a helipad. Behind it, tinted windows faced Nassau Harbor, with a panoramic view of Paradise Island nearby.

"Will this take long?"

"It shouldn't."

"I'll just leave you, then."

She also left the office door wide open, just in case. No point in leaving a repairman—white, at that—alone with all the photographs and trophies St. Jacques had accumulated in a quarter century of politics. You never knew when someone might decide to swipe that glossy black-and-white of Mel Torme and sell it for a five-spot to some tourist on the beach.

Schwarz knelt beside his toolbox, opened it and took a small screwdriver from the tray. In forty seconds he had cracked the box on St. Jacques's telephone and picked the wire he needed. Thirty seconds more, and he was finished hooking up the miniature "infinity device." He was on his feet again when Miss Efficiency looked in to check his progress.

"Have you found out what the trouble is?"

"Not here," he said. "I'll need to check your phone before I head downstairs."

"All right."

He wasted several moments in the outer office, going through the motions. There was no point planting anything on this phone, since St. Jacques would never use it or discuss his private business in the woman's presence.

"Clear," he told her, frowning for effect. "I'll try the trunk line next. With any luck I'll call you back within the next few minutes."

"Good. I hope so."

"Never fear."

He rode the elevator down and cracked the junction box a second time, restoring power to the lines in St. Jacques's office. For the purpose of a simple tap he could have done the work right there, but Schwarz wasn't content to simply eavesdrop on the politician's calls. With the infinity device in place he had the private office covered wall to wall, including interviews conducted face-to-face.

Schwarz plugged into the trunk and dialed, the tiny pager in his free hand pressed against the mouthpiece of his handset. He keyed the preset tone and waited, making sure. Upstairs, the telephone in St. Jacques's office didn't make a sound.

Not yet.

If he had company in the private office, though, their every word and sound of movement would have been picked up by the infinity transmitter, set to broadcast for a two-mile radius. The beam would reach his hotel room with ease, and they could also pick it up on mobile monitors, at any point within the unit's maximum effective range.

The Able warrior smiled in satisfaction, severed the connection, then dialed again. This time he used the public number, and the secretary answered on the second ring.

"Ministry of Tourism. May I help you?"

"I think we've got your problem covered."

"Yes, I see. Well, thank you."

"Anytime." He broke the link and told dead air, "The pleasure's mine."

*Niquero, Cuba*
*12:30 p.m.*

THE DSE WAS EVERYWHERE in Cuba, keeping track of counterrevolutionaries and assorted enemies of socialism, tracking their attempts to undermine the state. Miguel Ortega was the party's watchdog in Niquero, and he took his duties seriously, noting "humorous" remarks, subversive sentiments, along with mundane violations of the law. He didn't work with the police per se, his orders from Havana calling for a less obtrusive role. Ortega watched and listened, made his notes and filed reports with his commanding officer.

These days, the questions from Havana mostly dealt with rebels hiding out in the Maestras. They were known reactionaries, running dogs of the American imperialist forces, bent on overthrowing Fidelismo if they could. Of late, their inspiration came as much from Eastern Europe and the Russians, where once loyal socialists were busily dismantling the institutions forged in eighty years of struggle. If the Russians could abandon Communism almost overnight, the traitors said, why not Havana? Could the working people not exist without Fidel? Without the DSE?

State security was serious business to Miguel Ortega, and his recent failure to expose the rebels had been preying on his mind. Each week, there came new questions from Havana. Was he making any progress? Had he learned the names of any traitors who could be arrested and interrogated? When would he have something to report?

In fact it didn't help for him to know approximately where the rebels were. In the Maestras there were many places where an army could conceal itself. Had not Fidel himself conspired against the fascist pig Batista from those selfsame mountains? The informants whom Ortega cultivated in Niquero promised much but never quite delivered.

Not until today.

The peasant called himself Armando Duro, and he claimed to be a member of the counterrevolutionary force. He didn't look the type, but anything was possible, Ortega thought. At least his motive was believable.

Armando Duro wanted money. Word had reached his ears of the reward Ortega offered for substantial evidence against the traitors, and he wanted to collect.

First, though, the little man would have to prove himself.

"Two strangers," Armando Duro reported. "Men I never saw before."

Ortega sighed. "That hardly makes them traitors, does it?"

"Strangers," Duro repeated. "And they were talking to Raul Guerrero in his shop."

"Two customers, perhaps."

"Perhaps." There was a hint of mockery in Duro's tone that made Ortega want to reach across the desk and slap his face. "I think it is unusual for customers to wait inside a leather shop for half an hour, then be picked up in a car and driven out of town, toward the Maestras.''

''This Raul Guerrero, do you know him well?''

''Enough to know that he is one of those you seek.''

''As you have called yourself,'' Ortega said. ''Why should I trust you now?''

''Because I've seen the error of my ways.''

Translation: Duro saw a chance to profit by betraying those who trusted him.

''Where did they go, these strangers?''

''The Maestras,'' Duro said again.

Ortega scowled. ''I know that! Where did they go, specifically?''

The peasant shrugged. ''I see them come and go. Guerrero might know where they went, or he might not. Such matters are a closely guarded secret. I, myself, have no idea.''

''But I should pay you, all the same?'' Ortega's tone was ripe with scorn.

''For information on the rebels, yes.''

''For information *from* a rebel. You have signed your own death warrant here, today.''

The peasant licked his lips and shifted in his chair, brown fingers worrying the brim of his sombrero. ''But—''

''Enough!'' Ortega's open palm cracked against the desktop. ''Two nameless strangers came into Niquero and they leave within the hour. You, a traitor by your own admission, tell me this and ask for money in return. Perhaps you will remember something useful in Principe Prison.''

''This Guerrero—''

''He can join you. There is ample room.''

"I beg you—"

"I require a reason now, to spare you."

"Yes! The license number!"

"What?"

"I saw the license number on the car."

Ortega listened, then wrote it down. "If you are lying..."

"The truth, I swear it. On my mother's life."

"If you deceive me, Duro, I will make you wish that she had kept her legs together on the night you were conceived."

"You have my word."

"And you have mine. Go now, and when you think of running, think again."

Duro rose to leave, but there was still a spark of stubborn courage left. "About the money..."

It was so audacious that Ortega had to smile. "I'll be in touch. One way or another."

How would the Americans have said it? Don't call us...

But there were calls to make, oh, yes. Ortega had fresh leads—his first, in fact—and he'd waste no time reporting them, requesting help from his commander in Havana. This time, Miguel Ortega thought, the major would be glad to hear his voice.

It would be a refreshing change of pace.

# CHAPTER FOURTEEN

*Chigorodo, Colombia*
*Wednesday, 3:00 p.m.*

The helicopter ride from Panama City took ninety minutes. Colonel Antonio Delvalle was buckled in his seat and silently cursing himself for getting involved with these Colombians in the first place. It had seemed like easy money at the start, just look the other way and count your winnings while the smugglers took the risks upon themselves. But it was turning out to be a rather different game these days.

The past two days, to be precise.

The jealousy and tension had been evident between Barbosa and Velasco for a period of months, but that was all you could expect from narco traffickers. They lived in filth, survived on paranoia. No day was complete without a few psychotic episodes, imagining that some foe had breached their personal security.

A shooting war was something else again.

Stray murders here and there weren't a problem, independent operators being weeded out, defectors punished, thieves reminded of the risk involved when they were stealing from the drug cartels. From time to time Barbosa and Velasco quarreled over territory, making noises like a pair of schoolyard bullies, but they never took it all the way.

Since yesterday, Delvalle had more bodies piling up than he could handle, civil war between the narco traffickers on top of the continuing protests staged by Democracy in Action to embarrass the current regime.

And now the call from Santiago, "strongly urging" Delvalle to drop whatever he was doing and fly directly to Chigorodo for a private consultation. Delvalle had only made the trip once before, when he closed his original bargain with Santiago. Personal contact had been unnecessary beyond that point, a liability in fact.

But now...

Delvalle knew the problem, of course. His intelligence sources had advised him of the Rio Atrato ambush soon after the first Colombian military broadcasts were made. At least fifteen dead, with four vehicles destroyed, including two truckloads of merchandise bound for Panama.

Incredible.

Guillermo Santiago's private helipad lay close beside his outdoor tennis courts. A houseman met Delvalle on the pad and led him toward the rambling house, conspicuous consumption run amok. A glance told any new arrival Santiago was a very wealthy man. It took a second look, sometimes a third, to finally decide he had no taste.

The giant house appeared to be the work of several different architects whose styles and personalities couldn't be reconciled. Brick here and stucco there, with tall white columns in the front, evoking memories of the colossal American film in which Atlanta burned. There were several swimming pools—at least one built indoors—and a complete gymnasium. Inside the foyer a marble sculpture of Elvis Presley, twice life-size, regarded new arrivals with a brooding pout, his giant face as pale as death. Guillermo's taste in art-work ranged from European masters to a wall of "classic" movie posters mounted under glass. All vampire movies, as it happened, most of the posters featuring Christopher Lee...who could have passed for Santiago's brother, in the actor's younger days.

Two vampires, Delvalle thought. Given any kind of choice at all, he would have chosen Dracula and put his faith in garlic or a wooden stake.

Guillermo waited for him on the glass-enclosed ve-randa, with the air-conditioning turned low enough to raise a crop of goose bumps on Delvalle's arms. Or, was it a reaction to the very presence of this man who ordered death in wholesale lots without a second thought?

"Antonio, sit down. A drink perhaps?"

"No, thank you."

"Was your flight enjoyable?"

"It was...unexpected."

"So many things are unexpected nowadays. It keeps life interesting, I think."

Delvalle thought about the ancient curse: may you live in interesting times. At last he thought he under-stood the twist.

"I was advised of your misfortune," Delvalle said.

"*Our* misfortune," Santiago stated, correcting him. "Such incidents affect us all."

"Of course. I meant to say."

"I hope you might be able to assist me with this problem."

"How?"

Santiago frowned. "It must be clear to you our problems are related. This sudden violence cannot be coincidence."

"Barbosa and Velasco..."

"No, no." The drug baron waved one slender hand, a gesture of dismissal. "Fighting in the streets, perhaps. They might be rash enough to start a war in Panama, but they are not insane. Attacking me..." He let it go, dismissed the prospect with a smirk. "If either one of them had nerve enough to try, he surely would not burn the merchandise."

"Who, then?"

"The very question I would put to you. If these events *are* linked, then we must have a common enemy. Agreed?"

"But who?" Delvalle knew he sounded foolish, like an owl, but he could think of nothing else to say. "I mean, if it is someone from outside..."

"Outside." Santiago's frown was carving furrows in his face. "A possibility that we must not ignore. Who worries more about our business than Barbosa and Velasco put together?"

"The Americans?" The words were out before Delvalle had a chance to think about them. Facing Santiago from his chair, the colonel hesitated, shook his head. "It makes no sense."

"Because the Yankees have their Constitution?" Santiago's tone was mocking. "Where were all their rules and regulations when they came for Noriega, eh?"

"But this...without the military and the press," Delvalle said, "it seems improbable."

"But still a possibility. And if their government is not involved, the answer still may lie within America."

"Your competition," Delvalle suggested.

"Hardly that, considering the small percentage of the market they control. But if they seek a larger share..."

Delvalle saw it now, the prospect of a war between Guillermo Santiago and his gangland enemies in the United States, with Panama—Delvalle—caught between the two belligerents. It didn't answer all the question in his mind, by any means, but it could make a twisted kind of sense. And it would give him cause, if any more was needed, for anxiety.

"I could investigate," the colonel said.

"An excellent idea. Your contacts in intelligence."

"Of course."

"With all dispatch."

"I understand."

Santiago smiled. No vampire fangs were in evidence, but he could bite, oh, yes.

"I knew you would."

*Sierra Maestras, Cuba*
*3:30 p.m.*

IT WAS A LONG DRIVE from Niquero, back into the mountains. Rafael Encizo rode in silence, Calvin James beside him in the back seat of an old sedan that creaked and grumbled as the road began to climb. Their driver concentrated on the task at hand and didn't try to keep them entertained.

Though born in Cuba, Encizo had never been to the Maestras, seat of so much revolutionary history. It had been here, he knew, that Castro hid and plotted to destroy Fulgencio Batista, with covert assistance from the White House and the CIA. Fidel hadn't been a Communist in those days—or, at least, he'd claimed that he wasn't—and the Americans considered him a fair alternative to the regime in power. Castro promised liberty, agrarian reform, a kind of Cuban populism that would clear away the rot of the Batista government while leaving great American investments more or less unscathed.

Once he had taken power, though, the mask came off. In fact, Fidel declared, he was a die-hard Marxist after all. His closure of the Mafia's casinos in Havana was the prelude to a sweeping campaign that nationalized agriculture, mining and industry throughout Cuba, with little or no compensation to the American power brokers who were suddenly stripped of their holdings. The exodus to Florida began, and Soviet advisers soon arrived to teach Fidel the fine points of managing a one-party "republic."

Almost overnight, a new breed of rebels had been drawn to the Maestras, plotting yet another coup. Once more, the CIA was on their side, red-faced with the embarrassment of having helped install a Communist regime ninety miles from the Florida Keys. Fidel would never wholly crush the organized resistance to his rule, but it would wax and wane with time and circumstance. These days, with communism crumbling worldwide, a new generation of rebels had begun to sniff the wind, detecting the aroma of potential victory within their grasp.

And when it came, Encizo asked himself again, what would it really mean? Would the victors finally secure democracy for Cuba, or would history repeat itself with yet another despot seizing power?

In front of them a young man stood beside the one-lane track, his face deadpan as they approached. The driver slowed and finally stopped a few yards short of where the young man held his ground.

Encizo stepped out of the car, James close behind him, carrying their duffel bags. When they were clear, the driver put it in reverse and started backing down the mountain, disappearing on a curve some fifty yards away.

"You think he plans on backing all the way down to Niquero?" James asked.

Encizo shrugged. "His problem."

As the Phoenix warrior spoke, two other men emerged from cover, one on each side of the road. They held weapons, one of them an army-surplus M-1 carbine, the other a Kalashnikov. Encizo watched the first young man reach underneath the loose tail of his spotless peasant shirt and draw an automatic pistol from its hiding place.

"Terrific," James muttered. "Now we're looking at a firing squad."

"An escort," said the young man, who appeared to be the trio's leader. "You are armed?"

"We are," Encizo replied, "as you have doubtless been informed."

"You won't mind letting Pablo and Ricardo hold your bags until we reach the camp."

It didn't come out sounding like a question, and the Phoenix Force warriors passed their duffel bags to waiting hands, the pistols they had worn beneath their lightweight jackets tucked inside before the bags were zipped shut. They still had folding knives, their combat training in the martial arts, but none of it would matter in the face of automatic weapons fired at point-blank range.

Encizo made himself relax, as the young man guided them along a narrow forest trail, their escorts bringing up the rear. The woods weren't precisely jungle, they were too high up for that, but it was close enough. Trees grew close together, right up to the trail, with tangled undergrowth and insects buzzing into their faces with every step. As far as the humidity was concerned, he figured it was somewhere in the eighties, anyway. Sweat soaked the back and armpits of his chambray shirt before they covered fifty yards.

"Nice weather for a hike," James observed.

To which the guard immediately on his heels replied, *"Silencio."*

It took nearly an hour to reach their destination, planted in a forest clearing strung with leafy netting ten feet overhead as camouflage. The rebel camp was tents and people, with a slit trench well down slope for the latrine. Mobility was everything, and it was obvious they wanted to be ready for departure at a moment's notice. Strike the tents and pack them up if there was time, or run and leave them if the enemy got past your outer guards somehow and took you by surprise.

And it wasn't one camp, he saw now, but a string of three, each visible between the closing trees. The clearings were connected, more or less, by narrow trails, and that was good enough. Encizo listened for the river sounds but couldn't hear them. Still, he knew there would be running water close at hand.

Beyond the layout, his attention focused mainly on the guns. Each man—and woman, too, he noticed several—was armed, a major violation of prevailing Cuban statutes in itself. Possession of a gun could earn you prison time, but bearing arms against the state was tantamount to suicide for any rebel captured by the army or the DSE.

A tall man moved to greet them, brushing past the others who stood staring at the new arrivals. He approached within ten feet of where Encizo stood with James beside him, studying both Phoenix Force warriors with the darkest eyes that the little Cuban had ever seen.

"I am Clemente Villa, leader of this troop," the tall man said at last. "I offer you our hospitality and hope that I will not be forced to kill you later on."

*Balboa Heights, Panama*
*3:42 p.m.*

THE TELEPHONE on Sergio Barbosa's desk had recently become his enemy. It brought him unrelieved bad news—or worse, no news at all—and he was sick to death of staring at it, waiting for his goddamned luck to change.

And he was tired of waiting. He had been sitting still for too long, hiding really, while his soldiers took a beating on the street. Eleven dead so far, and his accountants would be working through the evening with their calculators to evaluate the monetary damage he had suffered. Men could be replaced as easily as office furniture, and they were often less expensive.

At the moment Sergio Barbosa was concerned about the damage to his reputation, his loss of personal respect. If other *narcotrafficantes* came to think that he was weak, an easy mark, they would devour him like wild dogs ravaging an injured steer.

He thought about Velasco, the reports that told him Carlos had been taking hits as well. It was a riddle, and Barbosa had no head for riddles. When he was attacked for no apparent reason, logic told him to suspect the first, most likely adversary on his list of possibles. Velasco envied Sergio's success, his profit margin. There was no love lost between them. Thus, when Barbosa was confronted with a threat, Velasco's name immediately came to mind.

Who else would dare to challenge him this way?

There were a handful of competitors he ranked as small fry, nibbling around the edges of the business to support themselves, but none of them possessed the nerve or expertise to launch a series of attacks on par with what Barbosa had endured the past two days. There might be enemies outside of Panama—the Cubans or Jamaicans, for example—but they liked to do their killing in Miami, picking off a runner here and there. For full-scale warfare, it required more brains and nerve.

Velasco had the courage, certainly. As for the brains... he was about to learn that trifling with Sergio Barbosa was a grave mistake.

That morning, on the telephone, Delvalle had been nagging him to wait, allow the government to sort things out. The colonel emphasized that Sergio wasn't alone. Velasco had sustained his share of losses through the night, and if Barbosa hadn't been responsible for *those* attacks, how could he blame Velasco for the raids against himself?

It wasn't difficult at all. You simply closed your mind to any troubling questions that you didn't understand and ran on instinct.

Simple.

Alejandro, his houseman, knocked and stuck his head in through the door. "The men are ready, sir."

"Good."

He followed the houseman along a spacious corridor, the carpet thick beneath his shoes. They found two gunners waiting at the door, another pair outside to guard the threshold. Four cars were lined up in the curving driveway. Behind the tinted window glass, Barbosa noted faces turned in his direction, weapons showing here and there.

The drug lord's Mercedes stood second in the line. Counting himself and five men per car, that made twenty-one. It didn't constitute his total force by any means, but it should be enough for what he had in mind.

When he was safe inside the car, doors latched, the driver twisted his ignition key and brought the sedan to life. The other cars were idling now, the drivers waiting for their boss's signal. He nodded to his wheelman, their eyes connecting in the rearview mirror. On cue the driver lifted a dash-mounted microphone and spoke a single word, the lead car pulling out and gaining speed.

Barbosa didn't fear a raid against his palace in Balboa Heights specifically, though you could never tell exactly what a madman like Velasco might be thinking. Anything was possible, including an audacious move like this one, guaranteed to make Barbosa's enemy think twice about continuing his pointless war.

As if the foolish bastard really thought that he could win.

The traffic slowed them a little, entering the capital, but Sergio had time to spare. Velasco was a creature of habit, and it mattered little in the last analysis if he should vary his routine this afternoon. It was the gesture that mattered, a demonstration of contempt for one who waged war without reason, wasting precious time and resources in the pursuit of personal spite.

The gunner on Barbosa's left had an Uzi in his lap, double-checking the safety and load as they rolled through midtown traffic. On his right the soldier held two Model 61 Skorpion machine pistols, passing one of them to Barbosa. Its curved magazine held twenty rounds of 7.62 mm ammunition, the wood grip warm against his palm. Barbosa cocked the weapon, held it braced against one knee, his index finger well outside the trigger guard.

Soon, now.

Their target was a private club Velasco patronized each weekday afternoon from three to five o'clock. Velasco owned the place, which made the staff and visitors fair targets in Barbosa's mind. He didn't have a man inside the club to tell him if Velasco had arrived on this day, but someone would be there, enjoying cocktails or a meal prepared by the imported chef, pretending to be gentlemen, when they survived by selling drugs or filching cash from other people's bank accounts.

Illusions. Where would mankind be without them?

"There," the driver said, and Barbosa leaned forward for his first glimpse of the club. It would be on his left as they approached, and he reached up to find the crank that opened the Mercedes's sunroof, when it was open, breathing in exhaust fumes and the pungent city-smell.

Any moment now.

They could have parked and gone inside if he was bent on making sure, but this was more a gesture than a serious attempt to kill Velasco. That could wait. For now it was enough to let him know that he had failed to break Barbosa's spirit, make him cringe and hide like an intimidated child. A better man than him would be needed for the job of driving away Sergio Barbosa.

He stood, head and shoulders poking through the open sunroof, with his right hand wrapped around the Skorpion. Its four-pound weight was nothing, braced against the roof of the Mercedes. He would have to watch the recoil, with its rapid cyclic rate of fire.

The first car was already rolling past Velasco's club, a sudden blast of gunfire taking out the windows, etching several dozen pockmarks on the brick facade. Barbosa's car was next, and he began to fire immediately, milking short bursts from the Skorpion to make it last. The gunman on his right leaned past his legs to take a shot, but Sergio wasn't about to move.

He stole a glimpse inside the club through shattered windows, seeing bodies diving for cover behind pieces of furniture, each man scrambling to save himself. A startled face popped into view as they were passing, and Barbosa used the last rounds in his magazine to blast it open.

Rolling out of range, he held on, watching as the car behind him poured more automatic fire into the building, keeping heads down, peppering the walls and ceiling with a hail of bullets. The last car in line brought dessert. A grenade launcher poked through the driver's-side window in back, belching its first high-explosive round as the vehicle came into range. The blast was muffled, walls confining it, but Sergio could see the smoke come pouring out through empty window frames.

The second shot was an incendiary, finishing the job. Barbosa didn't fully understand the military chemicals, but he had faith in their ability to wreak destruction. By the time fire trucks arrived, the club would be a total loss.

Much like Velasco's effort to secure the country for himself.

A nagging doubt nibbled at Barbosa, but he dismissed it, satisfied to settle back and gloat. Velasco might not be inside the club, but he would get the message. Loud and clear, as the Americans would say. And he would reconsider any further moves against Barbosa in the hours and days ahead.

Or he would die.

It was as simple as that.

# CHAPTER FIFTEEN

*Sierra Maestras, Cuba*
*5:15 p.m.*

Once they had satisfied Clemente Villa of their mission and identity, things loosened up a bit around the rebel camp. There was a giant stew pot on the fire, and James could feel his stomach rumbling, though he wasn't about to ask the meal's ingredients. His training with the Navy SEALS had taught him to survive on grubs and fungus if he had to, but there were occasions when he found that ignorance was truly bliss.

Except where strategy in combat was concerned.

Clemente Villa had been waging war against the Communist regime for seven years, full-time. He stayed alive by planning out his moves and keeping one eye on security around the clock, in every situation that arose. He understood the risk of sellouts and betrayal, but his luck had held so far.

As for their mission to eliminate Luis Rivera, it didn't concern the rebel cause directly. Villa's people hated every member of the DSE, but some were worse than others. Villa recognized Rivera's name, but since the major's duties were primarily external—dealing with Havana's sympathetic contacts in Central America—their paths had never crossed.

Still, any blow against the DSE was worth a modicum of risk, and Villa's troop could claim the credit afterward if they desired. In fact, James thought, it would be perfect if they did, another layer of cover to disguise the work of Stony Man.

"You live here in the mountains all year long?" Encizo asked when they were seated on the ground, consuming bowls of stew that tasted even better than it smelled.

"We move from place to place," Villa said with a shrug. "A month here, three weeks there. The mountains have become our home."

"It must be lonely," James commented.

The rebel leader stared at him for several moments, chewing thoughtfully, before he spoke. "My family is here," he said at last. "All that remains. The Fidelistas killed my brother long ago, but I have different brothers now. We stand together, and we hit back where we can."

"What kind of progress are you making?"

Villa shrugged. "We gain a foot here, inches there. Some days we lose the ground we gained the week before. Fidel is conscious of our presence. It constrains him. For the moment that is victory enough."

James frowned and spooned more stew into his mouth. He recognized the fatalistic attitude, a mark of living on the edge so long that war became a way of life, perhaps the only life a man could recognize. It wasn't that you fell in love with war, exactly; on the other hand, you couldn't seem to live without it, either. It became addictive, validating your existence and defining everything you did, all that you ever hoped to be.

And if the Phoenix warrior recognized a measure of himself in Villa, it would come as no surprise.

"We'll need connections in Havana," Encizo said, getting back on track.

"Of course. We have friends there. They will assist you . . . to a point."

"We don't need backup gunners," James assured him. "Some logistics, information, this and that."

"Enough to get them killed," Villa said.

"Not if everybody does his job."

"You are not from the Company." The rebel leader spoke to James, and while it hadn't sounded like a question, the ex-SEAL felt compelled to answer.

"Not exactly. Sometimes, in a pinch, we help each other out."

"Cooperation."

"Right."

The rebel leader nodded. "I will send a message on ahead."

Encizo cleared his throat. "We'd rather not warn anybody in advance."

"You do not trust my people?"

"Nothing personal," James replied. "We all have little tricks we use to stay alive, you know?"

"Indeed. Two months ago—"

Before he could complete the thought, Villa froze, his eyes narrowing to slits, the bowl of stew forgotten in his lap. His face turned north, and James thought his eyes were closed, as if to channel full attention through his ears. He discovered that the background noises of the camp had died away to nothing in a flash.

A few more seconds passed before he heard the helicopter engines, seconds more until he satisfied himself at least two aircraft were approaching from a northerly direction, flying low and fast. Bodies were in motion around him, rebels scrambling to douse their cooking fires and grab their weapons, making ready to defend the camp.

The first chopper roared overhead, already banking for a comeback, and James recognized the Mi-24 Hind, a Russian gunship with plenty of lethal firepower on board. A second Mi-24 swept past on the left, some fifty yards away and started looping back as if the choppers had some kind of homing beam locked in.

It was about to hit the fan.

James's duffel bag was on the ground beside him, and he grabbed it as he scrambled to his feet, Encizo doing likewise. Villa got there first, already shouting orders to his troops as one Hind opened up with its twin-barrel 30 mm cannon, ripping through the leafy camouflage. The stew pot took an instant hit and toppled over, putting out the fire.

The first run seemed to be for cannons only, but the Mi-24s came back with UV-16-57 rocket launchers blazing, 57 mm warheads detonating on impact with the trees or ground. Between the helicopter engines and munitions going off, James found it difficult to follow Villa's shouted orders. Those who heard and understood were falling back into the forest on the south, assuming that a ground attack might follow from the same direction as the choppers had appeared.

The Phoenix warriors followed, having little choice. Three strides, and he picked out the whistle of an FAB-250 bomb. He threw himself facedown behind a tree and clasped both arms above his head.

The blast was close enough and powerful enough to bring a rain of shattered branches and detritus down on James's back. He heard the shrapnel thumping into tree trunks, and a big tree coming down somewhere immediately to his front.

The Hinds were circling, hunting, Russian-trained pilots and gunners taking their time like children flushing out an anthill.

James had the compact submachine gun out by now, for all the good that it would do. The Hinds boasted armor superior to anything else in the air, as witnessed by their service record in Afghanistan. A Singer would have done the job, but the ex-SEAL's PA3-DM was small improvement on a slingshot at the present range. Still, he felt better with the weapon in his hand, and if the gunships had a ground team coming in . . .

''This way!''

Clemente Villa tugged at James's sleeve, Encizo close behind them as they took off dodging through the trees. The camp was wasted—smoke, fire and crumpled bodies. The Hinds were ranging farther now, in search of targets, and there was time for James to wonder if their gear included thermal-imaging equipment that would stalk a living target through the trees. If they could seek out the rebels by body heat, there would be nowhere safe to hide.

The angle of descent was steeper here, and James nearly lost his footing as he followed Villa down the slope. He heard the river now, and in another heartbeat it was visible, a gleaming slash between the trees. James didn't know if Villa had a boat, but the rebel leader was their only guide just now. Around them, darting shadows in the trees were moving in the same direction, but the dodging shapes were few and far between.

How many dead or injured in the camp behind him? James had no way of knowing, but a casual estimate had placed Villa's strength close to forty guns on-site. So many targets for the circling, prowling Hinds.

The mountain stream was swift and narrow, overhung by trees that screened a clear view of the sky. Arriving on the bank, Villa led them several yards due north to reach a point where six canoes were lined up. Two other men were there ahead of them, and James heard others coming through the trees, but they were few...so few.

"We have no time to waste," Villa stated, stooping to reach for one of the boats.

"The others—" James began, and caught himself, the look on Villa's face enough to silence him. He helped with the canoe, Encizo pitching in, the other rebels picking out a second boat.

Behind them, farther off now, he could hear the gunships strafing as they scrambled into the canoe and let the current carry them downstream. In moments he could barely hear the guns at all.

Except inside his mind.

*Paradise Island, Bahamas*
*5:45 p.m.*

"OKAY," Schwarz said, "let's find out what we got."

The compact tape recorder was voice-activated with a twist, keyed to remote signals from the infinity device Schwarz had planted in Byron St. Jacques's office. Simple noises in the room—like squeaking chairs or footsteps—wouldn't activate the mechanism, but a human voice brought everything to life, regardless of the speaker's volume.

Magic, or the next best thing.

"Odds are the sucker never came back from his lunch break," Lyons said. "These island politicians make bankers' hours look like a stretch of hard labor."

"Nothing ventured," Gadgets told him, lifting the cassette deck from its place inside a dresser drawer to place it on the coffee table. Glancing at the footage indicator, he could see the tape had run for six or seven minutes, minimum. "There's something here."

"His secretary talking to her boyfriend," Lyons muttered.

"Not unless she took him in the boss's private office."

Gadgets punched the Rewind button, waited, keyed the tape to play. The first voice was indeed St. Jacques's receptionist, but she was speaking through the intercom.

"Mr. Mentzer on line one, sir."

A mellow, cultured voice thanked her, sounding closer to the hidden microphone. And then, "Thomas, good afternoon."

"You're hard to reach these days."

"That's Mentzer," Lyons said, confirming it from personal experience.

"The trials and tribulations of a public servant," St. Jacques replied, unable to suppress a chuckle.

"How you suffer."

"I survive," the politician said, still chuckling.

"Which brings me to the reason for my call. I have a customer who's interested in doing business at the standard rate."

St. Jacques was instantly more cautious. Schwarz could almost see him frowning as he gripped the telephone.

"I see."

"I don't suppose you want the details."

"Not just now." Too cagey to discuss their business on the telephone, regardless of security in place. "Perhaps another time."

"Of course. You'll want to check him through your sources, I suppose."

"As always, Thomas."

"Right. Chad Lewis, from the States. You want his passport number?"

"Please."

Schwarz glanced at Lyons, found him smiling as the dealer recited his passport number off, St. Jacques repeating it for confirmation.

"Anything that you can do to expedite the process," Mentzer said, "would naturally be much appreciated. Mr. Lewis strikes me as the sort who doesn't like to wait."

"It won't take long," St. Jacques replied. "If there was nothing else?"

"That's it for now."

"Thank you, Thomas. I should be in touch sometime tonight. Tomorrow morning at the latest."

"Fair enough."

The second call was shorter, St. Jacques speaking to an immigration officer, reading off the Lewis moniker and Lyons's passport number from the document prepared at Stony Man. When he was done, the tape fell silent, waiting.

Schwarz rewound again and primed the tape deck to receive new messages, returning it to the drawer where hotel maids were unlikely to disturb its operation.

"So, I guess we're off and running," Blancanales said.

"I told you he was hooked. When I started taking money to him last night, it was like he saw a chance to balance out the game or something. Maybe better. He's a cagey bastard, just like you'd expect, but greed's the driving force."

"Like any pusher," Blancanales said. Pol's personal contempt for drug dealers was nothing short of monumental, and the only time he tried to hide it was when working under cover on a mission. If their present target had been running down the street on fire, the Politician would have gladly offered him a cup of gasoline to douse the flames.

"And now we keep our fingers crossed," Schwarz said. "Have faith in the machine."

"It hasn't let us down so far," Lyons replied.

In this case the "machine" was the Stony Man operation itself, a complex network of communications, contacts, switchbacks, relays and the like that routed predetermined queries to a central switchboard in the Blue Ridge Mountain stronghold. Queries on a valid passport went to State, but any bite on Lyons's number—or the others periodically released from Stony Man—would come up empty, with resultant problems of the lethal kind for agents in the field. To solve the problem Aaron Kurtzman had invaded State's computer with a program of his own, referring queries on a given list of passport numbers, visas and the like to operators at a "sterile" front, where background information cleared by Stony Man would be released, albeit grudgingly, to callers with a "need to know." In that way covers were preserved and lives were saved.

The right lives, anyway.

"Assume St. Jacques's already made the call," Schwarz said. "He's in the system now, unless they shine him on with bureaucratic bullshit till the morning. Either way, we should be rolling by tomorrow."

"What about the money?"

All eyes turned to Perry Tate, a silent shadow seated in the corner near the door. The DEA man glanced from one face to the other as he spoke.

"No problem. I've got half a million standing by for earnest money. It's a confiscated stash, of course. You lose it somehow, no one's apt to have a cow. They won't be thrilled, you understand, but easy come..."

"You're covered all the way on this?" Schwarz queried.

"So far, so good. If anybody's tracking me, I haven't caught them at it."

There was momentary silence in the room, then Lyons said, "Okay. Let's wait and see. I think I'll take another run at the casino, try my luck. You want to join me, Perry?"

Tate relaxed a little, finally shrugging. "It couldn't hurt. Get seen with a high roller like yourself, it's bound to help my cover."

"Happy to oblige. It isn't every day I get to play celebrity."

"As long as you don't wind up on the boob tube," Blancanales cautioned. "Film at eleven, that kind of thing."

"No sweat. I'm on vacation here, remember?"

"Right. Vacation this."

Lyons grinned. "Forget it, guy. You want to play with me, you have to show the big guns."

"I suppose you've got a Magnum tucked away," the Politician said.

"I wouldn't be surprised."

Tate grinned and shook his head. "You guys are friends, I hope."

"We do all right," Lyons said, standing up and moving toward the door. "I need to change before we make our entrance, okay? It won't take long."

Schwarz watched him go, the door shut tight behind him, blocking out a brief view of the corridor. A feeling of anticipation gripped him, as it always did when they were on a mission, counting down the numbers, waiting for the crucial action to begin. In fact it had begun already, with St. Jacques. The rest would either happen or it wouldn't; there was little he could do to shape events from that point on.

But it could never hurt to try, hell no.

A nudge was all it took, sometimes, to keep the game on track or send it spinning out of bounds, whichever you desired. The situations varied, but the end result was always similar. Somebody dead, somebody else alive to tell the tale.

Schwarz hoped they didn't blow it this time.

Losing was a stone-cold bitch when you were betting everything you had.

*Panama City*
*6:05 p.m.*

BY ANY NORMAL STANDARD in the Latin tropics, it was still late afternoon, but businesses were closing throughout the city, workers drifting home or into taverns where they could relax. It was a time for catching people on the move if you were so inclined, and Bolan still had work to do.

The pot was simmering in Panama, but it hadn't yet reached a rolling boil. More heat was needed, and the Executioner had fuel to spare.

His efforts with Barbosa and Velasco were already paying dividends, according to the latest news reports, and it was time to raise the ante, take the game a step beyond the street-gangs-kicking-ass scenario. He wanted to involve the local VIPs, and there was nothing quite like starting at the top.

Or near the top, at least.

Jesus Avilla was dismissed from Bolan's calculations for the moment. He was dirty all the way, but in the city's present climate an attack on a politician could be misinterpreted, mistakenly assigned to any one of half a dozen "revolutionary" groups. For all he knew, Democracy in Action might be blamed and punished for the incident, instead of focusing the heat where it belonged.

Accordingly he chose the banker, Ernesto Montalvo, and timed his move to maximum advantage. When the target left his downtown office in a chauffeur-driven limousine, he had a tail, the Executioner pursing him through early-evening traffic, watching from a distance when the driver dropped him at an apartment house three miles from where the banker spent his days.

The girlfriend's place.

He knew about the banker's mistress from the dossier at Stony Man, the kind of trivia that hung a man unless he watched his step. When Montalvo's chauffeur was out of sight, the Executioner locked his car and started for the entryway. The doorman didn't recognize his face, but he accepted fifty pesos and forgot to ask the gringo stranger's business. Later on, if there was any flack, the doorman would remember he was in the washroom for a moment when the stranger slipped inside. A call of nature, it could happen to anyone.

This evening, it was happening to one Ernesto Montalvo.

And it was overdue.

He rode the elevator up to seven, turning left along the corridor until he reached the number he was looking for. A knock was risky, so he used the picks, a moment's work to beat the lock, keeping his fingers crossed that they hadn't engaged a security chain. The M-9 Beretta was in his hand as Bolan eased the door open on well-oiled hinges, music coming out to meet him. Strings and muted horns, some kind of instrumental lovers' number.

He shut the door behind him, softly, moving down a short, cramped hallway to the sitting room. No sign of life at first, until he saw a rumpled, silky-looking caftan on the floor beside the couch.

The banker wasn't wasting any time.

He checked the empty bathroom, going by, and found the bedroom door wide open, so the stereo could keep them company. It had already covered Bolan's entrance, and it wouldn't hurt if there was noise within the next few moments.

Standing in the bedroom doorway, the warrior watched them for a moment, feeling nothing. He wasn't the voyeuristic type, but he appreciated style and noted Montalvo's apparent lack of same. The little man was pumping breathlessly, about to finish by the look of things, and it was only six or seven minutes since he'd crossed the threshold. The man's companion made the proper noises, moving to his beat, but the expression on her face was bored, distracted.

It changed when she saw Bolan moving toward the bed, a scream prepared for lift-off when the pistol changed her mind. Instead, she lay there rigid while the Executioner tangled fingers in the banker's hair and lifted him from the saddle, flipping him over on his back. The banker's wide eyes were the biggest thing about him as he shriveled, staring up at Bolan's face and the Beretta in his hand.

"They tell me you speak English."

"*Sí, señor.*"

"So, speak it."

"Yes. I do. Speak English."

"There you go." The muzzle of his automatic came to rest on Montalvo's nose, making the banker cross his eyes. "I hate to interrupt your coffee break, but we've got business to discuss."

"B-b-business?"

"Right the first time. You've been dealing with some gentlemen who don't have long to live. I thought you'd want to know."

"Wha—what gentlemen?"

"Avilla. Delvalle. Santiago. Ring a bell?"

The banker came up short on words, but the expression on his face told Bolan everything he had to know.

"They're going down," the Executioner went on. "You want to warn them, that's all right with me. There's nowhere they can hide. *¿Comprende?*"

"*Sí.*"

He poked the banker's flaccid stomach with the muzzle of his automatic.

"You should really try to stay in shape."

That easy, going out, and he was finished with Montalvo for the moment. If they met again, it would be over the length of time it took to squeeze a trigger.

Just like that.

The doorman smiled at Bolan as he left and snapped a quick salute in his direction. The Executioner returned it, moving toward his car, too far away from his new friend to see the license plate. He was confident that all concerned would hear about his chat with the banker within the hour.

Soon enough.

And in the meantime, he had other calls to make.

The Executioner was blitzing on.

# CHAPTER SIXTEEN

*Panama City*
*7:40 p.m.*

Colonel Antonio Delvalle hated working nights. He had drawn his share of sleepless duty as a young soldier, coming up through the ranks, but a colonel has certain privileges, including the assignment of obnoxious graveyard shifts to his subordinates. Except, that is, when crisis situations call for special expertise.

Like now.

The Santiago ultimatum—and it could be seen as nothing else, all things considered—made it clear that delegation of authorities wouldn't suffice in the present situation. A handful of Delvalle's trusted subordinates were directly involved in his dealings with the drug cartel, as were one or two of his superiors, but the relationship was by no means general knowledge. Violence in the streets focused unwelcome attention on the local cocaine trade, and if it escalated to the point where new investigations were demanded by the legislature, then Delvalle would be seriously compromised.

But it would never go that far, he realized. Guillermo Santiago and the politicians had too much to lose. If necessary, they would find themselves a scapegoat, silence him to circumvent the need for public trail—with its attendant risk of a confession or a bargained plea—and let the public think one venal man had been responsible for an unforeseen, unpredictable crime wave.

A man like Delvalle, for instance.

The colonel had other ideas, none of them incorporating martyrdom. His first imperative was restoration of the peace between Barbosa and Velasco, for the gangs were certainly at war by now, regardless of whoever was responsible for the original attacks.

Delvalle didn't buy Guillermo's argument concerning the Americans. He couldn't rule it out, of course, but in his own mind such a drastic course of covert action seemed improbable. More likely, Santiago was unwilling to admit that his competitors in the United States had power to reach out and challenge him at home. The drug baron's ego was a fragile thing, and it might one day get him killed, but it wasn't Delvalle's place to tell him that.

Instead, the colonel concentrated on a strategy to save himself.

Step one was meeting privately and separately with each of the identified combatants, buying time. If he could talk Barbosa and Velasco into laying down their guns, however briefly, he'd have a chance to scrutinize the early incidents more closely, search for proof that outside elements were trying to foment a shooting war in Panama.

And if there were no outside elements involved, then he'd have to start from scratch. The best scenario would be a small-time independent dealer, playing off one major trafficker against the other for his own advantage, hoping that Barbosa and Velasco would eliminate each other, leaving open territory for a would-be drug tycoon. In that case, once the culprit was identified, it would be relatively simple for Delvalle's troops to run him down and solve the problem permanently, meting out swift justice from the muzzle of a gun.

But if Barbosa or Velasco was responsible, then he'd have a choice to make. Which dealer was potentially more valuable—and more manageable—in the long run? Which could he more readily afford to lose, in the interest of peace, harmony and self-preservation?

Should it come to that, Delvalle knew that he would make the choice and see it through to execution. If the evidence was strong enough, he saw no reason to consult Guillermo Santiago first. When the Colombian assigned Delvalle to complete a task, his orders carried the authority to use initiative along the way. Santiago could live with Delvalle's decision and like it, or he could start to do his own dirty work for a change.

Velasco first.

It made sense to Delvalle, since Barbosa had been first to suffer an attack on Tuesday, kicking off the round of violent incidents that still continued unabated, brand-new victims chalked up by the hour. Delvalle couldn't picture Sergio Barbosa planning an assault against his own troops, even to divert suspicion from himself. It would require intelligence and subtlety that Barbosa did not, in Delvalle's opinion, possess. Velasco was Barbosa's major competition, and his placement at the head of any suspects lists was thus assured.

The meeting had been relatively simple to arrange, Delvalle mentioning that a refusal to discuss their common problem would have drastic repercussions for

Velasco and his troops. Right now, the dealer was on roughly even footing with Barbosa, but Delvalle could shift the balance of power on a moment's notice, committing his troops to the battle on one side or the other, as he chose. Neither smuggler could afford a head-on clash with the Panama Defense Forces, and anyone insane enough to tough it out would recognize Guillermo Santiago's guiding hand behind Delvalle's move.

Case closed.

Before Velasco tried to fight Barbosa plus the army *and* his chief supplier in Colombia, he would be well advised to have his head examined. While he might be slow in some regards, a wild man when it came to honor and revenge, Velasco couldn't be mistaken for an idiot.

Three minutes on the telephone, most of it listening in silence while Delvalle told him how things stood, and Carlos had agreed to meet. Delvalle let him choose the place, an ego stroke that he could well afford. Velasco wouldn't try to harm him in the present circumstances, when there was nothing to gain and everything to lose.

The colonel knew the nightclub by its reputation only. He had never been inside to mingle with the pimps and prostitutes who waited there for gringo tourists to arrive with money in their pockets, looking for excitement and a chance to say that they had "been around."

Tonight would be a first.

Delvalle's driver stopped across the street, a zone where parking was forbidden, but their military plates would keep police at bay. One thing you had to say for Noriega, he had trained his lackeys well, and their conditioning hadn't broken down entirely once El Presidente was removed from office to a Yankee prison cell. The local officers still knew their place and recognized the established chain of command.

The colonel's driver left the car, stepped back to open his boss's door, standing at rigid attention as Delvalle brushed past him. Both men wore civilian suits, a concession to Delvalle's covert mission, but their military bearing instantly set them apart from the street denizens of this seedy neighborhood. All eyes were on the colonel as he moved to cross the street, an easy forty feet to reach the entrance of Velasco's club.

Unless you had to make the crossing under fire.

The first shot struck the ground in front of him, a crack and whine against the pavement several inches from his polished shoe. There was no sound of gunfire, but Delvalle recognized his danger instantly, dropping to a crouch and turning toward the car, a panic rush of pure adrenaline imparting greater speed.

The second round was almost on his heels, another ricochet. The colonel said a silent prayer of thanks that his assailant was no marksman, sprinting now, his driver looking startled, then aghast. The back door of the car was closed. Precious seconds were wasted while Delvalle stretched out his arm, reaching for the handle, wondering if he could make the grab and throw himself inside the car in time.

Round three was well ahead of him and wide of the mark, punching through the trunk of the car with a hollow twanging sound. Delvalle had his right hand on the handle of the door now, jerking at it, cursing when his fingers slipped.

He got it on the second try and threw himself head-first across the seat. A bullet followed him and drilled the window of the right-hand door in back, perhaps a foot above his head. Most of the glass was blown outside, but several jagged shards caught in his hair and stung his scalp.

The left-hand door stood open behind him, leaving his flank exposed, but Delvalle was frozen, unable to turn back and close it. His driver slid behind the wheel a heartbeat later, cursing as a bullet struck the left-front fender and exploded through the headlight in a spray of shattered glass. The colonel heard the engine roar to life, and then the vehicle was moving, burning rubber from a standing start, accelerating down the block and out of range. Momentum slammed the door behind him, and a parting shot took out the wide back window, dropping more glass on the colonel's huddled form.

Delvalle's mind was racing as they turned a corner, then another, until they were finally beyond the line of fire. He thought about Velasco, wondering if the Colombian was really mad enough to risk his life on such a move.

And if he was, how would the dealer react on learning he had failed?

Delvalle cursed the fear that kept him huddled on the seat, below the line of sight from anyone outside the car. Velasco still had much to answer for, but he couldn't assume the dealer's guilt without more evidence. The sniper could easily have been dispatched by Sergio Barbosa . . . or by someone else.

The colonel had gained nothing for his sojourn to the wrong side of the tracks, and now he found that he was running for his life.

*Paradise Island, Bahamas*
*7:50 p.m.*

NICKY DEAN was getting used to freedom, and he liked it fine. Eleven years inside a cage was too damn long, but there was still a silver lining. Something could have happened just as easily to screw up his parole and make him serve the twenty that a goddamned bluenose judge had given him to start with. Someone could have found his stash and ripped him off while he was in the joint. Hell, any half-assed con with an imaginary grievance could have slipped a shank between his ribs and finished it before Dean even knew that he was dying.

In the joint, that kind of thing went on around the clock, day in, day out. You woke up every morning grateful for another sunrise, even if you couldn't really see it from your cell. The morning wake-up clamor of a prison meant that you had made it through another night, nobody squirting gasoline between the bars while you were sleeping, following the juice up with a match.

Before he took his fall in Lauderdale, Dean used to think the streets were hard, but they were nothing when you stacked them up against the joint. He couldn't say about the country-club reports where Wall Street swindlers did their time, but dealers from rank and file were sent to maximum, a fucking zoo with keepers who were prone to look the other way when rabid animals began to fight among themselves.

Eleven years, and he had won some not-so-minor victories along the way. For starters Nicky Dean still had the asshole he went in with, even if he had to shank a couple guys to keep it. He was no one's punk and never would be. If you let it happen once, it meant that you were marked for life, and living as a punk inside the joint was no real life at all.

Another victory of sorts, he had avoided all the racial bullshit going down inside the walls between the "aryans" and "black guerrillas." Fighting all the goddamn time about the color of your skin was stupid. Fucking wasted effort, when a man with brains could organize himself and turn a profit on his situation, setting up a pipeline from the streets to bring all kinds of merchandise inside. The guards—a few of them, at least—were willing to cooperate if you could make it worth their while, and once word got around that you could make delivery on time, it was a decent way to go.

Not anything like being free, of course. Dean hated every day inside, regardless of the coin he managed to accumulate. He never once forgot the judge or prosecutor who had sent him up, the scheming undercover agents who had busted him when he was running hot and pulling down an easy three, four hundred thousand free and clear. It wasn't like he had it made or anything; he wasn't set for life, by any means, but Nicky Dean was getting there, before the roof fell in.

Now, he was free and on vacation, soaking up some sun, enjoying life. A man of leisure, checking out the Paradise Casino. Relaxing and living it up for a change, after paying heavy dues. The last thing he expected was a blast from the past ... until the pig walked in.

A man didn't forget a face that sent him up for twenty years—a big mean bastard, smiling at him when they made the deal, flashing his badge when the heat came down and sticking an automatic in Dean's face, asking him if he wanted to try his luck. A guy like that, you knew he'd love to take you down and call it line of duty, just because you were making more than civil-service pay without a time clock marking off your life in bits and pieces. Loving it, the way he clamped the handcuffs on and prodded Nicky toward the car.

Now, here he was.

The kind of money federal agents made, he knew the bastard couldn't afford Paradise Island on his own dime. That meant he was working, maybe the dude beside him, seated at a corner table in the lounge. The agent hadn't spotted Dean yet, and the ex-con meant to keep it that way. Slouching lower on his bar stool, shoulders hunched, he watched the two men from the corner of his eye, nursing his drink and wondering how he could best turn the situation to his own advantage. Payback, at the very least, and if he had an opportunity to profit on the deal ...

Three scenarios came to mind, off the top. First up, the big guy could be working with the other dude, scamming some third party, which initially ruled out the direct approach. A second possibility, the other dude might be Big Guy's target, willing to pay for some timely advice, but the only way to check that out would be to wait and see. Last option, the other guy could turn out to be some kind of go-between, connecting the narc with a local target, pocketing a finder's fee. In that case he would have no relevance to Nicky Dean at all.

Like anything, it was the timing that would nail him if he didn't watch his ass. Jump in too soon, he wouldn't know the players, maybe spill his guts to some damned Fed and buy himself another couple years for violating his parole. Hang back too long, and Big Guy just might drop the net before Dean had a chance to warn his target. Not that it would damage Nicky, watching someone else go down, but he would miss the chance to pay an adversary back for all the hassles he had suffered in the joint. Those opportunities were few and far between. He didn't want to screw it up.

Especially if he had a chance to make some money in the bargain.

The trick was waiting for a chance to do it right, pull off the sting without real danger to himself, pick up some money in the process. All he had to do was watch and wait, find out exactly what was going on.

He got his break ten minutes later, when a black man joined the the narc and his friend at their table. Dressed to kill, this one, with the look of major money. If he wasn't the big guy's mark, Dean figured he would have to be the next best thing.

Okay.

The wheels were turning rapidly in Dean's mind, propelling him in the direction of a plan. Unless they had already set some kind of deal and they were ready for the bust, he still had time. Could the narc bust a mark outside of the United States?

Relax.

It was a simple thing to watch and wait, find out who Mr. Money was and speak to him in private, even if

Dean had to risk a beating in the process. Make him listen for his own sake, waiting for the gratitude to overflow and manifest itself as cash.

No sweat.

Unless the three of them were shacking up or leaving town together, the ex-con reckoned he would have his chance that night.

He settled back to watch and wait.

# CHAPTER SEVENTEEN

*Havana, Cuba*
*Thursday, 5:10 a.m.*

The all-night journey from the wasted camp in the mountains had exhausted all concerned. They'd paddled for an hour in canoes to start, prepared at any moment for the Hinds to sweep in low behind them, spewing armor-piercing rounds and rockets. But the gunships never came. Once they had ditched the boats, it turned into a waiting game, another ninety minutes waiting for Clemente Villa's contact to arrive with a sedan that had been well beyond its warranty when Calvin James was borne.

James sat in back, with Encizo, Villa and their driver in front. The rebels spoke in Spanish, Villa briefing his companion on the raid, apparent losses and the urgent need to double-check security from top to bottom. When he finished, he had turned to Encizo and James, an expression on his face that drew on equal parts of rage, suspicion and remorse.

"We've used that camp for seven months," he said. "Too long, perhaps, and yet . . ."

James knew what he was thinking, knew it would have been the first thing on his own mind if the situations were reversed.

"You're wondering if we did something wrong," he said in fluent Spanish. "Well, I can tell you no one trailed us from our landing to Niquero, or from there on to your camp. We double-checked our gear for bugs and homers in Jamaica. Nothing. If you think we sold you out deliberately, I guess you'd better spit it out."

The rebel stared at James for a moment, frowning, then finally shook his head. "If I believed that, I would be forced to kill you."

"Only way to go with traitors," James replied. "The point is that we didn't sell your people out. Which means the choppers found your camp by pure dumb luck, or—"

"Someone else betrayed us," Villa said.

"It looks that way to me."

"How many people knew where we were going?" Encizo inquired. "Outside the camp, I mean?"

"Raul Guerrero and the man who brought you to the camp."

"That's it?" James pressed.

"Unless . . ."

"I'm listening."

"There is a chance you might have been observed," said Villa.

"Another way to go, Guerrero or the driver could have let it slip."

"I trust them both."

James shrugged. "Your call. Let's say they mentioned it to someone else inside the group who didn't need to know."

"I will investigate. First though, we must count our losses, find out who is left."

Their destination on the outskirts of Havana was a ranch-style house with poorly tended trees out front and a wooden fence around the yard in back. They made one drive by, Villa checking out the neighborhood, then a second pass before he finally cleared the driver to approach. Stray chickens scattered as they pulled into the unpaved driveway, fresh dust settling as the engine died.

James had the duffel strap across his shoulder with the bag unzipped, his right hand in the bag and wrapped around the submachine gun's pistol grip. He noticed Encizo had done the same, prepared to cut loose at the first sign of a setup. You could never be too careful in the hellgrounds, least of all when it appeared your luck was running on a downward turn.

A man of middle age came through the front door of the house, hands empty, moving toward their car across the scruffy yard.

"Hello, Paolo," Villa called, already stepping from the car. He shook hands with the stranger, told him something Calvin couldn't hear and jerked a thumb in the direction of the car. When they were finished, Villa turned back toward his passengers and said, "This way."

"I hope we get it right this time," James said.

"At least we're in Havana," Encizo replied. "But such a price."

"Somebody owes on that one, big-time," James agreed. "Thing is, it might not be our tab to pay."

The house was cool inside, or cooler than the yard, at any rate. Four other men were waiting for them, all with weapons close at hand. James saw an M-1 carbine and a Thompson submachine gun, plus two

AK-47s obviously liberated from the Cuban military. There were solemn introductions all around, nobody jumping in to make them feel at home.

All things considered, James didn't blame them for their attitude.

How many dead in the Maestras, just that afternoon? It might be days before they got a final count, if ever, and the loss of every man or woman was a telling blow against the revolutionary front. They lived and died on dedication, and today it had been mostly dying. Tension in the room was thick enough to stop a bullet, and the Phoenix warriors let Clemente Villa do the talking for a while.

He started with a detailed recitation of the raid for his assembled comrades, leaving nothing out. The man named Paolo had some information for him from the south, news gathered since they fled the mountains, but it added little to their knowledge of events. The DSE was on alert, more so than usual, and grilling their informants for potential leads on any known "reactionaries" scattered by the airborne raid.

James wondered if the dragnet would extend from the Maestras to Havana, knowing even as the thought took shape that there was nowhere safe in Cuba for them now. If they were stopped for any reason, they would have to pray their bogus documents could stand more than a cursory inspection. With the weapons they were carrying, a search would wrap it up. Case closed, next case.

Somebody fetched beer from the kitchen, passing bottles around the circle. It was stronger than the brew that James was used to in America, but at the moment he could stand the extra kick. It tasted fine.

"We have been hiding long enough," Villa told them all a moment later. "It is time to fight, repay the Communists for the losses we have suffered."

"That's the eight of us, you mean?" James asked.

"We aren't alone," the revolutionary leader told him. "This is merely what you see. By nightfall, other members of our cadre will be in the city, ready to proceed."

"I hate to break the mood," James replied, "but two of us have a specific job to do, if you recall."

"Luis Rivera." Villa spoke the name as if it left a foul taste in his mouth. "I don't forget. None of us will forget. He is as good a place as any to begin."

James thought about it for a moment, glancing at Encizo, picking up the wiry Cuban's shrug. It was a change of plans, but what the hell? With reinforcements maybe they could salvage something from the mission that had gone awry and still come out of it alive.

Or, maybe not.

James sipped his beer and met Villa's level gaze.

"So, what's the plan?" he asked.

*Panama City*
*5:30 a.m.*

THE WAKE-UP CALL WAS thirty minutes early, but it still found Jack Grimaldi sitting by his window, fully dressed. He scooped up the receiver on the second ring, already thinking that it couldn't be the desk clerk. Nothing in the damned hotel had been on time so far, much less ahead of schedule.

"Yes?"

"I understand the weather's clear today."

The sound of Katzenelenbogen's voice sent voltage racing down Grimaldi's spine.

"That so?"

"Why don't you meet us at the big house later on?"

"Say when."

"Our goal is 1930 hours, give or take."

"I'll see you there. Good hunting."

"That's affirmative."

The line went dead. Grimaldi cradled the receiver, smiling. Still thirteen hours, but at least he had a goal now. Anything beat waiting in his room for Bolan to report.

The Panamanian authorities had trouble on their hands, and then some. Much of it was Bolan, but the big guy's targets had begun to duke it out between themselves, without his help, and things were heating up. Aside from the sporadic raids and drive-by shootings, members of Democracy in Action were denouncing the police for their reaction to a protest march that left two dozen demonstrators in the hospital. More violent footage, clubs and tear gas, bodies writhing in the middle of the street.

It was Grimaldi's kind of town.

He thrived on action, and the closest thing to purgatory he could think of was the waiting that preceded combat. Not that he was nervous in the strict sense of the word. Grimaldi's confidence was boundless, damn near legendary, but his patience threshold left a lot to be desired.

It came from flying jets and helicopter gunships over Nam, he told himself. In those days you were either quick or you were dead, and it was still the same in everything that counted. Sitting still and waiting was the trick that got you killed more times than not. Grimaldi understood that it was different with the infantry, where setting up an ambush was the stock in trade, with soldiers trained to lie immobile by the hour, letting ants and spiders use their bodies like a superhighway, waiting for the one shot that would drop your man.

But when the heat was on and there were VC as thick as fleas around the base camp, or that ambush blew up in your face and you had casualties, it was the speed that counted. Death from above or a second chance at life, take your pick. Whichever it was, the ground forces needed it now, if not sooner, and you could stick your lame excuses where the daylight never reached.

This day it would be death. The men of Phoenix Force were going for the "big house," simple code for Santiago's fortress in Colombia, at Chigorodo. The flight would take him roughly twenty minutes, once he picked his war bird up at Albrook Air Force Base, and that meant he had time to kill, but it was different now. At least he had a target and a deadline. Only Katz could call the mission off from this point on to zero hour minus sixty seconds. After that, no one on earth could save the "big house" from a dose of hell on wings.

Grimaldi knew the risk involved in Katzenelenbogen's plan. A U.S. warplane striking at civilian targets in Colombia and ducking back to roost in Panama would qualify as an outrageous act of war, assuming anyone identified Grimaldi or his plane. Colombia had coastal radar, and he figured some of it was bound to overlap their border with the isthmus, but it was a chance that he would have to take. The dealer's stronghold lay just forty miles across the border—less than sixty seconds as the jet flies—and five minutes would complete the strike if he was dawdling. The nearest fighters the Colombians could scramble would be coming out of Monteria, and the pilots had to catch him if they wanted any part of Jack Grimaldi's action.

He thought of Bolan, wondering if he ought to try the big guy's room and tell him what was going on. Forget it. The Executioner would have been in touch if he was back at the hotel, instead of ripping up the town. In any case it was agreed in advance that Phoenix had his services on call. There was little he could do for Bolan in the city, nothing in terms of what the warrior did best.

He had a sudden image of himself, blazing through the heart of Panama City in an F-15, playing Top Gun. The smile on Grimaldi's face was reflex, disconnected from reality. He still had time to kill and didn't feel like eating breakfast yet.

The pilot rose, switched on the television set and sat down again. If nothing else, the breaking news should keep him entertained.

*Panama City*
*7:15 a.m.*

WAKING FROM a violent dream, Miranda Limachi's first thoughts were of the tall American. Belasko hadn't been in her dream per se, but it didn't require a psychoanalyst to find the link. The stranger had saved her life.

How many had he killed?

She wondered where he was right now, what deadly game he was involved with. In her heart and mind, Miranda knew that drugs were ruining her country. Not the same way they were ruining America, of course. Most Panamanians couldn't afford cocaine if they were so inclined. It was the traffic and corruption that surrounded it that undermined the government. So many greedy politicians with their hands out, desperate to be included in the feeding frenzy.

There could be no turnaround, no cleanup in the capital while drugs and politics were mingled in a noxious, deadly brew. And if the military officers in charge of interdicting traffic from Colombia refused to do their job, it must be done by someone else.

Miranda understood these things, but she was still put off by so much violence, even in a worthy cause. From childhood, almost from the cradle, she had been instructed in the ways of peace. when protest was required, it should be solemn and nonviolent. The Latin trend toward coups and revolutions was a curse that kept the workingman impoverished, virtually enslaved by military juntas of the right or left. In fact the politics made little difference when it issued from the barrel of a gun.

And yet she knew the dealers wouldn't leave her country voluntarily. Why should they, when the government of Panama had made them rich beyond their wildest dreams? It called for drastic action, and the American was capable of taking down his enemies efficiently, without remorse.

Miranda tuned the shower to a temperature that she could tolerate and stepped beneath its stinging spray.

Deliberately she made her mind a blank and concentrated on the steamy heat, dismissing politics and warfare from her mind.

She almost missed the sound, a muffled thump that emanated from her bedroom, just beyond the open bathroom door. At first Miranda thought it must be her imagination, but she turned the water off regardless, quick enough to catch the muffled sound of voices speaking in an urgent whisper.

Sudden panic flared inside her as she jerked the plastic shower curtain back and grabbed her robe. She was intensely conscious of her nakedness, a sense of vulnerability that was hardly assuaged once she covered herself.

Miranda scanned the bathroom for a weapon, anything with which she could defend herself. She whipped the medicine cabinet open, found nothing and started on the narrow drawers beside the sink.

She found a metal rat-tail comb.

It wasn't much, but it would have to do. A twist of facial tissue covered the sharp metal teeth and provided a handle of sorts, the five-inch gleaming spike protruding from her fist like a stiletto blade. Holding the makeshift weapon out of sight against her thigh, Miranda cautiously advanced until she reached the open doorway.

Three men waited for her in the bedroom, one face deadpan while the other two were smiling at her, dark eyes running up and down her body like insects, making her skin crawl.

"What do you want?" she demanded, afraid of the answer.

One of the smilers replied, "We want you, little one."

"And for what?" She was pushing it, stalling for time, still uncertain how she should react when they made their move.

"We can discuss that in the car," the smiler told her, pink tongue sliding out to swab his lips. "Perhaps you will enjoy our company."

"Perhaps if I was dead," she answered, standing fast.

"I thought of that," Deadpan said, "but our orders are to bring you back alive."

"And you expect me to cooperate?"

"It matters little, one way or the other."

Deadpan made his move before the others, stepping toward her, reaching for Miranda with his right hand while her own right whipped around and met his face. The handle of her rat-tail comb punched through his left cheek, scraped between his teeth and poked out on the right, a little spurt of blood on either end to tell her it wasn't some gross illusion from a stage magician's bag of tricks.

The stranger lurched away from her, Miranda glad to let him keep the comb, although she thereby left herself unarmed. The man raised both hands to his face, another moment lost before he understood exactly what had happened to him. When he tried to speak, his voice was muffled and distorted by the blockage of his tongue.

At last, Miranda and the others watching him, he gripped the comb in both hands and withdrew it from his face. More blood streamed down his cheeks and stained his jacket, soaking through his white dress shirt. He turned on his companions with a shout that spattered crimson in their faces, making both men wince.

"You idiots! Subdue her!"

It was over in a moment, even though Miranda fought them—kicking, scratching, biting, gouging with her thumbs. One of the men punched her in the stomach, just a tap when she considered it in retrospect, and suddenly she found she couldn't breath. It felt like drowning. By the time her lungs agreed to function in their normal manner, she was bound and gagged. The stranger with the punctured face took time to reach inside her robe and pinch Miranda's nipples, twisting them until the silent tears convinced him she was suffering.

"Enough," he muttered, as if speaking to himself, and found another pressure point between her collarbone and jaw.

The pain was less this time, and in a moment there was none at all, the darkness closing in to carry her away.

*Nassau, Bahamas*
*7:45 a.m.*

IT WAS AN EARLY START for Thomas Mentzer, but the man said his business was urgent, a matter of life and death. That would be true, at least, if he was wasting Mentzer's time, but it would be the caller's death...and that, the dealer thought, might prove amusing in itself.

Meanwhile, he was awake and he could spare the time to listen, satisfy himself that there was nothing in the wind before he had this pallid beetle crushed for waking him ahead of schedule. If there *was* some urgent matter he should know about, it wouldn't do for him to let it slide.

The white man had been trying too hard for a suntan, as they often did. He would have been fish-belly pale when he arrived on the island. Now he resembled something close to lobster red from lying in the sun too long, a lighter ring around each eye where thick sunglasses had provided some protection. Mentzer would have laughed at him another time, but at the moment he was curious, willing to listen.

Briefly.

"Your name is..."

"Nicky Dean. I'm from the States, you know?"

"Of course." As if he could have been mistaken for a native islander.

"I mostly live and work in Florida, but for the past eleven years I've been up in Atlanta. See, they got themselves a federal pen up there, you know?"

"A federal pen?"

"A prison, like."

"I see."

"You want to ask yourself, 'So what's this ex-con doing here, and why's he taking up my time?'"

"The question crossed my mind," Mentzer said, smiling thinly at his guest.

"Thing is, I figure I can help you out. You've got trouble coming, and you don't even know it yet."

"Such as?"

"One of the fellows you were drinking with last night, at the casino," Dean responded with a small, sly smile. "He's the fucking narc who sent me up."

The frown etched concentration lines between Mentzer's eyes. "Have you been spying on me, Mr. Dean?"

Dean lost his smile and raised both hands, a gesture of appeasement. "Hey, no way, man. I was drinking in the lounge, that's all. I spot this guy across the room and figure what the hell, it couldn't hurt to stick around and find out what he's doing. Maybe get a chance to pay him back for all the grief he caused me, dig it? Help somebody else out of a tight spot while I'm at it."

"You're an altruist, I take it?"

Dean responded with a shrug. "I never thought that much about religion, one way or the other."

Mentzer somehow kept himself from laughing in the man's face. "I mean to say, you do this favor as an act of charity."

"Well, sure. I mean . . . if it's important to you, and you feel like giving me some kind of a reward, hey, I'm not gonna throw it in your face, okay? I'm easy."

"There were two men at my table, Mr. Dean. Which one was your acquaintance from the States?"

"The big dude."

"Did you recognize the other man?"

"I never saw him before in my life, but if he's traveling with narcs, there's only two ways he can go. Dude's getting set up for a burn, or he's a cop himself."

"I cannot argue with your logic, Mr. Dean. The question still remains, why a narcotics officer would waste his time on me."

"Hey, I don't know a thing about your business, man. And I don't *wanna* know, you get my drift? I mean, your business is your business, all the way. I'm on vacation here, you know? I'm sure as hell not looking for Excedrin headache number three fifty-seven."

"Ah." Mentzer smiled across the broad expanse of his desk. "A wise man, as well as honest."

"Well, I didn't reach this ripe old age by jumping up and down on anybody's toes. Not strangers, anyway."

Mentzer stared at this man, ten years younger than himself, and resisted an urge to slap the man's face.

"Of course. Go back to your hotel. Relax and find yourself a woman. If your information is correct, I will be pleased to cover the expenses of your stay...say, two more weeks? Perhaps a little something extra on the side."

"All right."

"If it should prove to be erroneous . . ."

He left it hanging, but from Dean's expression, Mentzer knew he didn't have to spell the warning out.

"I didn't come up here to shine you on, man. This is straight, I swear to God."

"Then we should have no problem, Mr. Dean. Enjoy your stay."

"Yeah, right."

The tone of Dean's voice told Mentzer he would spend the rest of his vacation looking over his shoulder, and that was fine. The dealer had more pressing problems at the moment. It was obviously time for cleaning house.

# CHAPTER EIGHTEEN

*Unguia, Colombia*
*Thursday, 10:00 a.m.*

The easy way, Katzenelenbogen thought, would have been an airlift with Grimaldi at the throttle. Drop them close to Santiago's hardsite, hanging back until they closed the final quarter mile or so, and then coordinate the strike with everything they had.

But easy wasn't always wise, and it was seldom safe.

An airlift meant the risk of radar and a military response before they were fully in place on the ground. Grimaldi's solo flight might have the same effect, but Phoenix Force would have a chance to mark its targets first, and this way they weren't dependent on Grimaldi for a lift back into Panama. If something happened to the pilot—

No.

Katz cut the pessimistic vision off before it had a chance to put down roots. Grimaldi was a pro and then some. He could do things with a war bird most never thought about, much less attempted. In the time that they had known each other, since the Phoenix Project activated, Katz had never seen the man outclassed or outmaneuvered in the air.

If nothing else, they knew he would be waiting to assist them when the doomsday clock ran down to zero hour. Katzenelenbogen didn't know exactly what Grimaldi had in mind for his end of the action, but it stood to reason he would pull out all the stops and plaster Santiago with the kitchen sink.

So much the better.

There was only so much three men on the ground could do against an army, but the dealer had no air force of his own, unless you counted the civilian aircraft stationed at his ranch. One of Grimaldi's foremost tasks would be to stop Santiago from escaping in a plane or helicopter while the men of Phoenix Force were looking for him on the ground.

Provided that they ever got that far.

And if they were prevented, somehow, from arriving at the rendezvous on time, at least Grimaldi would be there to light the cleansing fire and give the dealer a foretaste of hell on earth.

They hadn't driven back to Panama City after the Rio Atrato strike, contenting themselves with an overnight stop in La Palma, on the Golfo de San Miguel. It cut their Thursday trip in half and gave the Phoenix warriors room to breathe once they had crossed the border west of Unguia.

McCarter was their pointman once they reached the town, his working knowledge of Spanish their key to picking up some kind of transportation they could live with. It wasn't impossible to walk the sixty-something miles between the border and Santiago's stronghold, but it would be easier if they could save some time and energy along the way, perhaps show up on time and with the strength to carry out their mission in top form.

The wheels turned out to be a military jeep of early 1950s vintage, with the fenders rusted through in spots, and patches on the fat spare tire. Still, there was power underneath the hood, and McCarter managed to negotiate a decent price, all things considered. There was no doubt that the seller had considered him a cocaine cowboy from the States, and that was fine with Katzenelenbogen. Anglo smugglers were a dime a dozen in Colombia, and one more looking for a bargain-basement ride would cause no lasting comment in the local bars. If opportunists pursued the gringo, hoping to relieve him of his money on the long drive south to Medellín, they would be in for a surprise.

The last one of their lives, in fact.

With wheels it was a simpler trek but still not easy. They would have two river crossings—the Atrato and Uraba—plus the miles of swamp that lay between Unguia and their target outside Chigorodo. Even so, there *was* a road that they could use until they got within a mile or so of Santiago's hardsite, thereby saving precious time. With any luck there would be ample opportunity for them to hide the jeep, check out their target, burrow in and wait for darkness.

Waiting was the hardest part of any hit-and-run campaign. Once battle had been joined, the action took care of itself with instinct kicking in. The waiting took a different kind of courage and determination, though, especially when you had to do it in the enemy's backyard, with hostile soldiers breathing down your neck. It was the kind of mission where experience counted double, and a green warrior's eagerness could get him killed . . . along with his companions.

Katz rode in back, with Gary Manning in the shotgun seat, McCarter at the wheel. They kept their weapons close at hand, with no real effort to conceal the hardware they were carrying. If they encountered enemies along the way, speed would be more important than discretion when it came to saving lives.

It stood to reason that Santiago would be on his guard, alert for any follow-up attacks, but Katz was banking on the arrogance of power to assist them with their strike. The drug lord would be shocked that anyone had nerve enough to challenge him so close to home, and while he mobilized his troops, he wouldn't seriously entertain the thought that anyone would dare attack his home.

Or so Katz hoped, at any rate.

No matter. They were on their way, no turning back. Grimaldi would be there with backup when they needed him, if he had to fight his way through the whole Colombian air force to keep their rendezvous. It was a relatively simple matter of concealment and evasion for the next few hours, picking out their fields of fire and lying low until the proper time arrived for them to strike.

And then, whatever happened, Katzenelenbogen knew it would be a night to remember.

For those who survived.

*Panama City*
*10:15 a.m.*

BEFORE HE MADE HIS MOVE against Jesus Avilla, long postponed until the other members of his venal clique were made aware of danger to their operations, Bolan thought it would be wise to touch base with his contacts at Democracy in Action and alert them to his plan. No details, naturally, but just enough to let them brace themselves for any possible reaction from the government.

He tried Miranda first, but there was no answer at her home. The second call reached Angelo Rodriguez at his storefront office, where police and soldiers regularly searched the desks and filing cabinets for "subversive" literature. They always came up empty, fundamentally because they missed the point. Democracy in Action *was* subversive to the ruling clique of greedy, money-grubbing politicians, but subversion in this case didn't involve a violation of established law. Rather, it attempted to revitalize the rule of law that had been trampled underfoot for years on end while narco dealers and their sycophants entrenched themselves in government.

A secretary took the call, repeated Bolan's code name, then left him hanging while she went to fetch Rodriguez. Bolan thought about the tension in her voice and wrote it off as normal . . . until Angelo came on the line.

"Where are you?"

"I'm on the move," Bolan replied. "What's happening?"

"Miranda," Angelo replied. "She has been kidnapped."

"When and where?" A heavy pulse kicked in behind the warrior's eyes, the makings of a headache if he let it take control.

"The time is not precise. This morning, early. She was taken out of her apartment. When she did not come into the office, calls were made. We got no answer. Finally I sent a courier to check on her . . . and she was gone. The boy found signs of struggle in her bedroom. Blood.''

"What else?"

"A call," Rodriguez said, "at half-past nine o'clock. A man's voice, no one I could recognize. He said Miranda would be killed if we continue to harass the government. Specifically they want the man or men who fired upon Delvalle. They believe our people were involved.''

"I'll handle it," the Executioner assured him.

"But Miranda—"

"Doesn't have a chance if you negotiate from weakness. If Delvalle's people are involved in this, they can't afford to let a witness live, no matter how they wrap it up. And if they're not, you're dealing with Barbosa or Velasco, maybe even Santiago."

"I regret the day we asked for help," Angelo said.

"I know the feeling. Stick around the office if you can. I'll be in touch."

With that he cradled the receiver and moved swiftly toward his car. He had a plan in mind, the general outline of a plan at any rate, and it was one the Executioner had used before.

In hostage situations, never yield.

It was a doctrine quoted frequently by governments, honored more in the breech than in observance. When a life was riding on the line, too many hardmen folded, handing over anything a predator demanded just to string the moment out and buy some precious time.

Mack Bolan had a rather different approach.

When someone whom he cared about was threatened by his enemies, the Executioner hit back. He didn't plead for mercy, soil his shorts, or promise anyone the moon and stars if they would please resist the urge to maim or kill. The only way to deal with savages was savagely, and Bolan was a man who wrote the book on that score.

He was driving when his mind began to drift, recalling other situations, dating back to Bolan's one-man war against the Mafia. He blocked that train of thought before it had a chance to leave the station, knowing there was nothing to be gained from reminiscing over times when he succeeded—or the times he failed—in an attempted rescue. Every situation was unique, his personal selection of an adversary's pressure points determined by a reading of events and circumstances.

There was only one firm rule that Bolan recognized for those occasions when an adversary tried to knock you down: hit back, hit hard and keep on hitting until the issue was resolved. You might not always win, but hostages were kept alive by their abductors for a reason. Dead, they lost their value to the enemy.

And if it went that far, then it was payback time.

Without the bargaining chip of Miranda Limachi's life, his enemies had nothing Bolan wanted, nothing in the world that would divert him from a battle to the death. Before this move they could have scattered to the winds, escaped, abandoned their illicit network in the middle of the night, and Bolan might have let them go.

Before.

From this point on, it was a brand-new game. The Executioner was fresh out of patience, and his enemies were standing on the wrong side of the firing line.

He had been playing with them, up until now. The rest of it would all be deadly earnest, no holds barred.

The Panama campaign was getting personal. He would do everything within his power to prevent more harm from coming to Miranda. If he failed, his enemies could look to God for mercy.

They would get none from the Executioner.

*Niquero, Cuba*
*10:15 a.m.*

RAUL GUERRERO WAS about to close his leather shop and start the long trip to Havana when he saw Armando Duro on the far side of the street. It was an odd sensation standing there, Armando watching him from fifty feet away.

What did Duro want? Had Villa summoned him to join the action in Havana? If so, Guerrero knew nothing of it, and his plans didn't include taking Duro with him on the long drive north and west to reach the capital.

He didn't fully trust Duro, even though they swore allegiance to the cause of Cuba Libre, shared an oath to see the Communists driven from their seats of power in Havana. There was something in the man's eyes that put Raul in mind of weasels lurking in the shadowed corners of a henhouse, waiting for a chance to rob the nest.

Of course, he realized that many of the rebels pledged to fight against Fidel were men with backgrounds that would bar them from the high-class social register. There were some "former" criminals among them, some of whom undoubtedly continued making money when and where they could, without regard to legal niceties. A rebel movement always drew its share of rogues and profiteers.

But Duro left Guerrero with a different feeling. There was something sly and devious about the man that kept the shopkeeper from sharing secrets with him, letting one of Villa's spokesmen tell Armando what he had to know when it was time. Guerrero had no evidence that would support a charge of treason to the movement, nothing but the feeling in his gut, and he wouldn't have troubled Villa with a personal complaint when there were more important matters on the leader's mind.

It might turn out to be a case of personal antipathy, no fault on either side. The fact that Duro made his skin crawl wasn't proof of anything.

Not yet.

Two men in matching leather jackets joined Armando. So it seemed, at any rate, although they made a show of window-shopping, neither man approaching Duro or addressing him directly. Still, Armando glanced across his shoulder as they stopped behind him. When he turned back toward Guerrero's leather shop, there was a new expression of determination on his face.

And something else. A trace of fear, perhaps.

Guerrero didn't recognize the other men, but he had seen their type before. If they weren't the DSE, they did a perfect imitation, from their close-cropped hair and jet-black leather to the attitude of smug superiority they carried with them like a badge of rank.

How many more outside, invisible from where Guerrero stood?

Too late to worry now.

He left the front door of the shop unlocked, proceeding quickly to the office-storeroom in the back. He took the big Colt semiautomatic pistol from his desk and checked its load unnecessarily, released the safety and cocked it as he walked back to the public portion of the shop. He found himself a paper sack and tore a hole in one side, to accommodate the pistol in his hand. From any distance it would simply look like he was carrying the bag—a personal delivery, perhaps—and if they let him reach his car without attempting to detain him, there would be no problem. He would have some extra time to think and forge a plan.

On the sidewalk he pretended not to see Armando, turning back to lock the door behind him, knowing it would be the last time that he ever saw his shop, regardless of what happened in the next few moments. Duro had betrayed him to the DSE, and there was no life for him in Niquero now. Perhaps no life in Cuba. Turning toward the alley where his ancient van was parked, Raul pretended not to hear the first time that Armando called his name.

"Guerrero! Hey, Raul!"

He waited for the sound of running footsteps, Duro closer when he raised his voice again.

"Raul! Where are you going?"

Swiveling to face his enemy, Guerrero saw the men in leather turning from the window of a bakery across the street. The two of them were crossing now, and from the look on Duro's face, Raul knew there were more behind him, probably emerging from the alley where his van was kept.

"I need to speak with you a moment," Duro said.

"Of course."

His first shot blew a cloud of tan confetti into space and set the paper bag on fire. Guerrero saw the bullet strike Armando in the stomach, just below his sternum, stunning him with its explosive impact. Raul had time for one more shot, a good one to the traitor's face, before a gun butt slammed into his shoulder from behind.

At once Guerrero's shooting arm went numb, his fingers losing purchase on the Colt and smoking paper sack. They struck the sidewalk with a crack, and Raul was stooping, reaching for the weapon with his left hand, when a strong arm locked around his throat from behind, cutting off his wind. A hard knee rammed between his legs, the pain detached from stark reality somehow. It brought him down, but in the seconds of surviving consciousness, Guerrero seemed to stand outside himself and watch the hectic scene.

At least, he told himself, Armando Duro had been duly paid for his betrayal of the holy cause.

When darkness overwhelmed his conscious mind, it came as a relief.

*Nassau, Bahamas*
*11:00 a.m.*

THE MORNING MEET had taken Lyons by surprise, but he was ready to proceed. He'd gotten a call from Mentzer, saying he was ready to discuss the proposition in more detail, but he had to see the earnest money first. For the amount of cash and product Lyons had proposed, there could be nothing left to chance.

So be it.

Perry Tate was riding shotgun, serving as the local go-between, while Schwarz and Blancanales scoped the meeting from a distance. It wasn't supposed to be a hit. They wanted Mentzer's link with the Colombian machine on tap for that, but Julio Marti wasn't about to show himself until his front man gave the go-ahead.

The meet was set for Windsor Park, on Mackey Street. Lyons approached from the north, taking his time. Beside him, Tate was whistling softly, tunelessly, watching the shop fronts and houses roll by. If he felt any kind of nervousness about the meet, it didn't show.

"You packing?" Lyons asked him.

"Absolutely, man. I don't leave home without it."

Fair enough. The Able Team leader had his own Glock-17 tucked in the waistband of his slacks, a reassuring pressure at his back, but it was good to know this wouldn't be the only gun on their side if it hit the fan. Experience had taught him anything could happen at a drug deal, even in the early stages. With a cool half-million tax-free dollars riding on the line, there was a risk from so-called friends and unknown enemies alike.

Trust no one but your proved comrades when the stakes were life and death. It was a simple rule, and Lyons had survived this long because he never let his guard down on—or off—the job.

Some famous thinker had described eternal vigilance as the price of liberty. For Lyons it was simply life insurance.

"There."

He saw the park ahead of them as Perry Tate stopped whistling and pointed. Slowing, Lyons pulled into the public parking lot and killed the rental's engine, waiting for another moment at the wheel.

"Let's take a walk," he said at last, already looking forward to the meet with Mentzer. Reaching in the back seat, Lyons grabbed the briefcase filled with hundred-dollar bills, a hundred notes to the bundle, fifty packs in all.

They started across the grass toward an ornate bandstand, a hundred yards due west. Tate walked beside him, looking casual, but Lyons felt the DEA man checking left and right as they proceeded, missing nothing with his eyes.

The bandstand was their destination, picked by Mentzer as a place where they could sit and talk while the dealer counted Lyons's money, leaving with it if they made a deal. The sticking point would come with the demand for a personal meeting with Julio Marti, but Lyons felt that he was in a decent bargaining position. A half million down, no strings attached, and more where that came from if they went into business. Marti would be drawn out of his hole by greed, and all they needed was a nibble at the bait.

One meet to put him on the spot, and they could wrap it up.

At fifty yards they saw a figure waiting for them on the bandstand, sitting on a bench, his features masked in shadow. Trees closed in on either side, a backdrop for the bandstand during concerts underneath the open sky.

In retrospect it would be difficult to say who saw the gunners first. Tate hissed a warning, pivoting to face a pair of figures on his right, as Lyons confronted two more on his left, emerging from the trees.

A trap!

In front of them the dark shape on the bandstand shifted, leveling a weapon. They could turn and try to run the gauntlet, but the odds against survival were immense. Lyons made his choice in something like a heartbeat, reaching for his pistol as he went to ground.

The big ex-LAPD detective fired a shot in the direction of the bandstand, dropping prone before the echo died away and submachine guns filled the air with angry, swarming bullets. Leaving Tate to hold the right flank, Lyons chose a moving target at the tree line, leading with his sights, and triggered two quick rounds at twenty yards.

The gunner stumbled, went down on his knees, still firing blindly as he toppled onto his back. The second triggerman was firing on the run, no real attempt to aim, but he got lucky with a burst that punctured Lyons's briefcase, drilling into stacks of hundred-dollar bills.

He gave the runner three more strides, then stopped him with a bullet in the chest. It might have been a fatal shot, but Lyons wasn't taking any chances. As the man began to fall, he fired twice more, the bullets ripping in on target, finishing the job.

A burst of Parabellum manglers ate into the sod in front of Lyons's face, perhaps a foot off target. He rolled away, heard bullets slapping at the briefcase from a new direction and fired two rounds in the general direction of the bandstand as he veered off from the hostile line of fire.

The shadow man was on his feet and pivoting to bring his prostrate target under fire. A well-placed round from Lyons's Glock drilled through his shoulder, spinning him around. His profile was a decent target, even so, and Lyons fired twice more, the semiauto pistol bucking in his fist. He saw both rounds strike home, the shooter's jacket rippling on impact, and the dead man went down on his face.

A cry from Perry Tate brought Lyons spinning to his right in time to see the DEA man staggering, a string of submachine gun bullets ripping through his abdomen from front to back. Across the bare expanse of lawn, one gunner stretched out on his face, the other firing steadily as he began to swing his weapon toward Lyons.

There were six rounds left in the Able Team leader's pistol, and he used them all in a second and a half. Four hits he was sure of, and the last man on his feet slumped forward, frozen for a moment on his hands and knees, as if he meant to try some push-ups, finally dropping forward on his face.

All done.

Reloading as he rose, Lyons scanned the trees for any further sign of hostile movement. Perry Tate was dead before the Able Team warrior reached him, and it made no sense to drag his body from the scene. Instead he grabbed his riddled briefcase, ran back toward the parking lot, waving Schwarz and Blancanales off as they piled out of their car.

Too late for any help.

The hit had gone down so fast that there had been no real time to think about it.

But he was thinking now.

About revenge.

# CHAPTER NINETEEN

Aaron Kurtzman had been working on a turkey sandwich when the word came in from Nassau. Guarded phrases, even with the scramblers, just in case. The Able warriors didn't stay alive by overlooking small details.

And from the way it sounded, they were in the shit already, swimming hard against the tide.

The word came up with Carmen Delahunt, an FBI computer wizard who had traded in her federal badge to work at Stony Man. A divorced mother of three, she had been tracking fugitives at the Bureau's National Center for Analysis of Violent Crime, in Quantico, when Kurtzman made her an offer she couldn't refuse. In their first week together she had given Bear a demonstration of the classic redhead's fiery temper, but they mostly got along. Today, when she delivered the report from Nassau, there was worry in her eyes, compassion in her voice.

"At least the team's intact," she said after Kurtzman had a moment to digest the news.

"But compromised," he replied. "We don't know if their cover's blown, but someone obviously has them marked. They'll have to wrap it up ASAP or cut and run."

"I don't see Able running."

"You got that right."

So, they were midway through the second full day of the operation, Kurtzman told himself, and it was time for things to break. A job like this, the longer Bolan and his people hung around, the more risk they ran. Two days could be a lifetime in the hellgrounds, and the Stony Man commandos were renowned for lightning raids that left their targets in a bloody shambles. In and out before the savages had time to grasp exactly what was happening.

But sometimes there was necessary groundwork to be done.

Like now.

His appetite was gone, and Kurtzman pushed the plate away.

"You're done with that?" Carmen asked. When he nodded, she retrieved the untouched half sandwich, trying on a hefty bite for size. "Not bad."

"No other word?" It was a pointless question, knowing Carmen would have told him off the top, but Kurtzman felt compelled to ask.

"Just Nassau. All we have from Panama is news clips off the satellite, and nothing from Havana."

"Damn it."

"Could be one time when the rule applies," she said.

"Which rule is that?"

"No news is good news."

"Maybe." Kurtzman didn't look or sound convinced. He knew that these things had a way of suddenly unraveling. A leak in the Bahamas meant there was a possibility of Mentzer or Marti communicating with associates in Panama. One thing led to another, and you never knew where it was going to end . . . until it blew up in your face.

"They'll have to wrap it up," Carmen said.

"Right. No matter what. I'm out of here."

He wheeled himself out of the mess hall and on to the computer room, Carmen catching up before he pressed his thumb against the small screen set beside the coded access sliding door. They entered together, and Akira Tokaido turned from his place at the command console to face them. He was chewing bubble gum as always, but the earphones for his mini-CD player were around his neck instead of welded to his ears.

"I was about to page you," he said.

Kurtzman felt the pulse begin to throb behind his eyes. "What's up?"

"I've got a rumble from the CIA. Their people have been intercepting Cuban military chatter via satellite. It's ninety-nine-percent routine. They do it all the time. Thing is, Havana has a flap in progress, mounting raids against an unnamed group of 'counterrevolutionaries.' What I'm picking up from Langley is that they've already busted out a camp in Oriente province. Major casualties." Akira saw the question in Kurtzman's eyes and hastened to add, "No mention of foreigners yet, one way or the other."

"It could be coincidence," Carmen suggested.

"And I could be running the marathon Saturday," Kurtzman replied. "But the odds are against it."

"Okay. What's the drill?"

"Sit and wait," Kurtzman said. "It's the pits but I don't see an option."

"You want me to contact Hal?" Tokaido asked.

"Damn right. He wants everything fresh off the wire. It's his ulcer."

"I'm on it."

"And stick with that Langley connection as close as you can."

"Got it covered."

Kurtzman scanned the bank of terminals and monitors, his chosen battlefield. He missed his legs then, in a way that had nothing to do with self-pity or simple regret. It would have been a different game if he could help his comrades in the field directly, take some of the heat upon himself instead of sitting safe behind the lines.

Spilled milk.

He blanked his mind to yesterday and focused on the here and now. He couldn't change the past, but there was still a chance to have some impact on the present and the future.

But first, he had to watch and wait.

*Paradise Island, Bahamas*
*12:15 p.m.*

"THEY HAD US SPOTTED going in," Lyons said bitterly.

"I worked that out myself," the Politician replied. "The question is, who spotted you and how?"

"It doesn't make much difference now. I'm burned, regardless. The way I see it, we've got one shot left to clean this up."

Blancanales didn't have to hear him say it. When the odds were against you, there were two ways you could handle any given situation. One was cut and run, if you could find an opening. Slip out and live to fight another day. It worked, sometimes, but always left a sour taste behind.

The other route, you got your act together PDQ and started kicking ass. Again, there were no guarantees of coming out alive, much less victorious, but when you pulled it off you felt a damn sight better.

Either way, the price of failure was identical.

"We still don't have a fix on the Colombian," Gadgets reminded them. "If we take St. Jacques and Mentzer down but leave Marti in place, we might as well forget the whole damn thing."

"Okay," Lyons said, "we need to flush him out. We've tried the money angle, now we need to find another way."

"I'd say that's right." Blancanales stared at the briefcase on the bed beside him. They had opened it upon returning to his hotel suite, examining the damage. Roughly half of the ten-thousand-dollar bundles were intact, the rest resembling shredded paper from a rat's nest where the Parabellum rounds had done their worst. A quarter of a million dollars had been literally shot to hell.

"I'd like to take whatever's left," Schwarz said, "find out if Tate had any kind of family and stick it in the mail."

"Suits me," Blancanales agreed. "The DEA won't miss it, one way or the other."

"Screw 'em if they do," Lyons snapped. "It seems to me that one of Mentzer's people grabbed the case and got away in the confusion. The more I think about it, I'm convinced that's what went down."

"Okay, next question." Blancanales frowned. "How do we find Marti?"

"One way to go," Lyons said, "is that we could assume the hit was aimed at Tate. Call Mentzer back and ask him what the hell he thinks he's doing, treating customers this way. He wants the money and the deal, we strike a bargain on the phone. No meeting with Marti, no contract."

"So, he agrees to anything," Schwarz said, "and sends another team of shooters in his place. It's suicide."

Lyons forced a crooked grin. "One minor hitch."

Schwarz rolled his eyes. "I always knew you had more guts than brains."

"Another thought," Blancanales said, cutting through the banter. "We can squeeze St. Jacques until he squeals. If he can't get a meeting with Marti, we're up the creek."

"And when they huddle..."

"We revise the playbook," Lyons said. "I like it."

"Better than a suicide mission?"

"You can't have everything."

The Politician checked his watch. "I'm betting St. Jacques's out to lunch right now."

"I never bet against sure things," Schwarz said.

The young receptionist confirmed it, telling Blancanales that the minister was expected back at half-past one. If there was any message in the meantime...

None.

"One-thirty," he informed the others as he dropped the telephone receiver in its cradle.

"Do you think he knows about the rumble at the park?" Schwarz asked.

"If he's on top of things, he'd better."

"What's the angle, then?" Lyons asked.

"Hit him straight, no bullshit," Blancanales replied. "If he doesn't know that Mentzer's people blew it, he's behind the times. Whatever, once he knows *we* know about his various connections and we've got him marked to fall with Mentzer and Marti, smart money says he'll want to talk. I wouldn't be surprised to see him call a meeting with the others, try to work things out."

"Or save his own ass, anyway," Schwarz said.

"Whatever."

"I've been thinking," Lyons said.

"Uh-oh." Schwarz grinned and shook his head.

"Don't be a smartass, Gadgets."

"Testy."

"Let's suppose they weren't all Mentzer's guns."

"Why not?"

"For one thing only two of them were black. The others looked Hispanic."

"Like Colombian, for instance?"

Lyons shrugged. "It works for me."

"Which means you've got Marti's attention, as it is," Blancanales said.

"Me, or Tate."

"Or both of you."

"Or both, that's right."

"We'll find out soon enough," the Politician told his comrades. "Come one-thirty, I've got a surprise for the esteemed minister of tourism. I want to let him look at gambling from a new perspective, find out how he functions when he has to bet his life.''

*Havana, Cuba*
*12:35 p.m.*

WITH THE AFTERNOON HEAT, the house began to swelter. Eight or nine new members of the rebel party had arrived, and it was getting crowded, three of them intently puffing on cigars that mingled with a smell of sweat to foul the air. Two men were on the windows constantly, alert to any sign of uniforms or strangers on the street outside.

"How many more are you expecting?" James asked Villa, while they shared a midday meal of stringy beef and refried beans.

"Another five or six," the rebel leader replied. "Some others have a different place to meet. Say twenty-five, if none of them are intercepted on the way."

James didn't like the sound of that, but let it go. If any one of Villa's men was picked up by the army or the DSE, it wouldn't take the experts long to pick their subject's brain for every useful scrap of information he possessed. Including the location of his contacts.

As if in answer to his thoughts, Villa said, "We shall be moving in a little while. I have another place in mind where we can wait."

"How long?"

"My eyes are on Rivera. We must strike him at the moment when he least expects it, when his guard is down."

"With last night's raid," Encizo said, "he should be feeling confident."

"I hope so," Villa answered. "Let his pride destroy him."

"You keep track of DSE commanders?"

"When we can. They are not the only ones who study how to spy and infiltrate. In Cuba, since the Fidelistas came to power, subterfuge has been a way of life."

"How long have you been fighting Castro?"

Villa was about to answer when the walkie-talkie on the couch beside him came to life with static, followed by a burst of rapid Spanish. James missed part of it but caught enough, and he was reaching for his submachine gun when the lookouts on the windows sounded warnings.

"Chief! Quickly!"

"Soldiers!"

Just like that, and every man was scrambling for his weapon, rank cigars forgotten as they crowded toward the windows, several gunners peeling off to check the rear.

Outside, an armored car was nosing in against the curb, at least three dozen uniforms dispersing to the cover of surrounding trees and hedges, ancient cars and homes. The soldiers obviously knew what they were there for, quickly staking out their fields of fire.

Villa rattled off four names, with orders for the "lucky" ones to hold the enemy at any cost and buy some time. "The rest of you," he snapped, "out through the back! The vehicles!"

It was a sucker play, James thought, but the alternative was standing fast and waiting for a larger force to bring the house down around their ears. There would be reinforcements on the way, perhaps already waiting in the neighborhood, and once the soldiers met resistance they would unleash everything they had, including hand grenades and rocket launchers if it came to that. The house might stand for ten or fifteen minutes if their luck was very, very good.

He hit the kitchen running, Encizo just in front of him. Clemente's plan to drive away was something else, exchanging one set of close quarters for another, but James reserved judgment, waiting to see what lay in store for them outside. If they were cut off from the rear, surrounded, it would be every man for himself.

Behind him, a crash of rifle fire ripped through the house. A symphony of weapons answered from the yard, and James heard bullets striking home, some breaking glass while others drilled the walls. One of the rebels fell as James looked back, his three surviving comrades keeping up a steady stream of fire into the yard and street beyond.

Their vehicles were parked in back, a spacious yard, but soldiers were waiting. Their automatic weapons opened up the moment one of Villa's rebels showed himself, his body jerking from a dozen hits before he fell.

"Cut off!" Villa snapped, firing three rounds through a window set above the sink.

"Not yet," James said. "I count five guns out there. With cover fire and a concerted rush, I'm betting we can drive them back and get a fair shot at the cars."

"Perhaps."

"If you want to stop and think about it for a minute, it could be fifteen or twenty."

"Very well." The rebel leader snapped another order, and four men took up positions at the windows while the others braced themselves to rush the yard and take their enemies by storm. James found himself in the attacking party, with Encizo at his side.

Another heartbeat, and they hit the threshold, two men charging through with two more right behind, and so on. Some of them were taking hits, one going down at once, but then the gunners in the windows opened up to cover them, the soldiers ducking back to save themselves. James marked one sniper, hosing his position with the PA3-DM and breaking for the vehicle they had arrived in. Just a few more yards...

A soldier showed his head, a careless move, and James took it off with half a dozen Parabellum rounds. A bullet plucked at the Phoenix warrior's sleeve, but he was at the car now, piling in, a driver snug behind the wheel. Encizo had his window down and he was firing at the soldiers with his submachine gun, pausing briefly to reload. There was no sign of Villa as the engine roared to life and they were moving, peeling out, the back tires spitting grass and gravel as they dug for traction.

They rolled toward the wooden fence where two of the opposing troops were waiting for them, firing as they closed the gap. A bullet starred the windshield, then another, but they missed the driver and he kept his nerve, a lead foot on the gas. James estimated they were doing close to thirty miles an hour when they hit the fence and kept on going, lumber scraping on the doors and roof as they plowed through. A soldier sprawled across the hood, eyes wide and staring at them. Someone in the front seat shot him through the windshield, and he fell from view.

But there were more to take his place, James saw immediately, as they raced across a neighbor's yard and through another fence to reach the street. A wall of uniforms and smoking weapons drilled bullets into the sedan. James hunched his shoulders, got a burst off through the open window on his right-hand side, but mostly he was ducking as they ran the gauntlet, roaring down the block.

All right.

For just a moment he believed that they were clear, and then the jeeps fell in behind them, two of them with mounted automatic weapons, keeping pace and laying down a screen of deadly fire. The trunk caught some of it before the window blew in back, and he was sitting in a pile of jagged glass.

He fired a wild burst through the window, trying for the driver of the nearer jeep and missing by at least a yard. The left rear tire exploded, steel rims digging into asphalt seconds later. The old sedan began to swerve, momentum fading in the stretch. Their pursuers caught the scent of victory and crowded closer, ready for the kill.

The driver obviously knew that it was hopeless, swerving hard left through another yard and putting several mangy dogs to flight. Behind him, James tried another close-range burst, rewarded when the jeep's main gunner clutched his side and slumped across his weapon, clinging fast to keep from being thrown out of the open vehicle.

James didn't know exactly what their driver had in mind, and he was unprepared for their collision with the front porch of a wooden, four-room house. The impact jolted him and thrust a blade of silver pain between his shoulder blades.

All this, he thought, and now having to deal with whiplash. Shit.

Straight across the sagging porch and through the front wall of the house, their juggernaut relinquishing its grip on life once they were in the Spartan family room. An old man gaped at them in stunned surprise, his wide eyes going wider as the troops unloaded, brandishing their arms.

"Out back!" one of the rebels snapped. "Split up and make your way to Rosalita's tavern if you can. See Bolívar!"

The rest of it was dodging, running, as the jeeps stopped short of following their prey inside the house, machine guns cutting loose at close to point-blank range. James veered out of his way to knock the old man sprawling, well below the line of fire, and kept on running toward the kitchen, through it and out the back door to the yard.

How long before foot soldiers picked up the pursuit?

He had his answer seconds later, as shouted curses and a rapid burst of gunfire came from the house. A bullet whispered past him on the left, another on the right. In front of him he saw Encizo hit the old man's fence and scale it in a flash. The next man up was halfway there when he stopped dead, spine arching, a scarlet blossom bursting between his shoulder blades.

He jogged hard left and hit a different portion of the fence, hands grasping, feeling splinters gouge his flesh, the submachine gun slapping at his rib cage on its

makeshift sling. The blunt toes of his shoes found
traction and his strong legs worked like pistons, going
for the altitude. He needed only seconds, just another
foot or so.

The gunner missed him by an easy eighteen inches,
but the burst of automatic rifle fire ripped through the
boards supporting James's weight and dropped him six
feet to the hard-packed earth. He landed on his side,
the PA3-DM beneath him, feeling ribs give way. A gasp
of pain escaped between clenched teeth as he rolled
over, groping for the weapon, knowing it could be his
only chance.

Disoriented by the impact of his fall, James took a
moment to discover he was lying on the same side of
the fence where he had started. Six or seven feet away,
the rebel who had died before his eyes lay faceup on the
lawn, his back still arched from the explosive power of
the bullet that had snipped his spine.

Four soldiers were advancing on the spot where the
Phoenix warrior lay huddled in the dirt, one hand
wrapped tight around his submachine gun's pistol grip.
They knew what they were doing. There was too much
open space between them for a single burst to drop
them all at once. James reckoned he could take one
down for sure, perhaps a second if his luck held out
that long, but two were bound to kill him where he lay.

And if he let it go, then what?

Interrogation. Names, dates and places. How much
damage could he do, when the authorities had raided
every rebel hideout he had visited? He had no names
except Clemente Villa's, and for all James knew, the
counterrevolutionary leader could be dead by now,
perhaps in custody himself.

It was a choice of live or die, and he had something like a second and a half to cast his vote. At last, reluctantly, he stretched his arm out to its full extension and dropped his submachine gun on the grass.

The soldiers moved in close, still covering their captive. They were smiling when a sadist wearing sergeant's stripes reared back and slammed his boot into the bridge of James's nose.

# CHAPTER TWENTY

Bolan's third strike since the news of Miranda Lima-chi's abduction was a cutting plant where Sergio Barbosa's people "stepped on" their cocaine to stretch the quantity. At that, a buyer in the States would still be getting merchandise that ranged from eighty-eight to ninety-two percent in purity. Enough to cut another six or seven times and drive those profits through the roof when it eventually hit the street.

Big business, right.

His first stop after speaking to Rodriguez on the telephone had been a small marina where Ernesto Montalvo kept a sleek $200,000 pleasure boat. A member of the crew was cleaning up when Bolan got there, and he offered no objection when the Executioner suggested he should take a swim. It might have been the MP-5 K submachine gun Bolan carried, or the grim expression on his face that did the trick. In either case he held the swabbie long enough to find out that the guy spoke English...sort of. The warrior gave the message to him once and had the guy repeat it word for word before he took his dive.

"I want the girl, alive and well. Until I have her, no one's safe."

He used a three-inch wedge of Semtex, molded to the bulkhead in the forward cabin, well below the waterline. Two minutes on the timer, and he watched it blow from dockside, twenty yards away. The blast was muffled, but it did the job, the boat on fire before it settled deck-deep in the water, belching thick, dark smoke.

He'd left a simple warning at his first stop, but he knew the word would get around. Bad news was useful, that way.

Bolan's second target of the morning was a stylish brothel patronized by diplomats and businessmen of several nations. It was owned by one Jesus Avilla, confidant and aide to the respected president of Panama. Avilla made sure that the operation was protected, and he paid his madam bonuses for any useful information gathered on the clients entertained within those walls. Avilla didn't deal in blackmail, but it helped to know the weaknesses of friends and adversaries when it came to talking cash for trading rights and other economic privileges.

Avilla's brothel wasn't open when the Executioner arrived. He didn't stand on ceremony, circling around behind the building, opening the back door with a kick. A kitchen was on his left, occupied by three young men dressed in white, and an older man who directed them in preparation of the midday meal. He let them see his submachine gun, herded them out back and left them to their own devices. If they went for the police or any other help, so be it. Bolan meant to finish up his work within the next few moments and be gone.

To that end he went quickly up the stairs to reach the landing on the second floor. Directly opposite, twenty feet from where he stood, a crystal chandelier hung from the ceiling, overshadowing the parlor down below. A short, precision burst from Bolan's subgun brought it down, the sounds of gunfire and the crashing impact of the chandelier enough to rouse the house.

He counted fifteen girls and women altogether, some of them still in their teens, and the madam pushing forty. There was one man in the lot, a weasel with a long mustache who glared at Bolan like he couldn't wait to strike. But he did nothing, keeping both hands in his pockets and a grim expression on his face. The madam and a handful of her girls spoke English, passing Bolan's message to the others when he told them to evacuate the house. The man hung back a moment longer, practicing the evil eye, and the Executioner let the MP-5 K stare him down. The guy was running as he hit the stairs and almost lost it halfway down.

Alone, Bolan moved along the landing, dropping incendiary sticks in every other bedroom, another at the head of the stairs. He left his last two in the spacious parlor, one tucked underneath the cushions on a couch, the other in a well-stocked liquor cabinet. He could smell smoke as it left the house and brushed past three young women standing with their madam on the lawn. Again, he left his message, knowing it would get back to Avilla by the time he traveled half a mile.

"I want the girl, alive and well. Until I have her, no one's safe."

And now, Barbosa's cutting plant.

It was a drab four-story building half a block from the waterfront. There was a lookout on the street, but Bolan managed to avoid him with a quick run up the fire escape in back. The windows of the third floor were painted over as a hedge against prying eyes. No matter. His directions were explicit, and he knew exactly what to do.

The grenade was an American M-68 fragmentation model, with a timing fuse for backup if the first-line impact fuse should fail. He hung back several steps below the landing, yanked the pin and made his pitch. He had a bull's-eye on the center of a broad, black-painted pane, the glass not thick enough to detonate the impact fuse. The warrior gripped the railing on his left, ducked low and kept his eyes shut as the hand grenade went off inside, a storm of jagged glass erupting from the windows overhead.

Inside, it came to mopping up. Two gunners had survived the blast, and both of them were on their feet as Bolan entered through the window, ready with his submachine gun, eyes and lungs protected from the haze of cocaine dust by goggles and a surgeon's mask. Half blind and reeling from concussion, the shooters tried to take him out, but the Executioner got there first, a tidy figure eight dropping them in their tracks.

He made it to the door and out along the landing, just in time to catch the sidewalk sentry pounding up the stairs, a shiny automatic pistol in his hand. Before the gunner recognized his danger, Bolan stitched him with a 4-round burst across the chest and slammed him backward, somersaulting down the stairs and landing in a boneless heap.

Reversing to the makeshift cutting plant, he found a couple of Barbosa's lab rats wounded, gagging on the clouds of noxious dust, but still alive. He chose the one who seemed to be less badly injured, dragged him to the landing where he had a chance to breathe. Without the smoke and drifting powder, Bolan was surprised to find he had a gringo on his hands. He slapped the pasty face until he saw some kind of hazy recognition in the eyes.

"Wake up," he snapped. "You've got a chance, if you can do exactly as you're told."

"I hear you, man."

"I've got a message for your boss. You pass it on, you live."

"Let's hear it."

"I want the girl, alive and well. Until I have her, no one's safe."

The lab rat gave it back to him verbatim through clenched teeth. Fresh blood was soaking through his slacks from shrapnel wounds, but there was nothing to suggest a severed artery or major vein.

"I've got it, man. I won't forget."

"So, live."

He ditched his mask and goggles, and went out through the front, the submachine gun tucked beneath his jacket. Spectators were gathering, but no one tried to stop him as he made off through the crowd.

Three targets down. How many to go?

As many as it took.

*Albrook Air Force Base, Panama*
*12:40 p.m.*

THE CO WAS EXPECTING Jack Grimaldi, but he didn't like it much. Displeasure turned down the corners of his mouth beneath the bristling mustache that he wore, but he was used to taking orders, some of which ran solidly against the grain. The brass tag on his chest identified him as Colonel J. Reardon. The look on his face told Grimaldi he was pure bad news for anyone who tried to cross him in performance of his duty.

"Garrett?"

"Right."

The colonel didn't offer to shake hands. In fact he kept his distance, circling back around his desk and lowering himself into the high-backed swivel chair. Grimaldi hooked a plastic chair up to the desk and sat without an invitation, facing Reardon eye-to-eye.

"You pack some kind of weight in Washington," the colonel said at last.

"I follow orders, just like everybody else."

"I might feel better," Reardon said, "if I had some idea of what those orders were."

"If you've been on the horn to Washington—"

"They told me it was need-to-know.'

"In that case—"

"Ours is not to reason why," the colonel finished for him, glaring hard enough that Grimaldi was glad looks couldn't kill. "You're checked out on the Fighting Falcon?"

"That's affirmative. I keep my hand in."

"And you want to supervise the arming, so I'm told."

"Affirmative, if that's all right with you."

"I'll tell you what's all right with me," Reardon said. "For the record I don't care for spooks, civilians mucking up my base with cloak-and-dagger errands, much less total strangers checking out a multimillion-dollar aircraft for a night run off to God-knows-where. I guess we know whose ass is on the line if you fuck up."

Grimaldi's smile was thin and humorless. "If I fuck up, at least you'll know I won't be coming back to bother you again."

"The plane's my worry, Mr. Garrett." Reardon frowned again. "Or should I call you 'Sir'?"

"Not even close."

"All right, then. Since we understand each other, let's go meet your bird."

"Suits me."

"I wasn't asking, Mr. Garrett. Come along with me."

Grimaldi missed the air-conditioning as soon as they had stepped outside. It was a fair walk to the hangar where his F-16 was waiting with its service crew. Inside the shady cavern, sheltered from the tropic sun, Grimaldi let his eyes adjust before he made a walking circuit of the fighter.

She was fifty feet in length, from needle nose to tail, with a wingspan of thirty-one feet. The single Pratt & Whitney F100-200 engine was an augmented turbofan with a maximum rating of 23,830 pounds. In practice, that meant the fighter had a cruising speed of 915 miles per hour at sea level, improved to 1,350 miles per hour at an altitude of 40,000 feet. The prototype had made its maiden flight in 1974, as a technology demonstrator, but within a year it had been recast as a slightly larger, more capable multirole aircraft for tactical service. With continuous revisions and modifications, it continued in service as one of the front-line fighters used in Operation Desert Storm.

More important, the Fighting Falcon was a single-seater, ruling out troublesome witnesses who might have qualms about attacking a civilian homestead.

The F-16's basic armament was an M-61 20 mm gun mounted to the left of the cockpit, with 515 rounds of belt-fed ammunition in a tight pack. Externally the bird had a maximum capacity of 12,000 pounds, with a wide variety of rockets, bombs and guns to choose from, depending on its mission. Grimaldi had brought a shopping list along, and he presented it to Colonel Reardon after finishing his visual inspection of the aircraft.

"You don't ask for much," the colonel muttered.

"Only what I need."

Reardon rattled off the list. "Six Maverick AGM-65E laser-guided ASMs. One LAU-3/A rocket pod with incendiary loads. One MK 82 retarded bomb. One Paveway KMU-351 smart bomb. Two Sidewinder AIM-9Ls. No kitchen sink?"

"Not this time."

"Well, I've got my orders, Mr. Garrett. This could take a while."

"We have all afternoon, and then some.

Grimaldi had chosen his munitions with an eye toward the intended target, as depicted in the aerial photographs he had reviewed at Stony Man Farm. They had a lot of ground to cover at Guillermo Santiago's hardsite, but the manor house would be his nerve center, and most of Grimaldi's action would be air-to-ground. The twin Sidewinder air-to-air missiles were insurance, a hedge against the aircraft—planes or helicopters—that he might encounter over Santiago's property. The dealer would have nothing that could touch an F-16 in terms of combat, but Grimaldi didn't mean to let his target slip away, in any case.

The bulk of his munitions were designed for striking targets on the ground. The Paveway smart bomb and Maverick air-to-surface missiles were laser-guided, homing in on targets illuminated by a laser tracking beam from the delivery aircraft. The retarded bomb, by contrast, came equipped with air brakes that opened on release, slowing the payload's descent and allowing low-level attack craft to reach a safe distance before detonation.

He would supervise the loading even though Colonel Reardon's people undoubtedly knew their jobs. It was a small investment for Grimaldi's peace of mind, and he had time to kill, before his part of the killing began in earnest.

Soon enough.

The waiting was a part of it, anticipation tuning up his eagerness for contact with the enemy.

Not long, now.

Not too long at all.

*Panama City*
*12:45 p.m.*

"I DON'T KNOW ANYTHING about this goddamned woman!" Sergio Barbosa snapped. "What does he want, this gringo?"

Watching his lieutenants shrug in helpless ignorance, he had an urge to kill them where they stood. They were incompetent, the lot of them, and he could only blame himself for failing to detect their weakness earlier. It might be too late now, unless he found some way to save the game himself.

"Velasco," he decided, thinking aloud. "The bastard wants me to believe the Yankees are involved. Confuse me with this story of a missing woman." With a snarl he turned to face his three subordinates. "But I am not so easily deceived."

"No, sir," they replied as one.

"I know Velasco from the days when we were children, picking pockets in the streets of Medellín. He was a sly one then, and nothing changes. He has always envied my success, believing only he should rule the roost. But I have other plans. I want all troops on standby. They must be ready on a moment's notice. When I give the signal, nothing must be left undone. See to it!"

His three lieutenants turned and left the room, leaving Barbosa to consider strategy.

Of course, there could be only one response to someone like Velasco. The direct approach, and never mind Delvalle's efforts to convince Barbosa that tranquility would be restored if he sat down and faced his enemy across some table like a diplomat. The only sure road to prosperity and peace would lie across Velasco's grave.

Delvalle had an inkling of that now, with the attack upon himself, but he was still a politician in a soldier's uniform. The colonel took his orders from Guillermo Santiago first, and then from his superiors in the armed forces. It was a delicate balancing act, and lately Delvalle had been showing signs of strain. It would be anybody's guess how long he could maintain his double life, but if he tried to interfere with Sergio Barbosa's business he would be committing suicide.

Barbosa swore this to himself.

As far as he could tell, Velasco had begun this war for selfish purposes, but he wasn't about to finish it. Barbosa meant to fight for what he had and to expand his territory if the opportunity arose. No one could blame him for responding vigorously when his life and livelihood were threatened by a vicious scavenger.

In fact, he thought, Velasco might have done him a tremendous favor, after all. It could have taken months to think of an excuse for wiping out his competition, but Velasco had supplied the answer on his own, a gift from heaven as it were. This way, whatever moves he made would be a clear-cut case of self-defense.

And if he wound up dominating the narcotics trade in Panama, so be it.

All things come to those who wait.

MIRANDA TUGGED the bathrobe close around her, wishing she had something else to wear. So far, beyond the violence of her abduction, no one had molested her. She had a headache and a queasy stomach, but she managed to console herself with thoughts of the attacker she had scarred, perhaps for life.

It could have been much worse, she realized. The fact that she was still alive said something, but she didn't know precisely what. Somehow, she had more value to her captors as she was, but that could change without her knowledge, since she had no real idea of why she had been kidnapped in the first place.

Hooded with a pillowcase before she left her flat, Miranda had no fix on where she was. The drive had taken roughly half an hour, but for all she knew they could have gone in circles, winding up a block or less from where she lived. The room in which she found herself was windowless, a single chair its only furniture. The walls were thick enough to make her prison nearly soundproof—scratch the cheap apartment buildings in her neighborhood—and they had locked her door from the outside. She had an empty closet with the door removed, a plastic bucket for her toilet and the terry robe she wore. The carpeting beneath her feet was old and dirty, like the walls and ceiling of her cell.

She thought about Belasko, wondering if he had missed her yet and whether her abduction was connected to his war against the cocaine dealers. She supposed that she would find out soon enough, if she had any active role to play in what would follow. The alternative was silence, waiting helplessly while her abductors flipped a coin, deciding whether she would live or die.

The proximity of death was something new and frightening. From the beginning of her struggle with Democracy in Action, she had known there might be danger, risks that she would have to bear, but it had always been remote, impersonal. A whiff of tear gas or a clubbing in the chaos of a demonstration. Threats from members of the opposition party applied to anyone and everyone around the office. Never had Miranda felt so singled out, so much in jeopardy as now.

So helpless.

She was pacing when the sound of footsteps in the outer hallway stopped her, frozen in her tracks. Her stomach growled, reminding her that she had gone without food since the night before. A small thing, when she thought of what might lie before her, but her body craved sustenance all the same.

The footsteps stopped outside her door, replaced by muffled voices for a moment, then a key turned in the lock. She watched the knob turn, taking several backward steps until her buttocks and shoulders met the wall.

No place to run or hide.

Miranda recognized the man at once, though she was only used to seeing him in photographs, and then in uniform. Somehow, illogically, he seemed more dangerous this way, without the epaulets and campaign ribbons on his chest. It made her concentrate on his unyielding face, the unforgiving eyes.

"We need to talk," Delvalle told her. There was nothing in the way of introductions, but he might have realized that none was needed. When he waved her toward the straight-backed chair, Miranda hesitated, finally stepped forward and sat.

"Why am I here?" she asked. "Why was I taken from my home?"

"You wish to play charades, so be it." Delvalle was holding his temper in check, at least for the moment. "I give credit where credit is due."

"Pardon?"

"At first I thought we had a simple street war on our hands," Delvalle said. "It took some time for me to understand that there was more involved. Subversion of the lawful government in fact, as perpetrated by your band of left-wing revolutionaries."

"Subversion? Left-wing? I don't know—"

He crossed the room in two long strides and slapped her face, his weight behind it, spilling Miranda from her chair. She felt her robe splayed open, riding up her thighs, but she required a moment to collect herself.

"No lies," Delvalle cautioned, leaning down to grab one of her arms and hoist her back into the wooden chair. "I know about Democracy in Action—such a name for Communists who plot to undermine the nation of their birth. Your link to the Americans who scheme against our government is also known."

He was guessing, Miranda thought, but she didn't push her luck. "Democracy in Action speaks for Panamanians," she said defiantly. "As for America—"

She saw the open hand coming this time, but she was too slow to dodge it. The blow sent her sprawling, and this time Miranda tasted blood in her mouth.

Delvalle waited, let her contemplate the pain for a moment before he bent and lifted her again.

"Your plan will not succeed," he told her, speaking through clenched teeth as if he were in pain. "I have loyal eyes within your nest of traitors. They have given you to me, and you will give me the Americans. It is a simple trade—your life for theirs. Unfortunately you are running out of time."

Her lips were swollen, throbbing. When she tried to speak, Miranda found it difficult. "Democracy in Action is a native movement," she informed Delvalle. "If you fear the people, it can only mean you have betrayed them and the country you are sworn to serve."

This time, Delvalle struck her with a clenched fist, just above one eye. The impact drove her over backward in the chair, Miranda's skull rebounding from the carpet and the floor beneath. When he addressed her next, the colonel's voice was small and fuzzy, sounding like it came from miles away.

"If it amuses you to suffer, my dear, I don't mind," he said. "We have all night."

# CHAPTER TWENTY-ONE

*Havana, Cuba*
*1:05 p.m.*

Finding Rosalita's tavern was the easy part, but going in cold was a whole different story. In the past eighteen hours Rafael Encizo had twice seen the Cuban rebels routed from "safe" locations by government troops, and Calvin James had been lost in the second attack. Encizo had no way of knowing whether James was still at liberty or even still alive, but he always made a point of expecting the worst. That way, if he was "disappointed," it always came as a pleasant surprise.

If James was dead, the grieving would come later, after Encizo completed his assignment and escaped from Cuba. If he failed—and that was still a possibility, the odds against him growing steadily—then someone else would have to do the job and mourn them both.

Meanwhile, Encizo still had work to do.

He asked a vendor on the sidewalk for directions to the tavern, brushing past pedestrians and pushcarts on the way. He was intensely conscious of the duffel bag across his shoulder and the submachine gun tucked inside, the pistol wedged against his spine. An ambush on the open street would mean a shootout, innocent civilians in the line of fire and killer odds against him.

Encizo had no good reason to believe the tavern was a setup. The rebel who supplied him with the name had clearly been sincere, caught up in running for his life from government commandos. Even so, if agents of the DSE had cracked two hideouts in the span of one day's time, he had to wonder if the tavern might be watched, staked out by Castro's personal gestapo in an effort to complete the roundup.

How many rebels were still at large? Encizo had no way of knowing. Of a dozen at the "safe house" in Havana, he had seen two die and estimated there were four or five more dead, at least. If any had escaped the tap, besides himself, they'd be hiding in the city or its suburbs. Running for their lives...or waiting for a chance to meet at the cantina?

Rosalita's had been open for an hour when the Phoenix warrior got there, circling the block on foot as if he had to find an address that was stubbornly eluding him. He checked the alleys, shops and recessed doorways, roofs and vehicles pulled in against the curb. At length he satisfied himself that any ambush must be waiting in the bar itself, and there was only one way he could find that out.

The tavern had no more than half a dozen customers so far, but liquor, smoke and perspiration had combined to form a special atmosphere that met him on the threshold, causing him to flare his nostrils for an instant. It was almost feral, like the smell inside some animal's secluded lair. He half expected one or more of the drunks to turn and snarl a warning at him as he entered, but they concentrated on their drinks, immune to trivial distractions.

Encizo proceeded to the bar and found a seat, his duffel resting on the empty stool beside him, with the muzzle of his PA3-DM aimed toward the street door. Anyone who tried to take him now was in for a surprise, no matter what the final outcome.

He was ready when the bartender approached, fondling a towel that looked in need of washing. He was short and whip-thin, with a mustache that drooped to form parentheses around a narrow, bitter mouth. His eyes were dark, expressionless, accustomed to the men who wandered in to drown their sorrows in the middle of the afternoon.

"What can I do for you?"

"I need to speak with Bolívar," Encizo replied. "A good friend told me I could find him here."

A spark of something flashed in the man's eyes, but Encizo couldn't have given it a name. The bartender considered his request for a moment, finally said, "Wait here," and turned away, retreating to a door marked Private at the far end of the bar.

The code was simple. Any Latin knew Simón Bolívar as the George Washington of South America, liberating much of the continent from Spanish rule in the early nineteenth century. Bolivia was named in honor of the "Great Liberator" who also left his indelible mark on Colombia, Peru and Venezuela. As a password for a group of freedom fighters in the area, his name would be ideal.

The bartender was gone for several moments, and Encizo waited on his barstool, one hand inside the duffel bag. If there was someone waiting for him in the back room, other than a contact with the rebel forces, he wouldn't go down without a fight. It troubled him to think of Calvin James, not knowing if his comrade was alive, but there was nothing he could do about it at the moment. The remaining Phoenix warrior had a job to do, and he wasn't about to let it slide.

He saw the bartender coming back, his face no more expressive than before he left. This time, he stood before Encizo, wiping at the bar top with his dirty towel. "Go through the door in back. Someone is waiting for you there."

"A friend, I hope."

The man shrugged. "Perhaps."

"If not, I might be forced to visit you again," Encizo warned. "One final time."

He left his stool, the duffel bag across his shoulder, one hand still inside. He felt the bartender watching him as he moved along the bar to reach the door marked Private, reaching for the knob. No turning back, once he had crossed that threshold.

Done.

The corridor was narrow and dimly lighted. A man stood at the other end, alone. His face was masked in shadow, eyes downcast.

"I've come to speak with Bolívar," Encizo said.

"You've found him," Clemente Villa said. "Come. We still have much to do, if you intend to help your comrade."

*Nassau, Bahamas*
*1:35 p.m.*

THE CALL CAME in on Byron St. Jacques's private line. He had returned from lunch a mere five minutes earlier. He wasn't expecting any calls, but only ten or fifteen people on the island had this number, and none of them appreciated being put on hold. He lifted the receiver on the second ring, prepared for anything.

Almost.

"Hello?"

"St. Jacques." It didn't come out sounding like a question, and he didn't recognize the voice.

"Who is this, please?"

"A nightmare walking, Byron."

"I beg your pardon?"

"It won't do you any good, the kind of shit your buddy Mentzer tried to pull this morning."

St. Jacques felt his stomach tightening, an angry fist below his heart. His palm was slick with perspiration where he gripped the plastic telephone receiver.

"I'm not sure I understand," he said, relieved to find that he could still control his voice.

"Then you're behind the times," the caller told him. "Mentzer had a deal with me. A cool half million just to talk. He could have played it smart, but he got greedy. Him and Julio Marti."

"These men—"

He was prepared to bluff it out, denying any knowledge of the too-familiar names, but St. Jacques never got that far.

"I guess you heard about the little party out at Windsor Park," the caller said.

The shooting, six men dead, had been a conversation topic over lunch. A brief one, to be sure, since all of them were clearly hoodlums and the motive was unknown, but it came back to St. Jacques now. He should have known Marti would be involved. And as for Mentzer...

"I recall some mention of a shooting," he allowed.

"I bet you do. One question, Byron—did they run the idea past you in advance or take you by surprise."

"If you are seeking to imply some link between this office and—"

"I'm not implying shit," the nameless voice assured him. "What I'm saying is, your playmates blew it. I was set to deal, put up the going rate for first-rate merchandise, but now I've changed my mind. Somebody tries to take me out for no good reason, I start thinking we should try a new arrangement. Cut the dead wood first and start from scratch, you get my drift?"

"I am afraid that you misunderstand—"

"My only question now," the stranger said, "is whether you're deadwood or someone I can use. I have to tell you, though, these half-assed friends of yours are going, either way."

"Perhaps if I had some idea of what we were discussing—"

"Fine. You want to play dumb, that's all right with me. The folks I represent have got no use for morons, I can promise you."

Thus far, St. Jacques had played it safe, a show of ignorance in case the call was being taped. But now his curiosity kicked in, and he couldn't restrain himself.

"Who *do* you represent?" he asked.

"Just tell Marti that New York plays for keeps. That's all they need to know."

"New York." The words had taken on a bitter taste in St. Jacques's mouth.

"You heard me right."

"If I should meet these gentlemen you speak of... could you say the names again?"

His caller laughed out loud. "Forget about the Oscar nomination, Byron. You're not even close, and no one's taping this, unless you've got a wire on your end."

"I would never—"

"Then you're in the clear, I'd say. Unless you try to fuck me over. Pass the word just like I told you. While you've got them on the line there, maybe you should tell them both goodbye."

"Assuming there was some response..."

"I'll be in touch. Believe it."

Suddenly the line went dead. He listened to the dial tone for a moment, like a sharp drill boring deep into his brain, and then he cradled the receiver. St. Jacques felt an urge to wash his hands, as if the telephone had somehow been infected with a virulent disease. Instead, he palmed a handkerchief and blotted at the perspiration on his forehead, cheeks and hands.

New York.

He knew what that meant, and he didn't have to ask Marti or Mentzer for interpretation. In the old days, when Sir Stafford Sands had opened up the island to casino gambling, the money flowed from New York City in an endless stream. Some of the men who brought it had Italian names, while others looked like Jews. Their ethnic backgrounds were irrelevant when you considered what they had become, the kind of men they were, and what they did to those who interfered with their designs.

More recently, the men from Bogotá and Medellín evoked a similar response. Their clothes were custom-tailored and their nails were manicured, but you could never really clean the bloodstains off a killer's hands. Such men were dangerous to everyone around them, but they scattered money to the winds with such apparent disregard for cost that it was difficult—impossible—to turn them down. A man would be insane to turn away, when there was so much tax-free money to be made.

Months later, when you had to count the cost, it was too late.

Like now.

St. Jacques had no idea what kind of ambush had been staged at Windsor Park. He didn't question for a moment that Marti was capable of murdering six men or sending out six men to die on his behalf. If Thomas Mentzer was involved—a probability, in view of his association with the slick Colombian—then both of them had put St. Jacques at risk. It was their fault that strangers called him on his private line and threatened to eliminate him like a piece of... what?

Deadwood.

Ideally Byron would have liked to put the matter out of mind and let the others sink or swim alone. Unfortunately he had no doubt that the caller from New York would act upon his threat, and St. Jacques didn't mean to sacrifice himself, all that he had worked for, on behalf of two cheap dealers in cocaine. They would be easily replaced, especially if New York brought down its own man to coordinate the action. Any quarrel between the Yankees and Colombians would hopefully be settled somewhere else.

But first St. Jacques had calls to make and messages to pass along. Marti would probably demand a meeting, which was fair enough, considering the odds that it would be his last.

The politician's hand was trembling when he reached out for the telephone, but he was smiling all the same.

There still might be a way to profit from the situation if he played his cards right. Gambling was a part of politics, and Byron St. Jacques was accustomed to betting the limit.

This time, no matter how the cards were dealt, someone would have to pay the tab in blood.

*Panama City*
*1:40 p.m.*

WITH SEVEN STRIKES behind him, Bolan took a breather and arranged to meet with Angelo Rodriguez on the sly. The spokesman for Democracy in Action had been terse and cryptic on the telephone, accepting Bolan's call, but he had something urgent on his mind. It was not something he was willing to discuss by telephone, and the Executioner granted him a face-to-face.

And here they were.

The small garage was used primarily for auto body-work, but it was closed this afternoon. The Executioner approached with caution, understanding that the meet could be a trap, although it didn't have that feel. Sometimes you had to trust your gut and forge ahead, no matter what was riding on the line.

Like now.

A lookout spotted Bolan, let him in, and locked the door behind him. Picking out familiar smells of motor oil and gasoline, he crossed the silent office cubicle and passed through a connecting door to the garage.

Rodriguez came to meet him, two young strangers hanging back to flank an open grease pit in the middle of the floor.

"Forgive the setting," Rodriguez said. "It was all that I could think of for the privacy... and afterward."

"What's going on?"

At first he thought there might have been a message from Miranda's captors, but the grim expression on Angelo's face told him there was no cause for celebration yet.

"Returning from an early lunch, I found someone inside my office, going through the private files."

"One of your people?" Bolan asked.

Rodriguez nodded, swallowing the foul taste of disgust. "A trusted aide, in fact. André Molina, curse his name."

"He's here?"

"This way."

Rodriguez led him to the near edge of the grease pit. Staring down into the gravelike opening, Bolan saw a young man, bruised about the face and clearly frightened, cringing in a corner of the pit.

"What has he told you?"

"Everything he knows, I think," Rodriguez answered.

"Are you sure?"

The leader of Democracy in Action glanced at his companions, one of them nodding while the other cracked the knuckles of his hamlike fists.

"I'm sure."

"Let's hear it, then."

"He is a spy, of course. Recruited by the Panama Defense Forces with a promise of tuition payments, possibly employment when his work was done. The army still believes that we are Communists because we want drug dealers thrown in jail despite the bribes they pay."

"Go on."

"This piece of cow dung managed to ingratiate himself around the office. I myself appreciated his enthusiasm, working overtime and weekends. No one ever had to ask him. He would always volunteer. Such dedication to the cause. I know Miranda trusted him, as well."

"Enough to tell him what was going on?"

"Perhaps." Rodriguez didn't look convinced. "More likely, this one eavesdropped on our conversations, maybe on the telephone extension now and then. He does not know why you are here, or who you are, but he had told the army we are working with a gringo—maybe several—and Delvalle must have put the rest together on his own."

Bolan felt the short hairs on his nape begin to rise. "Delvalle took Miranda?"

"So it would appear. Molina cannot be positive, but nothing else makes sense. Barbosa and Velasco have ignored us until now. It is the government that watches every move we make."

"I guess that moves Delvalle to the top spot on my list," the Executioner replied.

"And this?" Rodriguez nodded to the young man in the pit.

"Your call." The warrior wouldn't make it easy for them, one way or the other. Some jobs had to go the hard way, or they didn't go at all.

"He has betrayed us," Rodriguez said.

"That's a fact."

"And knew what he was doing when he did it."

"Right again."

"To serve himself."

"I'd say that fits."

Rodriguez frowned. "Our movement is—has been— devoted to nonviolence. It is hard for me to do what must be done."

"The day you feel it getting easy," Bolan told him, "then you'll know you've gone too far."

"It is my job," Rodriguez said, and as he spoke he drew a small revolver from the waistband of his slacks, where it had been concealed beneath his shirt. His two companions backed away, both staring, sounds of hopeless pleading from the pit. He braced the gun in both hands, took his time to aim and squeezed off two slow rounds.

All done.

"Delvalle next," Rodriguez said, determination in his voice.

"He won't be quite that easy," Bolan told him. "You're not about to catch him in a pit, for one thing, and he won't be on his own."

"We'll take him, all the same, and win Miranda back."

The Executioner was wise enough to know that killing off Delvalle and his men wouldn't ensure Miranda's safe return. He was humane enough to keep it to himself.

Instead he told Rodriguez, "Let's just take it one step at a time."

*Havana, Cuba*
*2:00 p.m.*

IT TOOK A BIT OF TIME for Calvin James to figure out that he hadn't been shot. His memory came back in bits and pieces, followed by a rush of everything at once, requiring him to sort it out, prioritize the input and make sense of what he could recall.

The fence. A burst of automatic fire that clipped the aged boards and dropped him sprawling in the yard. The fall had winded him and slowed him down. The DSE commandos were on top of him with boots and rifle butts before he had a chance to fire.

It felt like being shot, though, when he sat there, strapped into his metal throne, and tensed his muscles, cataloging injuries. His body was a crazy quilt of bruises, scrapes and sprains, some minor cuts, but nothing that would kill him short of an infection left untreated, turning into gangrene.

And you could have gone all day, James told himself, without that notion cropping up.

In fact he didn't know if it was day or night outside his cell, a concrete box with one beige-painted metal door, a single light bulb burning in a cage above his head. It was the kind of room where you would logically expect a drain set in the floor, but James couldn't crane his neck to verify the guess.

No matter.

If he bled too much and there was no convenient drain, the pricks would simply have to mop it up.

It never crossed his mind that he could get out of the room without experiencing pain. His chair was made of welded metal, bolted to the floor, and leather straps secured his chest, waist, wrists and ankles. Add to that the fact that he was naked, and the scene was tailor-made for an interrogation in the Spanish style. If his inquisitors possessed the necessary skill, James knew he might survive for days, just praying for the end.

Enough of that!

He wouldn't contemplate the various techniques of torture, thereby softening his own defenses before a hand was raised against him. Rather, he considered ways of spinning out the ordeal, buying time for Rafael Encizo to escape or make the tag, assuming he was still alive.

And if he wasn't, then what?

Scratch two Phoenix warriors and go back to start again.

But in the meantime, while a ghost of hope remained, he had to stall for time. Begin by lying, offering cooperation to the enemy and spilling any half-baked line that came to mind. He was a mercenary, hired by wealthy exiles to investigate the possibility of stalking Castro on his own home ground. It had been tried before, of course, but if at first you don't succeed ...

They would suspect he was American, of course. It would take time to prove it, even with the latest drugs, but even that concession wouldn't jeopardize the team at Stony Man. Americans of one sort or another had been drawn into the covert war against Fidel for more than thirty years. In some families it was an honored tradition, handed down like a gold watch from father to son. Today you are a man; now go and kill The Beard.

The key was plausible deniability. When you were on the grill and had to tell them something, anything to buy some time, you made the lies as realistic as you could, inventing details, never deviating into science fiction.

In front of him the beige door opened. Three men entered, boot heels clicking on the concrete floor. Two of the men wore uniforms, an officer and an enlisted man. The third was decked out in a spotless lab smock, with a stethoscope around his neck.

"I guess you still make housecalls," James said in Spanish, not expecting them to laugh or even understand the reference. The trio let it slide without blinking an eye.

"You are an enemy of Cuba," the officer said, like reading from a dusty script that dated from the early 1960s. Missile Crisis time. "It is required for us to ask you certain questions. You will answer with the truth or suffer pain."

"I'll do my best," James replied.

"Your name?"

"Sylvester Brown. I never liked Sylvester much, myself. Why don't you just call me Brownie?"

"You are pleased to joke."

"I find it helps me pass the time."

"Perhaps," the officer suggested, "we can find another way."

# CHAPTER TWENTY-TWO

*Chigorodo, Colombia*
*7:20 p.m.*

Night falls swiftly in a tropic forest. Twilight is a luxury the hungry predators cannot afford. They have been waiting all day long, and darkness is the feeding, killing time.

For Yakov Katzenelenbogen, a predator lying in the tangled undergrowth a hundred yards from the perimeter of Santiago's hardsite, nightfall also meant that it was time for hunting. He had traveled from the Blue Ridge Mountains of Virginia to destroy one man, and anyone who tried to interfere with that appointed mission would be marked for death, as well.

The hours of watching had been helpful, to a point. He had confirmed at least a partial layout of Santiago's estate as depicted in aerial photographs, scanning the parts he could see with field glasses from his secure vantage point, and he was busy counting heads throughout the afternoon. In short order Katz had begun to recognize many of Santiago's soldiers, giving them personal nicknames to differentiate one from another while he kept an eye out for new men. "Crabby" seamed to scratch himself incessantly when there was no one else around. "The Beak" had a nose that would have put Durante in the shade. "Brows" had eyebrows like a werewolf, grown together in the space above his nose.

And so on.

He had counted thirty-seven individuals so far, without a glance of Santiago. That made roughly ten to one against his three-man force, and Katzenelenbogen knew there must be others who, for one reason or another, avoided the grounds he could see. House troops, for instance, or patrols assigned to other sectors of the large estate.

Killer odds, without a little help from Jack Grimaldi's one-man air force.

Anytime now.

Glancing at his watch again, he gave Grimaldi five more minutes. Jack was known for his precision on a strike, and if you told him 1930 hours, you shouldn't expect the guy to show at 1928 or even 1929.

Katz thought about the list of things that could have gone wrong back in Panama. Grimaldi might be catching flack from someone at the air force base. Worse yet, he might have been caught up in Bolan's action since their early-morning conversation, maybe even hurt or killed. There would have been no way for the pilot or Bolan to communicate, assuming they were still in any kind of shape to use a radio.

The gruff Israeli recognized what he was doing and he cut it short. Despite his years of field experience, the battles he had lost and won, Katz still experienced the pregame apprehension of a green recruit. These days, he balanced out the butterflies with logic and the lessons of experience, but Katzenelenbogen doubted whether they would ever disappear entirely. If they did, he thought, it would be time to quit. A man who had no second thoughts at all when facing odds of ten-to-one or greater had to be a stone-cold psychopath.

Or maybe he was simply dead inside.

The sound came out of nowhere, a suggestion of some aerial disturbance well across the border into Panama. Katz waited, making sure, before he reached for the compact walkie-talkie on his belt. He didn't speak—there was no way of telling whether Santiago's men had radios, or what their frequency would be if so—but it was safe to tap the button twice, transmitting static whispers to his comrades on the firing line.

He rose from his prone position to a crouch, tucking the AKS-74 under his arm. A few more seconds remained until Grimaldi put the ball in play. The airborne thunder grew louder with every heartbeat, closing from the west.

Manning and McCarter would be moving in by now, the darkness masking their approach. Katz went to join them, pushing all thoughts of death and defeat from his mind. He had a job to do, and he'd give it everything he had.

Guillermo Santiago didn't know it yet, but he was running out of time.

INSIDE THE GREAT HOUSE, Santiago sipped a glass of whisky in his private study, brooding. He was still no closer to uncovering the bastards who had torched his border convoy, and from all reports the shooting war in Panama was escalating by the hour. His first attempts to reach Barbosa and Velasco had been fruitless, and he gave up trying after that, convinced that one or both would have their lines tapped by the Yankee DEA or someone else. Guillermo faced an epic list of charges in the States already, and he had avoided extradition by the relatively simple means of bribing anyone and everyone that he could reach. Police and military officers in Chigorodo were prepared to say they checked his rancho twice a week and found him absent every time. Of course, they couldn't lock up a man they couldn't find.

Until the ambush of his convoy, Santiago had enjoyed a feeling of security at home, whatever else might happen in the world around him. Now he had to reconsider that position, wondering if anyplace on earth was truly safe.

If fear and cash together weren't adequate for his protection . . .

Santiago cocked his head, distracted by the powerful, distinctive sound of a jet aircraft. Soft at first, but rapidly approaching—was it from the west? He found it difficult to calculate. Perhaps if he was outside, in the yard . . .

No matter. It was strange enough to put him on his feet, his drink forgotten as he moved to stand before the giant window that faced northward. His ranch didn't lie on a flight path for commercial airlines, and the military seldom passed this way unless the idiots in Bogotá demanded photographs of his estate to fatten up their files. As if they could expect to find a truckload of cocaine parked in his driveway for the world to see.

The first explosion shook his house from its foundation to the third-floor rafters. Santiago raised an arm to shield his face from glass, the picture window suddenly disintegrating, but the shock wave swept him off his feet. He fell against a chair, sharp corners gouging at his ribs and back before he hit the floor. Dust filtered down around him, and a life-size portrait of himself slid down the wall and keeled over on the carpet.

Smoke alarms were going off at several points inside the house, their shrill, insistent clamor working on his temper like a dentist's drill on naked, unprotected nerves. He came up cursing, rushing toward the exit, one hand wrapped around the doorknob when a second blast ripped through the house. He barely heard the jet's whine overhead as he was driven to his knees.

Clinging to the doorjamb, Santiago struggled to his feet. Outside his study, in the corridor, the smoke alarms were even louder, shrieking at him. Two men stumbled past him, moving toward the stairs with automatic weapons in their hands.

Defenders of the castle, Santiago thought. Too little and too late.

He tried to think of someone on his list of enemies who had the influence and contacts to command an air strike, and his thoughts kept coming back to the Americans. But it would be an act of war to violate the airspace of another sovereign nation, blasting at civilian targets from the sky.

Another thunderous explosion erupted, this one from the grounds. He barely felt it, moving toward the stairs on wooden legs, dust filling up his sinuses. No matter who was trying to destroy him, Santiago could recover and repay their treachery in kind—but only if he lived to fight another day. Escape was his priority, by any means available.

The helicopter.

It was doubly risky, in the middle of an aerial attack, but what was his alternative? He wouldn't stay inside the house and wait for it to burn down or collapse on top of him. His one hope lay in flight, and there was no more time to waste.

He reached the stairs and started down. The smoke was thick here, dark plumes wafting from the dining room and kitchen, filling the parlor and the entryway. He wouldn't use the front door, where an enemy was bound to concentrate his scrutiny. There was a better way, much closer to the helipad. If he could save himself some time—

The hand-carved double doors flew open, one of Santiago's gunners bursting in, wild-eyed. He gaped at Santiago for a moment, seemed about to ask his leader something, when the drug baron saw the man explode. A stream of heavy bullets drilled him from behind, a buzz saw shredding flesh and fabric, wild rounds chewing up the carpet, plunking through the doors and walls.

Santiago threw himself facedown and started scrabbling toward the nearby hallway on his stomach, digging with his knees and elbows. It was over in a heartbeat, and he could only guess at the number of rounds, the roar of a jet engine swallowing the sounds of gunfire.

In the yard, his men were firing back, but Santiago had a feeling it wouldn't be good enough. He had to get away, while there was time.

If it wasn't too late already.

If he still had any chance at all to save himself.

GRIMALDI CAME IN LOW and fast, four minutes from
the border to his target zone and he was right on time.
Somewhere below him, the warriors of Phoenix Force
would be closing for the kill, but they were waiting for
a sign from heaven.

Or from hell, depending on your point of view.

The Stony Man pilot armed the Paveway smart
bomb two miles out, and he was ready with the laser
optics from the moment that he got his fix on Santiago's palace. It was a clear match for the aerials he had
reviewed at the Farm, as if there could have been another ranch on this scale within a hundred miles.

He made his attack run at an altitude of two hundred feet, the laser lock on Santiago's mansion as he let
the Paveway go.

Grimaldi didn't have to watch the smart bomb do its
job. Pinpoint precision was the Paveway's trademark,
dating back to Vietnam and carried on with excellent
results through Operation Desert Storm. If you were
diving on a caravan, the laser-guided bomb would let
you pick and choose which vehicle you wanted to destroy. In this case all it had to do was find a house.

No sweat.

The pilot circled wide and came back to the attack,
this time approaching from the north. He found smoke
pouring from the house, a jumbled pile of garbage
where the south wing used to be.

"They just don't build them like they used to."

On his second pass, Grimaldi unleashed one of the
Maverick AGM-65E laser-guided air-to-surface missiles, picking off the dealer's pool house in a mushroom cloud of smoke and fire. It felt like kicking at an
anthill, watching Santiago's gunners racing back and

forth across the open yard, some of them pausing long enough to pump a few rounds at his F-16.

Good luck.

An air strike was clearly the last thing on Santiago's mind when he planned his defenses. If an enemy attacked him from the air, the dealer must have reasoned, it would be a helicopter bearing gunmen to assault the house and grounds, the kind of threat his sentries could dispose of with their rifles, submachine guns and grenades. An air raid in the standard sense was so implausible that Santiago's planners would have laughed it off.

And that was why it worked.

He used another Maverick on the third pass, targeting the house. Grimaldi had no way of picking out Santiago, but that wasn't his job. Distraction and destruction were the flip sides of the coin. Let Phoenix handle the precision work while he reduced the hostile odds.

The laser-guided missile came in underneath the eaves and blossomed into flame, a major section of the roof blown skyward on the shock wave. For an instant, there and gone, Grimaldi had a glimpse of little dollhouse rooms exposed before the smoke and fire devoured everything.

A line of flashy limos stood in the driveway, and Grimaldi used another Maverick on the middle car. It was a case of overkill, no question, but it felt right, watching the vehicles erupt like a string of giant firecrackers. Tiny stick figures were scattered by the explosions, and a flaming tire took off across the lawn, trailing sparks in its wake.

He headed back toward the house, picking out targets by firelight, triggering the 20 mm gun in short, deliberate bursts. One hundred rounds per second, give or take, but he could make one pass just for the hell of it. A gunner was on the front porch, squeezing off before he turned and bolted for the doors. Grimaldi hosed him and ripped up the whole facade of Santiago's house.

Take that.

He put the Fighting Falcon through a wide turn.

Coming back for more.

THE ONLY PROBLEM with a close-range air strike, Gary Manning thought, was that Grimaldi had no way of separating friends from hostiles on the ground. Of course it hardly mattered, one way or the other, since the smartest smart bomb still flattened everything within its killing radius, precision targeting aside.

So it was Manning's job to stay alive and kick ass to the best of his ability, without absorbing any of Grimaldi's shrapnel in the process.

Simple.

All he had to do was penetrate Santiago's hardsite, dodge or kill the sentries he encountered on his long run toward the house and try to find the man himself. It wasn't quite a needle-haystack proposition, Manning thought, but close enough. The house was burning now, and by the time he got there it would be impossible for him to make his way inside.

They could have let Grimaldi do it all, when you got down to cases. Sit back in the trees and watch while he delivered bombs and rockets to the narco baron's doorstep. Nuke the bastard, if he had to. Anything to get it done.

Except, they had to do it right, make sure that Santiago had been neutralized beyond a reasonable doubt.

A sentry veered toward Manning in the fire-lit darkness, calling out in Spanish, possibly mistaking the Canadian for one of his compadres. Manning hit him with a burst of 5.45 mm tumblers, spinning him around and dropping him before the gunner recognized his terminal mistake.

More running figures appeared on his left, and Manning loosed a burst in that direction, following up with one of the Dutch V-40 minigrenades. Its detonation was diminished by the thunder of a rocket slamming into Santiago's palace. Manning hit a shoulder roll to stay beneath the flying shrapnel, came up on the run and left his adversaries twitching on the lawn.

It seemed a long way to the house, but he was getting there. Some of Santiago's men were firing at Grimaldi's fighter, mostly wasted effort that would make them feel like they were doing something. Manning left them to it, using the distraction to his own advantage as he sprinted toward the house. A hundred yards remained, and what could he accomplish when he got there?

Santiago would be bailing out, if he was still alive. That meant an exit hatch, and with the limos wasted out in front the helicopter was his last, best bet. It didn't take a genius to decide their man would cut and run from somewhere on the north side of the house, if he was fit to run at all.

Manning changed his direction in midstride, keeping the house on his left and running parallel to the driveway that circled the mansion.

Soon now, and he would have an angle on the north side of the house, the helipad beyond. If Grimaldi hadn't already taken out the chopper waiting there, it would be Santiago's magic carpet. Up and out of danger while his men were dying on the ground.

But they were running out of time. Grimaldi couldn't spend much longer on the wrong side of the border, knowing military interceptors would be on their way. A dogfight with a "friendly" air force wasn't on the program, even if it meant the Phoenix warriors had to mop up on their own.

The big Canadian picked up his pace, saw more bodies scattered on the grass. Less danger, fewer men that he would have to kill.

But he was only seeking one man now, a dragon in a nest of vipers.

Just one shot, Manning thought. Just one decent shot.

IT WAS MCCARTER who spied Santiago running from the house, two gunners on his heels. The man had some kind of compact submachine gun in his hand—an Ingram or a mini-Uzi from its look—and his companions carried automatic rifles. They were just emerging from the house and breaking for the helipad when the Briton spotted them, Santiago recognizable by firelight at a range of forty yards. He had three targets on the move, but only one really mattered.

McCarter dropped to one knee, lining up his shot. He had his index finger on the trigger, tightening into the squeeze, when bullets started ripping up the turf around him, coming from his left. He spun in that direction, saw two gunners charging toward him, firing from the hip with automatic weapons.

It was do or die, and never mind Guillermo Santiago dashing out of range. McCarter let rip with the AKS, pushing off with his right foot at the same instant, lurching backward in a bid to spoil his adversaries' aim. The next two overlapping bursts came in where he had been a heartbeat earlier, one of the bullets tugging at his camouflage fatigues.

McCarter came out of his backward somersault with both hands on the AKS, a clear fix on his running targets. Six or seven feet of empty air stood between them, fixed snarls of exertion on their faces as they charged. It was a fluke that they had spotted him, McCarter realized, but anyone who drew a bead on Santiago in their presence had to be the enemy. They had that lesson fixed in mind despite the chaos all around them, which could only be traumatic for a pair of gunners used to sentry duty on a grand estate.

The left-hand target first. McCarter hit him with a rising spiral burst that spun the shooter. He was dead before he toppled over, but his trigger finger didn't know it yet, a last burst from the gunner's Uzi ripping up the grass around his feet.

And that left one.

McCarter's second adversary saw his partner die and tried to veer off course, still firing on the run. His weapon was an Ingram, probably the model 10 by its sound, the awesome cyclic rate of fire a handicap in any kind of duel where you were blocked from putting down your target in the first two seconds. When the little stuttergun ran out of ammunition, you could almost hear the shooter praying for a break.

Good luck.

The Briton tracked him with the AKS and watched him fumbling with the Ingram's empty magazine. Before he had a chance to ram in a fresh one, the tumblers found him, ripping flesh and fabric into crimson mulch. McCarter's target took a nosedive on the turf and stayed there, crumpled in a pose of supplication, with his knees bent under him, his buttocks in the air.

It was time for McCarter to reload, as he scrambled to his feet. Downrange, three runners had already reached the helicopter, Santiago close behind the pilot, with an extra gunner bringing up the rear. The Phoenix warrior heard the engine turning over, saw the rotor blades begin to move, slow motion for a start, as if the pilot couldn't quite make up his mind, then accelerating rapidly as McCarter sprinted toward the helipad.

Too late.

The bird was rising when he fired his first rounds from a range of fifty yards. Santiago's backup gunner saw him coming, laying down a screen of cover fire, the bullets mauling turf and forcing McCarter back. He saw them airborne, still technically within effective range, but it would take a fluke—a goddamned miracle—to bring them down from where he stood.

He tasted bitter failure as he brought the rifle to his shoulder, firing half the magazine in one long burst. No good. He followed with the final dozen rounds and watched his target soaring, heading north.

Going...going...gone.

GRIMALDI WAS PREPARED to leave, his air-to-ground munitions spent, when he saw Santiago's helicopter lift off its pad. He had deliberately avoided firing on the chopper, concentrating on the house with everything he had and leaving Katzenelenbogen's men to guard the aircraft, but their plans had fallen through.

Somehow, Guillermo Santiago had escaped the firestorm that was busily devouring his mansion. Somehow, he had made it to the whirlybird intact, and he was running for his life.

It never crossed Grimaldi's mind that Santiago's pilot might attempt to flee without his master. The drug lord ruled his soldiers with a mix of generosity and terror, paying well for loyalty and rewarding treason with a screaming death protracted over days on end. It was a savage but effective system, and it got results.

Grimaldi put the Fighting Falcon through a banking turn to port and instantly picked up the chopper's track. The whirlybird was running dark, no fear of running into a commercial aircraft here, above the trackless jungle, but the pilot couldn't beat Grimaldi's radar.

Neither, in his wildest dreams, could he outrun an F-16.

Grimaldi was a mile and closing when he armed the starboard Sidewinder, his visual display locking onto target acquisition. In a dogfight, with the men and aircraft fairly matched, it still might not have been a killing shot, but there was simply no way for the chopper to escape. Grimaldi spent the best part of a second wondering if Santiago knew he was about to die, dismissed the thought, and sent the AIM-9L along to do its work.

The blast reminded the Stony Man pilot of a giant, crimson flower opening before his eyes, the petals rippling in a miracle of time-lapse photography, spreading wide and withering before he had a chance to memorize their colors, store the imprint of their lethal beauty in his mind. This flower came apart in bits and pieces, burning streamers arcing toward the forest far below.

He stood the Fighting Falcon on one wing, avoiding the debris, and brought it back around until the aircraft's nose was pointed west. Below him, on the killing round, the Phoenix Force warriors would be mopping up, but one of them, at least, would certainly have seen the helicopter soar and die. With any luck at all, it just might be enough to let them disengage.

Whatever happened on the ground, Grimaldi's work was done. He was headed back to base and Colonel Reardon's disapproving stare.

His thoughts raced back to Bolan as he set a northwest course and gave the silver bird its head.

One battle was completed, more or less, but there was still a war to win.

# CHAPTER TWENTY-THREE

*Havana, Cuba*
*Thursday, 8:15 p.m.*

It was amazing, Calvin James decided, just how many different kinds of pain the human body could endure. Sharp and dull pains. Throbbing aches and lancing spears of white-hot agony that robbed a man of his ability to scream. The difference between a sprain, torn ligaments and broken bones. Internal pain and superficial trauma to the outer flesh.

And mental pain.

The worst of it, he thought, was holding on when any fool could recognize a hopeless situation. Who was left to help him now? For all he knew, the DSE had killed or captured Encizo, Villa and the rest. If some of them had managed to escape the trap, they had no way of knowing James was still alive, much less where he was being held. James didn't know himself, and if he did, what difference would it make?

The good news, of a sort, was that he had so little useful information to reveal. From all appearances the DSE knew more about their native rebels than he did, including the location of base camps and safehouses, the identity of Villa and his top lieutenants. James could do the movement little harm, if any, when he broke at last.

And break he must, at some point. James had been around the track enough to realize that no man could withstand long-term interrogation with his heart and mind intact. The pain was one thing, if you concentrated, focused on the goal line of unconsciousness, but once they started using drugs, the game was over. Courage and determination made no difference once the chemicals kicked in. Volition was beside the point.

But one way to beat the chemicals was death, and James was thinking more along those lines when his interrogators took a break for dinner, leaving him alone. Unfortunately he was still securely belted in his metal chair, that chair still fastened to the concrete floor. He had no hollow tooth full of cyanide, and he knew that it was virtually impossible for any man to suffocate himself by simply holding his breath. He might succeed in blacking out, but his inquisitors would simply find a way to revive him again when they returned.

The worst part would be giving up his link to Phoenix Force and Stony Man. Rivera and his flunkies didn't know the proper questions yet, but they were working on his background and connections. He had answered them in Spanish when he spoke at all, but once they verified that his ID was bogus, once they got around to focusing their questions on the States . . .

Admission of a government connection would be bad enough. Hot propaganda mileage for Fidel, just when the cold war was officially defunct. He didn't have the Soviets to back him up these days, but it would be a black eye for the White House at the very least. Worse yet, if they got into the specifics of the

Phoenix team at Stony Man, irreparable damage might be done.

James rubbed his wrists against the smooth arms of the chair, no edges sharp enough to break the skin, much less shear through an artery. If he could tip the chair, there would have been an outside chance that he could crack his skull or break his neck, but the designers of his prison had anticipated that plan.

No go.

That left provocation, the unlikely possibility that he could goad one of Rivera's cohorts into lashing out with force enough to land a killing blow. It was the most improbable of long shots, but it came down to his one and only chance.

*Nassau, Bahamas*
*8:25 p.m.*

RELUCTANT AS HE WAS to meet with Mentzer and Marti, St. Jacques was also wise enough to know their current business couldn't be disposed of on the telephone. The minister for tourism couldn't escape a meeting, then, but he could still control the time and place to some extent. He had selected the Ardastra Gardens for their privacy, rejecting Mentzer's first suggestion of an office building on the docks.

For this occasion St. Jacques wanted open air and flowers, to relieve the stench of dealing with his "business partners" face-to-face.

Of late he had begun to think his deal with Mentzer and Marti might be a serious mistake, despite the income he derived from licensing their traffic in illicit drugs. In the beginning it had all been gravy, St.

Jacques banking wonderful, absurd amounts of cash while his associates took all the risks. The government was riddled with corruption as it was, and someone else would surely take advantage of the gold rush if St. Jacques refused to help himself. Cooperating with the narco dealers was the only thing to do.

He told himself that he was harming no one—or, at least, no one that he would ever meet. If residents of the United States enjoyed cocaine, St. Jacques wasn't at fault. It was regrettable that some of them would overdose and die, while others robbed and killed to feed their habit, but America was rife with violent crime. The Yankees took a kind of perverse pride in their violent reputation, giving notorious criminals flamboyant nicknames in the press to make them seem more glamorous. There was historic precedent for shipping drugs through the Bahamas to America, dating back to the days of Prohibition when bootleggers docked their rum boats in Nassau and took on cargo for the run to Miami or New Orleans.

Still, St. Jacques had gone into the partnership with Mentzer and Marti believing he was safe, protected by his government position and a promise from Marti that any major "problems" would be handled well away from the Bahamas, preferably in the United States or out at sea. They had an image to preserve, not only for St. Jacques but for the islands as a whole.

The massacre in Windsor Park was bad enough, with six men dead, but now the minister of tourism was looking at the prospect of a gang war in the heart of Nassau, Yankees and Colombians at one another's throats. Already, his superiors were asking questions, and St. Jacques had promised them a swift solution to the problem. If he failed to make delivery on that promise, he was finished.

But at least he had a plan.

He would confront Marti and Mentzer with the threat he had received, together with the disapproval of his government. As businessmen with long experience among corrupt officials, they would realize that statesmanship—the brave facade of honesty and service to the public—must take precedence over business as usual when risks got out of hand. If Mentzer and Marti could strike a bargain with New York and thereby save themselves, St. Jacques would be relieved. If not, they would be on their own, with the police and courts against them in addition to their Yankee enemies.

It might look good, at that, for Mentzer and Marti to be arrested. The Americans were crowding Nassau these days, with their so-called war on drugs, the DEA investigating links between the narco traffickers and ranking members of the government. Of course they had no extradition power in the islands, but their findings sometimes surfaced in the press and caused embarrassment to wealthy men who thrived on privacy. If the administration could display good faith by toppling two major smugglers, it would be a long stride toward restoring confidence in government.

But there were problems, even so.

Marti and Mentzer would be furious if they were brought to trial. They might decide to testify against their turncoat friends in Nassau, even if that testimony wouldn't help them in a court of law. Revenge was sweet, and St. Jacques's business partners knew enough to bring him down, along with most of his immediate superiors. If prosecutors snubbed them, there was still the press, and by the time they finished talking, well, St. Jacques preferred to find an alternate solution for the problem, if he could.

He found it in the back seat of his chauffeured limousine, en route to meet Marti and Mentzer. Smugglers were notoriously violent, the Colombians especially. If he was forced to call for their arrest, it would be only natural for them to fight, resisting police. In such a case authorities couldn't be blamed for firing back in self-defense.

And dead men tell no tales.

The smile felt good on St. Jacques's face. It was the first one he could recollect in several days, and it was overdue.

Marti and Mentzer would be waiting for him. He would tell them what he knew and offer them a choice: cooperation or an end to their relationship. He wouldn't have to specify the kind of end he had in mind. Not yet.

And if he got another call from New York, St. Jacques was ready with a proposition of his own.

*Havana, Cuba*
*8:45 p.m.*

AT LEAST they weren't holding Calvin James inside Principe Prison. Villa had determined that much from his eyes inside Fidel's notorious Bastille, and it had narrowed down their search. No prisoners resembling James had been taken to the city jail that afternoon, and agents of the DSE would want more privacy in any case.

Which left El Rancho on the outskirts of Havana.

In official parlance the facility housed maintenance supplies and personnel, but it was actually employed for suspect grillings by the goons from State Security. Luis Rivera had a second office there, and Villa's lookouts verified the major's presence at El Rancho on this Thursday night. They couldn't guarantee that James would be inside, but Encizo thought it worth the risk. He was prepared to go alone, if necessary, but Villa had decided it was time to settle some outstanding debts.

Beginning now.

El Rancho covered fourteen acres, mostly open ground. The central feature was a concrete blockhouse where the DSE conducted business safe from prying eyes. When there were dissidents to be interrogated, covert executions to be carried out, El Rancho kept Rivera's secrets safe and sound.

They had eleven men in all, including Encizo and Villa. All of them were dressed in khaki uniforms designed to pass a cursory inspection, making them resemble soldiers. Crowded into a sedan and two old jeeps with military paint jobs, they were close enough to fool a sentry in the dark. At least, Encizo thought, they should get close enough to try a decent pistol shot.

From that point on it would be anybody's game, with no holds barred.

The drive took half an hour, with Encizo riding next to Villa in the back seat of the drab, four-door sedan. They had a jeep in front of them and one behind, like escorts for an officer. Inside the car Encizo kept his PA3-DM across his knees, a live round in the chamber and the safety off.

An unpaved track led off the highway, flanked by trees on either side. The jeep's headlights picked out a guard shack, a young trooper emerging to meet them. He wore a pistol on his belt and held a clipboard in his hand. Encizo couldn't hear him, but he saw the soldier's lips move, speaking to the driver.

He was in the middle of a question when he died, a silenced pistol bullet slapping home between his eyes. The impact pitched him over on his back, and one of Villa's people scrambled from the jeep to open up the gate.

Phase one.

They rolled along the drive in the direction of the blockhouse. There were two guards on the entrance, packing Cuban versions of the AK-47, both men squinting into headlights as the three-car caravan approached.

And they weren't alone.

Encizo made the sentry on the roof, hunched down behind a light machine gun, watching. When it hit the fan, in a few seconds, the rooftop gunner would command the high ground. If he held it, there was no way they would ever get inside.

The little Phoenix Force warrior gripped his submachine gun, one hand on the door latch as the car braked to a halt. One of the guards on the door was stepping forward, the other hanging back. They knew their business, dividing a potential enemy's attention, but they were outnumbered this time, with nowhere to hide.

The silenced pistol coughed again, and Encizo saw the lead sentry go down in a heap. His partner tried to get a shot off, but he never had a chance. Two automatic weapons nailed him where he stood and slammed him back against the concrete wall.

That tore it. Encizo was out of the sedan and firing with his submachine gun even as the lookout on the roof cut loose. Their muzzle-flashes might have been a mirror image, but the shooter on the roof was firing toward the jeep below him, picking off the driver as he sat behind the steering wheel. Another one of Villa's troopers tried to dodge the stream of fire and went down in a heap, the impact of his skull on pavement sounding wet and final.

Encizo spent several rounds to find the range, but then he had it, firing for effect. The gunner's head and shoulders were exposed above his weapon, all Encizo needed for a killing burst. He didn't see the rounds strike home, but there was no mistaking their effect. The sniper toppled backward and took his weapon with him, squeezing off a last burst toward the stars.

With guards outside the door hadn't been locked. Villa led the way, Encizo on his heels, three other men behind him. That left five to watch the vehicles and deal with any soldiers drawn from the perimeter by sounds of combat. If they found themselves outnumbered and outgunned, well, that was too damned bad.

Inside, they found an empty corridor protected by a television camera. Villa dropped it from its mountings with a rifle bullet, and the echo of his shot had instantaneous results. A door flew open halfway down the corridor, and a disoriented-looking soldier stepped into the hallway, brandishing a pistol.

"Mine!" Encizo barked in Spanish, squeezing off a burst before the rebel troops could sight and open fire.

His bullets cut the startled soldier's legs from under him and dropped him on his face, the pistol spinning from his grasp and out of reach.

Encizo reached the man in four long strides and knelt beside him, roughly turned him over on his back. The soldier's eyes were tightly clenched in pain, but they snapped open when Encizo wedged the submachine gun's muzzle underneath his chin.

"We're looking for a prisoner," he snapped, "a black man. He came in this afternoon."

The soldier thought of bluffing, the Phoenix warrior could see it in his eyes, but pain and something in Encizo's tone convinced him otherwise. Instead he raised one trembling hand and pointed down the corridor.

"Turn left," he almost whispered. "Third door. Number 103."

Encizo swung the muzzle of his PA3-DM against the soldier's skull and put him out, already moving as the man slumped backward into momentary darkness. Whether he survived the next few minutes was a question for the fates. Encizo's mercy was exhausted for the moment. He had no more left to spare.

A left turn at the junction of the corridor, and he was ready when the door to number 113 swung open, men in uniform evacuating the interrogation chamber. Neither one had a familiar face, but both of them were holding pistols, ready to defend themselves—or so they thought.

The sight of five men rushing toward them, armed with automatic weapons, broke the taller soldier's nerve. He turned and ran, three loping strides completed when converging streams of automatic fire reached out and brought him down. The dead man's comrade tried to make it back inside the room, but Encizo was quicker, stitching him across the chest and slamming him against the doorjamb. Sliding to the floor, the soldier triggered one wild shot before he dropped his pistol. The little Cuban heard someone curse behind him, turned and saw Villa down on one knee, clutching at his side.

"Go on!" the rebel leader gritted. "Finish it."

Encizo reached the open doorway, glancing inside before he stepped across the threshold. James was seated in a chair that faced the door, stark naked, bound with leather straps around the chest, waist, wrists and ankles. Just behind him, standing with an automatic pistol pressed to Calvin's skull, was Luis Rivera.

"An impasse, I believe," the major said.

"Not quite."

"You want this man alive, I think, or you would not be here."

"I came for you," Encizo told him. "One way or another."

"Ah." Rivera cocked the hammer on his automatic. "Then I really must insist you lay your weapon down."

"If I refuse?"

"A messy accident."

From James's looks, he had been through a string of "messy accidents" already. Encizo saw burns and bruises on his naked flesh, blood caked around his nostrils, one eye swollen nearly shut. For all Encizo knew, he might be dying, but it didn't change the job he had to do.

"All right," he said, agreeing with the man's ultimatum, crouching as he set the submachine gun on the floor. It was a gamble, every move from this point on, but he was running out of options. Conscious of the pistol tucked inside his belt, he waited for Rivera's face to break into a cocky smile, the automatic moving from its place at James's temple, swinging toward a different target.

Now!

Encizo drew and fired in one smooth, practiced motion, squeezing off two rounds at near point-blank range. The first round drilled Rivera's forehead, just above one eye; the second found his open mouth and punched him over backward in a lifeless sprawl. The major's single shot struck an acoustic ceiling tile, then his pistol clattered on the floor.

"You took your time," James said, his voice thick with pain.

"Letting you soften them up," Encizo replied, tucking away his pistol as he attacked the leather straps.

"I hope you've got some wheels outside," James said. "I don't feel much like jogging home."

"A car ride and a boat ride. But you'll have to dress for the occasion."

"Over there," James told him, nodding to a corner where his clothes were piled up in a heap.

"Okay, let's get you dressed and out of here."

The battered Phoenix warrior smiled.

"Sounds good to me."

*Nassau, Bahamas*
*9:00 p.m.*

"HERE GOES."

The small voice came to Lyons through an earpiece that he wore. It was a radio receiver, and the voice belonged to Gadgets Schwarz, announcing the arrival of the last man they were waiting for.

St. Jacques.

Marti and Mentzer had arrived in separate cars and left their drivers waiting in the parking lot of the Ardastra Gardens. It was well past closing time, but money talked in Nassau, and the gates had been unlocked when they arrived.

As for Lyons, he had simply scaled the wall.

The bug in St. Jacques's office had informed them of the meeting and its whereabouts. Arriving early, Able Team had staked out the gardens, made sure they weren't walking into yet another trap, then proceeded to prepare their own. With Lyons and Blancanales inside, Schwarz watching the only approach, they had it covered going in.

From his secure position in the verdant undergrowth, Lyons watched St. Jacques approach the others, moving confidently down the garden path. He had a politician's walk, bold strides, as if he were about to speak before assembled members of the press instead of huddling with low-life dealers to discuss the cocaine trade. Lyons gripped his Uzi submachine gun tighter, following St. Jacques until he reached the table where the others sat.

It would be Schwarz's job to take out the drivers. He had the AR-18 with a night scope, silencer and armor-piercing rounds to cover any action in the parking lot, but with a bit of luck he could be finished with a rapid one-two-three. No sweat.

And in the gardens, settling down to talk, St. Jacques and his companions didn't know that they were in a sandwich, pinned between Lyons on one side and Blancanales on the other.

They had talked about potential compromises, back at the hotel. Let St. Jacques walk, perhaps, if he agreed to blow the whistle on his various superiors, cooperating with the DEA. At last they knew it wouldn't work because the system thrived on secrecy, in Nassau as in Washington, Miami, L.A., or New York. St. Jacques would have an "accident" or else be stricken with amnesia by the time he was supposed to testify. This way, at least he'd be linked to Mentzer and Marti beyond a shadow of a doubt, and his superiors would have to fabricate a cover story on their own.

All things considered, Lyons thought, it was the best that they could do, but he was bound to let the bastards see him first.

He owed that much to Perry Tate.

Emerging from the undergrowth, he took a step in their direction, then another. Mentzer saw him now, his dazed expression registering shock. Was it the gun in Lyons's hand, or just the Able warrior's presence?

Julio Marti was turning toward him now, St. Jacques the last to realize that they weren't alone. A voice buzzed in his ear, the Politician asking Lyons what the hell was going on, but Lyons had no time to answer. He was on a roll.

"Surprise," he told the three men seated at the table. And he held down the Uzi's trigger.

# CHAPTER TWENTY-FOUR

*Panama City*
*9:00 p.m.*

Waiting was the hardest part, but grim experience had taught the Executioner to bide his time. The counterpunch against Delvalle had to be precise, a first-round knockout. That, in turn, meant waiting for the proper moment, even with Miranda in the clutches of his enemy.

She might be dead by now, Bolan realized, but he didn't think so. He couldn't explain his hunch, except to say Delvalle's people could have murdered her in the apartment without wasting time and energy to carry her away. The colonel wanted information or a hostage, maybe both. In either case they had a chance to find the woman still alive.

The odds went down, of course, if it was simply information that Delvalle wanted. It wouldn't take long to break Miranda using drugs or torture. She would tell Delvalle everything she knew and thus exhaust her usefulness. But if the colonel had a trade in mind.

Too late.

Delvalle had already waited much too long to make his bid. Intimidated by the Executioner's response, perhaps, he had been stalling, marking time, and now the wheels were set in motion for his own destruction.

There was no place he could run to hide where Bolan wouldn't track him down.

Of course Delvalle didn't know that yet.

But he would learn, when Bolan sprang his trap.

The warrior needed a diversion, and he counted on his adversaries to supply it for him. Fifteen minutes on the telephone, and it was all arranged.

He called Barbosa first, the houseman barely competent with English, finally passing the receiver to another member of the team.

"I want Barbosa," Bolan told the new man, speaking from a public booth and keeping both eyes on the street. "Just tell him it's a friend."

"He doesn't got no gringo friends."

"I'd say he needs one. Tell him I can name the man who set him up to get his ass kicked for the past two days."

A moment's hesitation. Then, "Hold on."

The warrior counted ninety seconds in his head before another voice came on the line.

"So, what do you want?"

"Barbosa?"

"If we're exchanging names, you better give me yours."

"I've got the names you want to hear, but mine's not one of them."

"Whose, then?"

"Carlos Velasco and Antonio Delvalle."

"Everybody knows those names. You haven't told me anything, yet."

"Suppose I told you that Delvalle and Velasco have decided you're expendable. They start to waste your operations, take a few shots at Velasco here and there to make it seem like someone's after both of you. Thing is, you don't fold quick enough to suit Delvalle, so he tries to frame you on a kidnap charge."

"It seems to me I heard something about a woman...."

"And her friends get word that you're responsible, so they go out and waste a few more of your operations. Nifty, eh?"

"What friends are these?"

"Guerrillas, Sergio. Delvalle has you squaring off against some hard-core revolutionaries, not to mention anything Velasco throws your way to wear you down."

"You know all this for sure, I guess."

"Let's say I've got connections."

"And you're telling me because we're such compadres?"

"Wrong. I want the girl back safe and sound. I want Delvalle."

"For Delvalle you might have to stand in line."

The line went dead, and Bolan smiled. One down and one to go.

His next call, to Velasco, was an instant replay of the first. Less argument perhaps, the dealer more than ready to believe that everyone had turned against him. Paranoia kicking in, with bitter rage to fuel the fire.

So far, so good.

The rest of it was Bolan's play, and he was standing on the starting blocks, with nothing else to hold him back.

MIRANDA TRIED TO EAT the food they brought her, but she had no appetite to speak of. She was also hampered by the pain of bruised and swollen lips, the cuts her teeth had made inside her mouth when she was beaten by Delvalle.

She was lucky, even so. The damage could have been much worse, but he grew tired of asking questions, either satisfied himself that she was ignorant or simply gave up caring.

He would never let her go. Miranda's common sense had told her that much. If the colonel needed her alive right now, to satisfy some personal objective, he would have to think again before he let her go. Alive, she was a danger to his reputation and position with the government. If nothing else, she could accuse him of abducting and abusing her—by no means an unusual event in Third World nations—but Delvalle's questions had revealed a major interest in the cocaine traffic flowing through the capital. And from the nature of his questions, it was obvious the colonel had no plans to cut off that stream of poison.

Would anyone believe her, if she had the chance to speak? It was a risk Delvalle couldn't tolerate. Why should he, when it was a relatively simple thing to make her disappear? Or, better yet, he could arrange her death to look like something else, a rape or mugging on the street, perhaps. No suspects would be found, and in a few days she would be forgotten, one more victim of the random violence that was far from rare in Panama.

How long?

It was a question she had tried to put out of her mind, but she couldn't prevent its coming back to haunt her. It was difficult to judge exactly how much time had passed since her abduction, but she knew it must be many hours—half a day at least. No matter what Delvalle had in mind, Miranda's instincts told her she was running out of time.

She thought about Belasko, somehow knew that he was looking for her, doing everything he could to get her safely back. She knew that there was something in his character, beneath the hard exterior, that spoke of sympathy and caring, that urged him to help a comrade in need.

The American might fail, but he wouldn't abandon her.

And knowing that, Miranda found the strength to eat a few more bites of stringy chicken served with plain, white rice. A plastic cup of tepid water washed it down.

When they came back for her, Delvalle or his men, Miranda was determined to resist. It was a hopeless situation, but at least the effort would restore some measure of her dignity. She thought of Mike Belasko out there somewhere, risking everything he had to set her free, and realized that she could do no less to help herself.

And if they killed her sooner than Delvalle planned, so what? Death seemed inevitable in the circumstances, and Miranda took heart in the knowledge that she had some chance, at least, to choose the time.

Whatever her interrogators sought from this point onward, they would have to take.

ANTONIO DELVALLE'S hardsite on the outskirts of the city was a walled estate, perhaps three acres, with his house positioned in the center of the compound. Bolan made his recon in the dark, picking out Delvalle's military sentries and examining their routines. The razor wire atop Delvalle's outer wall wasn't electrified, but special filaments inside each strip were linked to monitors inside the house, prepared to set alarms off if the wire was cut or moved.

The answer was an oak tree standing on the far side of the wall, thick branches reaching out across the barrier. Delvalle's people should have trimmed the branches back, but they were careless—or, perhaps the colonel had a soft spot in his rotten heart for trees. In any case it made a perfect bridge once Bolan tossed his nylon line around the thickest branch, secured it in a running noose and let the branch support his weight for several seconds as a test. When it didn't snap off or sag enough to touch the razor wire, he scrambled up the line, retrieved it and continued on his way.

It was a twelve-foot drop inside the compound, and he watched a pair of sentries pass below him, talking quietly to each other as they walked their beat. From where he sat the warrior had a clear view of Delvalle's house, perhaps two-thirds of his estate. The driveway and the gate were defended by another pair of men in uniform.

The soldiers had been much on Bolan's mind, enlisted men who followed orders, some of them at least presumably believing that Delvalle was a loyal and honest officer. He could compare them with policemen if he tried, demand the same immunity for them that he bestowed upon the most corrupt of law-enforcement officers. And yet . . .

Unless he reached Delvalle, there could be no doubt about Miranda's fate. Worse yet, until he was effectively removed, Delvalle would continue to protect the flow of drugs through Panama to the United States, and every man who stood behind him was, by definition, an accomplice to the vast, ongoing crime.

So be it.

He would spare Delvalle's troopers when and where he could, but nothing short of death would put him off the job that he had come to do. Miranda was an extra motivation, but his mission would have brought him to this point regardless, even if they had never met. His meeting with Delvalle had been destined from the moment that he got the call to rendezvous with Hal Brognola and the team at Stony Man.

And yet, he waited.

It would be a critical mistake to rush his move, proceed without allowing time for the diversion he had planned. A few more moments, one way or another, would determine what came next. If he misjudged Barbosa and Velasco, if they let him down somehow, then he would try it on his own.

But he could spare some time to watch and wait.

Another ninety seconds ticked away before he saw the headlights, three crew wagons rolling in a caravan formation, with the lead car nosing in against the gates. One of the guards stepped up to ask the driver's business, and an argument of sorts began. The voices were inaudible from Bolan's vantage point, but he could gauge the tenor of the conversation from the sentry's gestures, ordering the cars to back it up and move along.

The first shot sounded small and far away, a handgun, but it did the job. The guard went down, a boneless heap, and Bolan saw the lead car power forward, butting hard against the wrought-iron gate. It would require a few more tries, but the attackers showed no sign of giving up.

The sentries who had passed beneath him moments earlier came back the other way, both running toward the gate. When they were gone, with no more close behind them, Bolan jumped down from the tree and started for Delvalle's house.

He made it fifty yards of open ground, and he could stop a bullet anywhere along the way. No matter.

There was only one way he could do his job, and that was one-on-one.

BARBOSA SAW A LIMO pulling through the gates as they approached Delvalle's compound, one more car behind it, waiting to proceed. His mind began to click immediately, adding two plus two and coming up with five.

"Velasco! So, he meets Delvalle as the gringo said."

"But, chief—"

"Silence!"

Sergio cared nothing for the lame opinions of his second in command. The facts were obvious: a secret meeting called behind his back, so that Delvalle and Velasco could cement their plans to drive him out of business, out of Panama and straight into his grave.

He slapped the driver's shoulder, pointing with his index finger. "Stop them! Ram them, if you have to!"

Sergio had three cars filled with guns behind him, each man spoiling for a fight. He took the lead because it was the way a man should act, providing guidance for his troops. A riot shotgun stood upright between his knees, its muzzle pointing toward the ceiling of the passenger compartment.

Swift acceleration pressed Barbosa backward in his seat. The limousine surged forward, rubber smoking on the pavement, as his driver homed in on the last car passing through Delvalle's gate. They were within a dozen feet of impact when Barbosa saw sparks flying from the target limo, bullets glancing off the roof and hood.

Too late.

His own car rammed the limo broadside, drove it hard into the gatepost and held it there. Barbosa's troops were bailing out on either side to join the fight, and all of them could hear the gunfire now. A couple of them hesitated, momentarily confused, until a gunner started blasting them from Velasco's limousine, his bullets skimming harmlessly across the windshield of Barbosa's tank.

"Goddamn it!"

Sergio's lieutenant tried to hold him back, but it had gone too far. Barbosa slapped his hand away and piled out of the car, squeezed off a shotgun blast before he even had a target fixed in mind. It made him feel good, gunsmoke in his nostrils and the weapon bucking in his hands.

Just like old times.

He didn't know exactly what was happening between Velasco and Delvalle, but it hardly mattered now. He had a chance to clean the slate, and he wasn't about to let it pass him by.

In front of him Velasco's car was taking hits, one of his soldiers wriggling out an open window on the other side, collapsing as a stream of bullets cut him down.

Velasco's limousine was burning now, a tongue of flame erupting from below and following the fuel line toward the engine. Smoke was filling up the car and forcing desperate gunners to evacuate. Barbosa and his men were ready, waiting, firing into them at point blank range the moment they emerged from cover.

Three down. Four. Five. Six.

The wounded limo's fuel tank detonated, spewing flame across the hood of Sergio's own car. It didn' matter. He was caught up in the battle now, the heat that baked his face one more incentive to proceed. I symbolized the fire inside him, burning hot enough to char his enemies, destroy them all.

"I want Velasco!" he called out to anyone who might be listening. "The pig is mine!"

DELVALLE WAS RELAXING in his study with a pair of honored guests, enjoying vintage brandy, when all hell broke loose outside. Across the room, Jesus Avilla and Ernesto Montalvo nearly dropped their glasses at the sound of gunfire coming from the grounds outside. Delvalle felt a measure of his old control returning as he rose and set his glass on the coffee table, moving toward the door with measured strides.

"Wait here."

It was an order, but the two civilians didn't argue. They were men accustomed to political debates and civilized discussions in a corporate boardroom, ill equipped to deal with enemies who carried guns. They had arrived in answer to Delvalle's invitation, his assurance that their problem of the past two days was nearly solved. It was to be a celebration, but the colonel had a different notion now.

The sounds of battle drew him down a spacious corridor, across the living room and out onto the broad front porch. From there he had a clear view of a heavy vehicle battering against his gate, the driver bent on breaking through. Delvalle's troops were racing toward the gate, firing on the run.

There were so many questions in his mind—he didn't know who sent the car, how many guns there were inside—but only one thing mattered now. His enemies had come to kill him, repaying him with treachery after all that he had done to organize the cocaine trade in Panama. The first time anything went wrong, they turned on him like a pack of wild dogs.

Enough.

He backed inside and locked the double doors behind him. It would hardly slow his adversaries, but every second counted now, if he was going to escape. Delvalle had anticipated such a day as this, and he was ready. Moving back along the hallway to his study, he could feel the anger mounting, churning in his stomach, bringing bile into his mouth. Before he reached the study, he had drawn the pistol he wore beneath his jacket.

It was time to lose the deadweight that would hold him back. Beginning with the men whose cowardice now left him standing on his own.

"What's happening?" Avilla asked Delvalle, as the colonel stepped inside the room and closed the door.

"Who is it?" Montalvo demanded, looking drawn and pale.

"My plans have changed," Delvalle told them. "I am leaving now. You understand I have no choice."

"What are you saying?" Avilla snapped. "Have you gone mad?"

"In fact," Delvalle said, "I've never been more sure of anything."

And as he spoke, he shot Avilla in the face. His bullet pierced the politician's cheek, below one eye, and loosed a spray of crimson as it burst out through the back of his skull. Avilla toppled over backward, sprawled across the couch, blood soaking through the pale upholstery.

Delvalle swung the gun toward Montalvo and found the banker cringing, both hands raised in front of him as if his open palms could stop a bullet.

"Please!"

Round one punched through the banker's gut and dropped him to his knees. The second bullet struck his forehead with a smack and stilled his bleating cries of pain.

It took a moment with the safe. Delvalle's nervous fingers botched the combination once, and he was forced to start again. Inside, the hundred-dollar bills were neatly bound, ten thousand dollars to a pack, with twenty packs in all. It was enough to see Delvalle safely on his way and get him settled somewhere, give him time to tap his secret bank accounts.

The money went inside a briefcase, and there was only one stop left. The girl. She still might help him get away, and there was ample time to dump her body somewhere far from the estate.

Delvalle left his study with the briefcase in his left hand and the automatic pistol in his right. It was the first time in the past two days that he had felt some semblance of control.

It was time to take charge of his life again, remind his enemies that they were dealing with a man.

THE BATTLE AT THE GATE had drawn Delvalle soldiers from the house—or most of them, at any rate—but Bolan took no chances, veering wide around the back to enter through a set of sliding doors that faced the patio and swimming pool. He found himself inside a game room, with a billiard table, wet bar, and a dart board hanging on the wall.

Outside, a corridor left Bolan with a choice. He could proceed upstairs and search the upper floor, or he could prowl the kitchen, pantry, dining room and parlor first. In either case a search would take some time, and he could feel the doomsday numbers falling as he stood there, grappling with the choice.

A woman's muffled cry made the decision for him, drawing Bolan toward the kitchen pantry, where a door stood open on another set of stairs. This flight led downward to a cellar, dim lights burning down below. The perfect place to stash a hostage for a day or two.

He held the MP-5 K submachine gun in a firm two-handed grip as he approached the open doorway. Silence from the room below, but that meant nothing either way. An army could be waiting for him, or—

Again the voice, but closer this time, from a new direction. Bolan swiveled toward the kitchen door that led outside, into the night. It stood ajar, as if someone had lately passed that way in haste.

Miranda.

With Delvalle?

Bolan followed, leading with the H&K, prepared for anything. The house was bordered by strategic flood-lights, one of which looked down upon a parking area in back. Three vehicles were standing there, a military staff car and a pair of luxury sedans. Delvalle was about to make his mind up, standing with a briefcase in his hand and covering Miranda with a shiny automatic.

So.

"It's over."

Bolan didn't shout. There was no need, with less than thirty feet between them. As he spoke, the colonel froze, then raised his pistol slightly until the sights were leveled at Miranda's face. That done, he made a slow half turn until he had a view of Bolan and the submachine gun in his hands.

"I do not know you, gringo."

"I know you," the Executioner replied.

"You want the woman, yes? I do not think that I could miss at such a range."

"Same here, and I've got thirty chances."

"Ah." The colonel hesitated for a moment, finally getting to the question. "Why?"

"Why, what?"

"Why have you chosen me to persecute? Am I so evil?"

"You were bad enough," Bolan said. "If it's any consolation, though, you weren't alone."

"A man should not be tricked and trapped this way," Delvalle said. "An officer deserves respect and dignity."

"They don't come free of charge," Bolan told him. "You could start by putting down that gun and coming out of here with me. I can arrange a meeting with the DEA. If you agreed to testify—"

"Perhaps," Delvalle said, "there is another way."

Before the colonel finished speaking, Bolan saw him turn the shiny automatic on himself. Miranda screamed, recoiling from the splatter of the gunshot as Delvalle put a bullet through his brain.

"We have to go," he told her.

For a moment she was shaken, dazed. "I don't believe I know the way."

"Hang on," he said, and took her hand. "I'll get you through."

It was a long way back for both of them, he realized. One crucial difference, though—Miranda had a home, something she could call her own. For Bolan there would be only another battlefield, names changing with geography, but all the same when you peeled back the mask and concentrated on the flesh beneath.

There was a heartbeat underneath it all, a kind of grim vitality that he had recognized early on, at the beginning of his endless one-man war. Not human, necessarily, but universal. Something like a primal life force in the midst of violent death, which kept a warrior fighting on, as long as strength remained.

Without that driving force, he thought, it would have been a futile exercise with the hopeless outcome preordained. If that had been the case, would he have carried on the fight?

Of course.

"I'll get you through," he said again, and led Miranda from the killing ground.

It wouldn't hurt for him to spend a few more hours, possibly another day or two, before he started back. The war, he knew, wouldn't go anywhere without him.

It would be there, waiting.

And the Executioner wasn't about to keep it waiting long.

Past and future collide with deadly
force in the Middle East in

## David Alexander's

# NOMAD

## D E S E R T   F I R E

With his commando fighting skills and superior covert-
operations tactics, Nomad is a lethal weapon against
techno-terrorism's continued bid for power.

A brilliant research scientist turned psychotic guru
searches for power linked to hidden ancient energy
spheres, located somewhere in the Middle East. Nomad
stalks his quarry through space and time—final
destination, Iraq 1991, where this madman will join
forces with a powermonger whose evil vision will
unleash an orgy of death and destruction.

---

Break out for action with the next adventure of
the Peacekeepers in...

# 2030
### by MICHAEL KASNER

**In Book 2: JUNGLE BREAKOUT,** the Peacekeepers engage in guerrilla action against Asian warlords while trying to save a village of descendants of American POWs.

Armed with all the tactical advantages of modern technology, battle hard and ready when the free world is threatened—the Peacekeepers are the baddest grunts on the planet.

**America's toughest agents target a Golden Triangle drug pipeline in the second installment of**

# by DAN MATTHEWS

The scene has switched to the jungles of Southeast Asia as the SLAM team continues its never-ending battle against drugs in Book 2: **WHITE POWDER, BLACK DEATH.** SLAM takes fire in a deadly game of hide-and-seek and must play as hard and dirty as the enemy to destroy a well-crafted offensive from a drug lord playing for keeps.